TROUBLESOME RANGE

TROUBLESOME RANGE

A Western Story

by

PETER DAWSON

Skyhorse Publishing

First Skyhorse Publishing edition published 2013 in cooperation with Golden West Literary Agency

Copyright © 2007, 2013 Dorothy S. Ewing

"Troublesome Range" first appeared as a seven-part serial in *Western Story* (10/25/41–12/6/41). Copyright © 1941 by Street & Smith Publications, Inc. Copyright © renewed 1969 by Dorothy S. Ewing. Copyright © 2007 by Dorothy S. Ewing for restored material.

Skyhorse Publishing books may be purchased in bulk at special discounts for sales promotion, corporate gifts, fund-raising, or educational purposes. Special editions can also be created to specifications. For details, contact the Special Sales Department, Skyhorse Publishing, 307 West 36th Street, 11th Floor, New York, NY 10018 or info@skyhorsepublishing.com.

Skyhorse® and Skyhorse Publishing® are registered trademarks of Skyhorse Publishing, Inc.®, a Delaware corporation.

Visit our website at www.skyhorsepublishing.com.

10 9 8 7 6 5 4 3 2 1

Library of Congress Cataloging-in-Publication Data is available on file.
ISBN: 978-1-62087-724-1

Printed in the United States of America

TROUBLESOME RANGE

Peace Terms

"We'll give you a week. If you aren't out by that time, we'll run you out. We'll fire the building and dynamite your safe. And that's a promise!"

"There'll be a federal marshal in."

"Let him come. We've taken care of marshals before."

"You'll lose men."

"So will you."

The two men stared at each other over the length of the table, massive old Yace Bonnyman, belligerent as always and as always convinced he was right, and Fred Vanover, manager for the Middle Arizona Cattle Company, quiet under the strain and hostility of these past twenty minutes. It was to Vanover's credit that he hadn't lost his temper for he was alone here in this smoke-fogged room against Bonnyman and these other four Mesa Grande ranchers. Alone except for his outnumbered crew somewhere below on the street, and John Thorndyke, Middle Arizona's counselor, who had arrived late that afternoon by train from Phoenix.

Vanover now let his glance stray from Bonnyman's rugged face to that of the lawyer. Thorndyke wasn't enjoying this. His eyes were squinted against the lamp glare and smoke, and his face was paler than usual. He was scared, badly, not having liked Vanover's insistence that the two of them should meet the ranchers alone, without enough of their own men present to balance the odds. Vanover could see that Thorndyke wasn't going to be much help.

"We're willing to make certain concessions," he now said quietly.

"Concessions be hanged!" rumbled Bonnyman's uncompromising voice. "You close up shop or we run you out."

"Gentlemen, gentlemen." Thorndyke straightened in his chair, assuming what dignity was left him after hearing Middle Arizona so mercilessly raked over the coals these last few minutes. He gave Vanover a quick yet avoiding look, and went on: "I'm prepared to make you an offer, one I trust will meet with your approval."

"We're through with lawyers' tricks!"

Clark Dunne, in the chair alongside Bonnyman, reached out and put a hand on the older man's arm. "Let's hear what they have to say, Yace." He nodded to Thorndyke. "Go ahead."

The lawyer cleared his throat, and seemed to put starch in his voice, for when he spoke again his tones were firmer. "As I understand it, your objections concern the land company."

"Cattle company, land company, it's one and the same." Clark Dunne anticipated a new outburst from Bonnyman. "That's our prime worry. Another's the sticky loop your crew's been swingin'. Still another's your hirin' gun hands. Two can play that game, and, if you keep it up, we . . ."

"Stick to the point, Dunne," Vanover cut in, and now his look was angry. "I admit letting Harper hire a few men who know how to shoot. You've forced me into it. No use arguin' this rustling business because we think it's you, not us, that's doing it."

"How about Middle Arizona trying to grab the basin lease, trying to crowd us off our best summer range?"

"That was a tactical error," Vanover admitted, smiling thinly. "I had my orders from the main office, which were to bid on the lease when it was posted. So far as we could discover, no offer was ever made to lease it. It looked like a good proposition, so we made our offer and it was accepted."

"And we ran you out," stated Bonnyman.

"You had good grounds. I was never under the impression that we could make it stick. Others were. I was instructed to try, and failed. But to get back to the land company."

Dunne nodded. "I was going to say that you'd never have had even a toehold here if . . ."

"If it hadn't been for that worthless whelp of mine," Bonnyman put in bitterly.

Clark lifted a hand for silence. "Joe didn't know what he was doing, Yace," he said calmly. "We'll skip that. Thorndyke, your outfit got its start here through a piece of luck, through buying Joe Bonnyman's brand, in case you hadn't heard of it. There's no tellin' why Joe sold. But he did and Middle Arizona got its start. They couldn't get any more range by straight buyin', so they set up this land company that we all know is really a loan bank. They cut interest rates and loaned most of us money before we were wise to 'em. Well, they don't get to make their killin'. No court in this county is ever goin' to issue your outfit foreclosure papers. As Yace says, you're through. Close down the Land Office peaceful, or we run you out!"

"That suits us precisely, gentlemen," the lawyer agreed. "I'm authorized to do exactly that. But . . ."

"No buts," growled Bonnyman. "You cut it off clean."

"Let me tell 'em," Vanover said. He caught Thorndyke's relieved nod and went on: "This land company's been making money. It's no secret. And it's no secret why it was set up originally. We hoped to foreclose on several outfits and throw them in with the spread we bought from young Bonnyman and start a big operation here. But that's done with. We don't aim to increase the death rate for a few dollars' profit. On the other hand, the town needs another bank besides that branch of the Tucson National. Why not keep the Acme office open?"

Ed Merrill, across the table from Thorndyke, said explosively: "Why in thunder do we sit here lettin' ourselves be tied in knots by a bunch of fancy words?"

"Then here are some plain ones," Vanover drawled, feeling the intense hostility of them all. "We keep the Land Office open, and Middle Arizona will turn over its operation to any man you name."

He settled back in his chair, leisurely concentrating on his cigar, enjoying the awed silence that held even Yace Bonnyman speechless. His last few words had contained as much surprise as though he had brought out a sleeve gun after promising, as the rest had, not to come into this room armed. For the first time in nearly two years, Fred Vanover was feeling a let-down, with the weight of trouble he'd never wanted being lifted from his shoulders. Here, finally, was what looked like the end to the threat of a range war.

Clark Dunne was the first of the opposition to find words. "What's the catch?" he asked tonelessly.

"There is none. We're willing to do exactly as I said. It's no go on our opening up a big outfit in this country, so we take what we can get. Name the man you want to put in as head of Acme . . . to draw salary as president and to manage policy . . . and he can begin work tomorrow. Correct, Thorndyke?"

"Precisely."

"What about Harper?" Merrill asked, and the name of Vanover's immediate subordinate, now acting as foreman of Middle Arizona's ranch, brought set frowns to the faces of the others. "Does he stay on?"

Vanover shrugged. "I take orders from above. They may think he's still needed here. We'll have to prove to them he isn't before they order me to send him out."

"You'd better get that proof mighty quick," Merrill stated. "Otherwise, he's liable to meet with an accident."

"I'll keep Harper in hand," said Vanover.

Yace Bonnyman lifted a clenched fist, started to hit the table with it, didn't, and laid it out flat before him. It was obvious he'd been about to counter Vanover's decision, then thought better of it. His voice, when he spoke, was like a file being slowly run over a spool of barbed wire.

"Vanover, you work for a pack o' wolves, but I have no reason to doubt your personal word. Do I have it that this is straight, that you won't double-cross us?"

"I swear it, Bonnyman."

The old rancher got up out of his chair. He looked at his friends and neighbors, the men who had come here to make his fight with him, Ed Merrill of Brush, Charley Staples of the Singletree, Slim Workman of the Yoke, and finally Clark Dunne.

"If there's no objection," he said, "Clark gets the job."

The others nodded instant agreement, knowing what Yace was thinking. Clark was deeply involved with Acme by a loan. His outfit, built on a shoestring in the beginning, and only lately counted as one of the bigger brands, could stand a little financial bolstering. It was a tribute to Dunne himself, rather than to any facility at handling money matters, that these men chose him to represent them now. They liked him and wanted to see him get ahead. It was as simple as that.

Clark was flattered but uneasy under this suggested responsibility. "What do I know about finances?" he protested. "About . . . ?"

"You can learn," Bonnyman put in curtly. "Besides, all we want is someone to play watchdog."

"I'm supposed to be shippin' next week." Clark thought of another excuse. "What with pullin' the boys off the job to come in here tonight, I'm set back at least three days."

"We're all in the same boat," Slim Workman solemnly reminded him. "If this thing sticks, it's worth losin' two weeks of our gather. I'll send over a couple men to help out and your bunch'll be glad you ain't around. Well, what about it?"

Clark's glance went from one man to the next, as though his objections had been intended only to give him time to make sure they wanted him. And now this serious expression eased before a relieved smile.

"Sure I'll take it," he said. "Be glad to, and much obliged. Do anything to help end this ruckus. And it is ended, Vanover?"

"As far as we're concerned," Vanover replied.

"Good, then that's settled." Workman took a turnip-size watch from his pocket, his gaunt face mock sober as he looked at it. "Train time, Yace," he announced.

The others had a hard time keeping their faces straight as Bonnyman heaved a gusty sigh and rose from his chair. He reached for his Stetson hanging on the chair back. "Yeah," he said dryly, pretending not to notice their concentrated regard. "And I wish it wasn't. Want to come along, Clark?"

They all knew what he referred to. On his way out, Clark Dunne looked back from the door and gave them a wink, his sun-darkened face turned handsome under a broad smile. He and Bonnyman paused a moment on the landing of the covered stairway outside, sorting through the belts and holstered weapons piled on a caboose chair there. Yace selected his short-barreled .45 and thrust it into the holster at his left armpit, and Clark cinched a .38's heavy shell belt at his waist. While they stood there, they heard a mutter of subdued laughter in the room, and Workman called down to someone on the street.

When they reached the walk below, Clark fell into step alongside the older man. "Better spill some of the sand out of your craw, Yace." he advised. "After all, you sent for him."

"I know, I know." There was disgust in Bonnyman's tone. He glanced around and caught the familiar, pleasant cast of Clark's face and sighed explosively in irritation, but he added nothing to his self-indictment.

Clark was looking along the street. Evidently Workman had passed the word down, for the crews were on the way out. Close to thirty men had ridden in here tonight from the roundup chuck wagons in the hills above the mesa, primed for a shoot-out with Middle Arizona's outnumbered but tough outfit. Now, as they spilled from the saloons and the hotel and pool hall, and climbed onto their ponies, their shouts and rough laughter echoed along the wide street.

These men had been solemn and quiet on the way in; now, their long tension gone, they were like a bunch of kids unexpectedly released from the threat of having to stay after school. Clark saw Ed Merrill's Brush crew leave the Mile High hitch rack in a bunch, their ponies at a hard run before they hit the street's upper dogleg that marked that boundary of the business district. Someone down by the blacksmith shop set up a strident call—"Yoke, where's Yoke?"—and was answered by a shout from a cluster of riders milling in the dust before the pool hall: "Here, and come a-jumpin', Tex!"

"There's Blaze." Clark was looking across the street at a figure momentarily silhouetted in the Mile High's door. "Want me to call him over?"

"He'll be there," was Bonnyman's gruff answer, and from then on Clark let the silence hold, watching idly as Blaze Coyle, the Anchor foreman, spoke briefly to his men across there, and then turned down the walk the way Clark and Bonnyman were headed.

He's like an old range bull with spreadin' toes and sore horns, Clark was thinking of Yace as he matched the oldster's long stride. *Plenty salty yet, but not so sure of himself as he used to be, otherwise he wouldn't have called Joe down here.* The trouble was over now, and Clark was more engrossed in seeing how Yace was going to handle this immediate problem than in thinking back on how effectively Yace's bull-headedness had tightened the screws on Vanover and Thorndyke tonight.

It gave Clark a strange satisfaction in finding the old man humble at the prospect of this meeting with a son he'd driven out five years ago. Clark was fond of Joe Bonnyman, always had been, as fond of him as Joe's father was intolerant and unforgiving. He wondered if old Yace really hated his son. He didn't know.

Blaze Coyle was waiting at the head of the cinder lane that led to the station. Sparse-worded always, he caught the dogged look on his boss's face and fell in alongside Clark without a word. This red-headed cowpuncher knew the old man's moods and eccentricities as he knew the gaits and weaknesses of Anchor's ponies. Now, he sensed, was no time to try to get anything out of Yace, much as he wanted to know what had been decided at the meeting.

They crossed the loading area flanking the freight platform, and rounded the end of the building to step into the margin of light shed by the lantern at the waiting-room door, two overly tall men and one short one, old Bonnyman broad and massive in his tallness, Clark Dunne lithe and his stride effortless, Blaze spare and bowlegged, and looking as if walking didn't agree with him, which it didn't.

Down the siding the compressor on a helper locomotive that would boost the local over the pass was singing a rhythmic pant. There was the smell of coal gas on the chill breeze slanting in off the flats. Ghostly and indistinct on the southern horizon was a dark shadow looking like a towering range of mountains.

"Rain tomorrow," Blaze opined, knowing that shadow to be a storm cloud.

"Snow, more than likely. Is the gate shut on that upper tank?" Yace asked, his tone querulous.

"You ought to know. You rode up yesterday yourself to close it."

It was significant that Yace accepted his foreman's testy reply without protest. No other man of his vast acquaintance would have dared speak up to him in that manner. Fifteen years with Anchor had taken away Blaze's awe of both the outfit and its owner. That span of time had likewise increased Yace's respect for the abilities of his *segundo*, increased them to the point where he tolerated in the man certain tyrannies closely resembling his own. Most times he was amused by Blaze's acid comments; occasionally he'd intentionally prod the redhead into outbursts. He seldom stopped to reason that Blaze was only thirty-five, that his banty-rooster manner was at times plain insubordination.

Tonight Yace was too preoccupied with the coming meeting to take exception to Blaze's manner, even though he was irritated by it. He sensed that there were going to be some uncomfortable moments presently, and hoped he'd be up to them. The distant whistle of the train, the faint rail-borne rumble of its rolling trucks, made him want to leave this place and avoid facing his boy. He thought of Joe as just that, a boy, even though last month he'd penciled a circle around a date on the calendar and come to the startled realization that his son was somewhere celebrating his twenty-seventh birthday. Had he soberly considered this, let the idea of Joe's adulthood take firm root in his mind, he would have been better prepared for this reunion. As it was, he was confused and truculent, blaming not himself, but Joe, for the disturbing feeling that things were bound to go wrong when they faced each other.

An Unwelcome Prodigal

Joe Bonnyman's mood was the exact opposite of his father's as he scanned the night through the coach window and saw the lights of Lodgepole crawling up out of the darkness. It was good to be home again, to have put behind once and for all the feeling of being a pariah, of not being wanted. The last two years in an obscure bunkhouse high in the Tetons of Wyoming, working with a close-mouthed crew and an owner who had a peculiar liking for beef with assorted brands, heightened his sense of release. Few men up north had known Joe's real name. The law might not even remember that a lean, tow-headed man with an Arizona drawl had one night shot a crooked gambler in a saloon in Casper. All the same, Joe Bonnyman was glad to be back. He'd come perilously close to becoming a part of a life that was tawdry and predatory, to joining the pack he'd traveled with those two years in an existence that made a man a near animal, trusting chiefly in his ability to survive.

His father's letter curtly summoning him back to Lodgepole, "to help smoke out a nest of two-legged rattlers," had lifted from his shoulders the weight of the past five troubled years. He sensed with relief that everything must be all right with the old man, that Yace had forgiven the past and was taking him in again; there could be no other explanation for Yace's suddenly ending half a decade's silence. Joe had ridden out the day the letter arrived and sent a wire ahead half an hour before he boarded the train south.

He was up out of his seat, reaching for war bag and sacked saddle, as the coach rattled past the stock pens at the lower edge of town. Out on the platform with the conductor, the schooled impassiveness of Joe's lean, weather-burned face relaxed into a smile as he recognized familiar landmarks through the darkness—Sam Thrall's picket fence and wood shed, Oscar Nelson's two-story brick house with the storm porch at the back, the lighted rear windows of old Sally Baker's house.

"Some dump, eh," the conductor asked pleasantly enough as he shouldered past Joe, and climbed down to the swaying bottom step with his lantern.

"What's wrong with it?" Joe's tone held an edge of belligerence surprisingly like the elder Bonnyman's. He didn't stop to label the reason for that defensive answer, but it was backed by a deep-rooted pride in all he'd once called home.

The conductor shrugged and Joe forgot him as the cinder ramp unwound past the corner of the coach. He saw his father and Blaze and Clark standing under the ramp lantern, and wanted to yell, then thought better of it. Better go easy, was the way he crowded back the impulse. The old man probably thought he was still a little wild.

Joe tossed his saddle aground over the conductor's head while the train was still rolling; his swing down off the steps was one smooth uninterrupted motion, not awkward even for the weight of the heavy war bag. He saw Clark Dunne break into a trot toward him, away from his father and Blaze, and he let go the war bag and stood waiting, the flat planes of his face breaking under a wide grin. He was a medium-tall man whose profile gave him the look of having a light build, but whose full-front outline was made wide and blocky by an inordinately broad span of shoulder. The warm light in his dark-brown eyes made him almost handsome as he watched the approach of his friend.

Clark stopped abruptly two paces away, and both his smile and Joe's faded before mock seriousness in the beginning of a ritual Joe hadn't remembered until now. Suddenly they reached out and clasped hands in a quick stab, both applying instant pressure to their grips. Joe spread his feet widely and dropped his right shoulder a little as his upper arm muscles helped tighten the tendon of his fingers. He saw Clark's handsome face take on a flush, then a grimace of pain. Clark grunted, made a last, wringing effort to tighten his hold, and at the same time loosen Joe's. Then he was gasping a quick: "Lay off, dog-gone it! Enough!"

He jerked his hand free and they were both laughing, each rubbing a numbed hand to bring back the circulation. "Man, you've got your growth," Clark said. He sensed the approach of the other two and stooped to pick up Joe's war bag, adding a low-voiced warning: "He's primed for bear. Go easy."

Some of the warmth and friendliness left Joe's eyes, touching them with a surface brightness. It was the look many men over the past five years would have called his natural one, wary, close to distrustful.

Yace Bonnyman caught that look and found some satisfaction in it. He didn't offer to shake hands, but stood a moment regarding this son, who lacked half a head of matching him in height and some fifty pounds of meeting his weight.

"Hello, Yace," Joe said, and waited.

The old man let the silence run on another moment without replying, his glance carefully measuring his son. All at once he saw something that deepened his frown. It was an indentation midway the length of Joe's right pant leg, and Yace knew at once that the mark had been left there by the constant grip of a holster thong. It was what he was looking for, a flaw in the hard surface of this stranger who looked like his son, but whose bearing was disconcertingly cocksure, into which he could insert the sharp edge of his unreasoning scorn.

"Still the same hellion you were when you drifted out," he said flatly.

Joe's expression softened, became half a smile. *He doesn't want to eat his crow all in one piece*, he was thinking, and drawled: "Must be the bloodlines, Yace."

The quickly gathering fury on his father's face told him how much in error he'd been in judging Yace's remark as the blunt preliminary to a peace offering. The old man had been deadly serious. There was nothing to do but stand there and witness the almost visible snapping of the tightly drawn thread of his temper.

Blaze saw what was building and put in: "Somethin' to that. You'll have to admit it, boss."

Yace seemed not to have heard. Yet at the last moment, he did curb the impulse to lift his fists and maul this flesh and blood of his. It was because, at this moment, Joe's alarmed expression reminded him of Caroline's. He had buried his wife seven years ago, and the one sore spot in his conscience was the memory of how overbearing he had been with her at times. Her eyes had been dark, too, and the look he now saw in his son's, half fearful, half defiant, was a grim reminder of a part of the past he would have liked to live over and mend. So deeply was he shaken by this reminder of his one weakness, so nerve-shattering was the stemming of the flood of fury in him, that his shoulders sagged, and the breath escaped his lungs in an audible groan. He was abruptly aware of having to make a decision; he mustn't let them know how uncertain he was. But in trying to get a hold on himself he became even more confused. Blaze, knowing him better than the others, was shocked at the sight of the man aging before his eyes.

At length, Yace settled on the only line of action that occurred to him. Reaching into his pocket, he brought out his wallet and removed some bills. He held them out to Joe.

"Here's a hundred," he said. "Take it and get out. Go back where you came from."

When Joe made no move to take the money, Yace dropped it. Abruptly he turned from them and went out across the wide ramp. As he trudged out of sight around the station's far corner, Clark Dunne whistled softly.

"What came over him so sudden?" he breathed.

Enemies Meet Again

Joe stood staring into the shadows that had swallowed his parent, letting the shock of his welcome subside. In a moment he said: "Blaze, you ought to get him down to Phoenix and see a good doctor. There's something wrong with him."

Blaze gave a tired shake of the head. "Nothin' he didn't have when I first knew him. He's the meanest old fool I ever come across. I'm quittin' him, here and now."

That statement broke through the core of Joe's helplessness and put the final cap of irony on what had happened. He laughed softly, a mirthless laugh that brought Clark's glance sharply around on him.

"You were ready to quit when I left, Blaze. Still at it?"

"Jumpin' Jehoshaphat . . . enough's enough! I mean it, this time."

Because he needed something to steady him, Joe reached for tobacco and papers and built a smoke. He passed the makings to Blaze, and they went from the Anchor man to Clark. The time-tested ritual did something to ease the strain Yace's hot-headed action had put in all of them.

As Clark passed the Durham sack back to Joe, he said: "I've turned city man. Got a room at the hotel for the night. You can bed down with me till you find a better place."

Joe saw the money lying at his feet and stooped to pick it up. He looked at the wadded bills a moment, then handed them to Blaze. "It took more'n the sight of me to touch him off. What else is there?"

"That's what makes it so funny," Clark answered for the red-head. "Yace settled things with Vanover tonight. You'd think he'd have been off the prod."

"Vanover?" Joe frowned, trying to place the name.

"The Middle Arizona man," Blaze said dryly. "You know."

Joe nodded. Yes, he knew now. Vanover was the man who had represented the cattle company in the sale five years ago. Thinking back on that, Joe felt a momentary and keen shame. He'd gone out of here with $8,000 in his pocket, money that represented his legacy from a mother who had wisely judged her husband and son too alike ever to agree. She had made her gesture shortly before going to the grave, leaving Joe her thirty-section ranch on Troublesome Creek, wanting to insure his future. Joe had sold the layout to the cattle company after a bitter argument with Yace, knowing no better way to hurt his father. Had he foreseen the repercussions his act was to have, bringing on him the enmity of his neighbors and friends, ranchers who had fought to keep the cattle company from getting a foothold on the mesa, he might have acted differently. But the sale had been an accomplished fact before he became aware of what it represented. He'd drifted shortly after that. And he'd lost the last of the money that night in Casper when he had to leave the poker layout and the dead gambler in too much of a hurry to think about taking his sadly depleted stake.

"So that ruckus is still on," he said.

"Was, not is," Clark told him. "We had it out with Vanover and his lawyer tonight. Every man from the upcountry was in town. It finally wound up with Vanover's crowd pullin' in their horns. I came out of it with a job, president of a land company. You might say Yace rammed it down their throats." He gave Joe a sideward glance, trying to judge his friend's mood. "Who's thirsty besides me?"

"I am." Blaze spoke with ominous intensity. "And I aim to do something about it."

"Careful, Yace might not like that," Clark said in mock show of seriousness. He and Joe were both well acquainted with the red-headed cowpuncher's one failing, and the look he gave Joe was intended to convey that understanding.

But Joe was thinking of something else. "You . . . warmin' a chair in an office? What land company?"

"We'll get you caught up on things over a drink," Blaze said, and headed down the ramp after Joe's saddle.

As they passed the freight platform, Joe told them—"I'll come back after this stuff later."—and hefted his war bag up onto the planks indicating that Blaze should do the same with the saddle. There was a freight due shortly after eleven, Joe remembered, unless train schedules had been changed in his absence.

Joe had definitely decided to leave Lodgepole. He wasn't going back to the Tetons. No, he was through with all that. Somewhere south of here he'd find a riding job. There'd be no more gambling, he wouldn't wear a gun, and he'd begin saving his money. Now that the break with home was clean, now that nothing remained here to hold him, he tried to convince himself he was making a new beginning. Turning down the street along the dark aisle of cottonwoods, seeing the store lights up ahead, he had his moment of sharp regret, the rising up of a long-forgotten nostalgia for all this country held for him. But that feeling was brief. His father's open scorn had drained him of the last drop of sentiment.

He put all his bitterness into words as he sensed the full futility of his return. "Yace needed someone to make his fight for him, eh? Now that it's over, he can get along alone."

"It ain't quite that," Blaze said, wanting to explain exactly what had possessed Yace back there. In him was a stubborn streak of loyalty toward Anchor's owner. He felt personally responsible for the outcome of that meeting between father and son. But try as be would, he couldn't discover the real reason for this violent and final break; he could add nothing to his denial of Joe's claim.

They sensed that further words on the subject were futile. Joe changed it as quickly as he could, nodding across the street toward a new white-fronted building whose sign bore a familiar name. "Jensen's comin' up in the world."

As he spoke, Clark's stride slowed so abruptly that the other two looked around. They surprised the quick change of expression on his face. When he spoke, it was nervously: "Joe, there's someone you'll want to see." He tilted his head toward the broad verandah of The Antlers, beyond Jensen's saddle shop. "She made the trip in today on purpose to get a look at you. Don't disappoint her."

Across there, a girl's slim outline showed before the hotel's lamplit lobby entrance. Joe felt the turmoil within him subside quickly before a new feeling, one of mixed hesitation and expectation. Many times in these past harried years the image of Ruth Merrill had struck across his consciousness with freshness and clarity. Yet always in his thoughts of her was a blend of hot shame at having thrown himself so blindly at the one girl who had ever strongly attracted him; he'd offered himself and been held off, treated as her final choice only if she could make no better. Now the sting of that old defeat was in him again. But outweighing his instinctive rebellion at humbling himself once more was a live curiosity, the urge to experience again that old deep stir of feeling.

"Disappoint Ruth?" he said mildly. "Not me." He started obliquely over the wide span of the street.

The girl must have seen him coming, for she crossed the broad porch and paused halfway down the steps. They met there, he with hat in hand, she looking down at him. For a moment neither spoke. And Joe was grateful for that interval that let him ease the long hunger of his imagining.

He was conscious of a heightening expectancy as he took in the shadowed, near-perfect outline of her features. The prettiness he remembered was there, all of it and more, her ash-blonde hair adding a final striking touch to sheer beauty. He sensed some-thing else, too, something womanly and assured in the way she accepted the flattery of his glance. It was as though she put it aside and looked deeply into him, wanting to know, as he wanted to know of her, the changes the years had brought. Here was no girl relying on beauty alone for her attraction. Ruth Merrill had taken on the bloom of maturity. He was sobered by the thought of how much she could mean to a man.

"You're not the same, Ruth," he heard himself saying.

"Nor you, Joe. It's been a long time." Her voice was richer, more vibrant than he remembered it. Something in her tones, warm and low, seemed to hold a promise for him.

"I'd forgotten all this," he said awkwardly. "It's going to be hard to leave it."

"Leave? Again?" Interest was in her. But it was neither quick nor intense, and Joe knew he had misread the depth of her feeling as she first spoke. "Why, Joe?"

"Yace is on his high horse. His trouble's over and he doesn't need me."

"So you're going to a better place. Is there something so wrong with us that you . . . ?"

He was never to know the completion of her thought, for she paused without finishing it, and her glance ran coolly beyond him and across the street. A moment ago someone had called from over there; Joe was only now aware of it. Ruth smiled briefly, a smile neither warm nor distant, and said: "It's nice to have seen you. Don't let Ed make trouble." Then she was turning from him up the steps toward the lobby door. He didn't realize until she was gone that this was her good bye, that she was taking this parting casually.

"Bonnyman!"

Joe faced about slowly at the snappish quality in Ed Merrill's voice, hailing him a second time from across the street. He saw the man standing at the edge of the walk in front of the Mile High.

Until now, Joe had forgotten Ed and the old feud that lay between them, the culmination of which had come in his courting Ed's sister. The origin of their aversion to each other lay back beyond the reach of either's memory, in one of their first days at the country school. It had been fed by Joe's instinctive skill at all games, his love of a fight, his inability to harbor a grudge. Ed Merrill had always been best at a thing "next after that Bonnyman kid" even well into manhood. Joe's betrayal of the ranchers to the cattle company had only fed the fire of Ed's resentment; it had, in fact, elevated Ruth's brother to a station above Joe for the first time in his life and he had been one of Joe's chief tormentors five years ago.

This reminder of that old rivalry, the strident summons in Ed's call, whetted in Joe the edge of sharp anger. He couldn't define that anger, the feeling of recklessness that was suddenly in him, beyond knowing that Ruth Merrill's welcome had lacked warmth. He started across the street, feeling a strong impulse to settle once and for all any difference between him and Ed. It was that thought that put a tough and rakish look on his face as he ducked under the saloon tie rail and regarded Merrill. In his pale-blue eyes was a danger signal, if only Merrill had read it.

Ed Merrill had lately become a power on this range, and Joe sensed a new confidence in the man without knowing the reason for it. Old John Merrill, bedridden by something the doctor vaguely called "pulmonary constriction," had let his son gradually assume all the responsibilities of managing Brush Ranch. Ed was a big man, lord of a big spread, and well aware of it.

There was a surly arrogance in his glance as he looked down at Joe. "You never would take a hint, would you, Bonnyman?" he drawled.

"Hadn't it ought to be Mister Bonnyman?"

Merrill ignored the gibe. "You'll not hound Ruth any longer. Clark'll have something to say to this, along with me."

"Clark!"

Merrill seemed not to notice Joe's surprised exclamation, and went on: "I warned you away from her before we ran you out of the country. Or maybe you forget."

From the cobalt shadows farther along under the walk awning, Blaze Coyle's voice called solemnly: "All right, Joe?"

"All right." Joe's toneless drawl wasn't loud, but it carried well. "Go on in, Blaze. Order me a drink. Bourbon."

He waited until Clark's and Blaze's shapes had moved in through the saloon's batwing doors. He was trying to take in the full significance of Merrill's coupling of Clark's name with Ruth's. But that could wait.

"So you ran me out, did you, Ed?" he said mildly.

Now Merrill caught a hint of what was coming, and took a backward step. Even so, he was still sure of himself, and in the taut smile that came to his broad face seemed to be the sureness that two extra inches of height, his added poundage, and the justice of his argument were already balancing the scales in his favor.

"We ran you out," he stated.

Joe leaned back against the long pole of the tie rail, as though about to argue the matter further. His indolent gesture uncocked the other's wariness, and Merrill decided that what he'd been looking for a moment ago wasn't coming. Joe's move had been intended to do exactly that; now he let his weight go back against the springy length of the pole. The next instant he was using that added force to put speed behind his sudden lunge up onto the walk.

His feint with his left was wasted; Merrill wasn't ready. Then Joe's right clipped the rancher below the cheek bone with a force that sent the bigger man staggering backward across the walk and hard against the saloon's wall. Merrill had but a split second to lift his guard and steady his reeling senses, for Joe pressed in on him. As Merrill's hands came up, Joe whipped in two blows that drove the wind from the other's lungs. Merrill struck out wildly, savagely. He missed and was slammed back into the wall again with a bleeding mouth and a stinging ear.

Joe fought with relentless accuracy, goaded by Merrill's reminder of his disgrace. Here seemed to be the target of all his hates, the embodiment of his long frustration, and he set about calmly and expertly to whip the man. The taste of blood seemed momentarily to steady Merrill, and for an interval he stood clear of the wall, almost toe to toe with Joe, landing blows, but doing little damage. Then, abruptly, he weakened, and it was as though he had decided that defeat would come when his back was to that wall again, for he swung sideways from it and gave ground along the walk.

Shortly Joe found himself abreast the darkly curtained window of the Mile High. Its broad sill was knee high. Jeff Olander owned the saloon and one of Joe's last memories of five years ago was of a group of his friends, or men who had been his friends, turning their backs when he entered the place, and even Olander refusing to drink with him. Now a taut smile came to his face as he thought back on Olander's indictment, and slowly, slugging, dodging, and weaving, he maneuvered Merrill around so that the man's back was to the window.

Suddenly he gave no thought to protecting himself, but only to driving each fist home in Merrill's face. The brutality of his attack made Merrill give ground. Then the rancher felt the window at his back and tried to side-step. In that precise instant Joe's updriving right fist caught Merrill on the point of the chin. Pain shot the length of Joe's forearm as he deeply bruised a knuckle. But he had the satisfaction of seeing Merrill lifted up on toes, then fall backward. The man reached out with both arms as the sill of the window caught the backs of his knees. The window cracked in a dozen places, making a jangling, high-pitched sound. Merrill fell inward in a smother of shattered glass, caught the heavy curtain, and dragged it down from its rod as a bright rectangle of light cut the gloom on the walk. The breath left his lungs in a low groan as he hit the floor inside. His head snapped back hard against the planks, and his high-built frame went loose as consciousness left him.

Arms cocked at his sides, his breathing labored, Joe stared in through the glassless opening to see his father, Charley Staples, and Slim Workman staring in a paralysis of surprise the length of the room from a back table. Blaze and Clark were at the bar, and it was obvious that the breaking in of the window was the first indication they'd had of what went on outside. Two other customers stood farther back along the rough pine counter, their attitudes clearly indicating the line of flight they had picked to the alley door. Jeff Olander, his round face slack in amazement, had been caught with a dripping glass in one hand, a towel in the other, and stood transfixed in that posture so symbolic of his trade.

Joe took all this in at a single sweeping glance as he stooped to pick up his Stetson, which had a moment ago fallen to the walk, stepped over the window's low sill, and sauntered across to join Blaze and Clark. No one else in the room moved. A full shot glass of whiskey sat alongside Blaze's empty one; Clark, too, had finished his drink. The extra was the one they had ordered for Joe. He took it, emptied it at one toss, and drawled: "Let's get out where the air's better."

They put their backs to the room, Blaze and Clark taking on a measure of the disdain with which Joe scorned to look in the direction of the prostrate Merrill. It was a gesture that held Olander and the rest, even Yace Bonnyman, speechless. Joe, flanked by his two friends, pushed the batwings wide, and they stepped through and out of sight onto the walk.

The doors had long stopped rocking on their double hinges before Olander found his voice. His beady glance went to Yace Bonnyman and his voice intoned: "Someone's got to square with me for that window."

Yace was still eying the doors. He nodded soberly, as though the saloon owner had interrupted a portentous and awesome thought. "Put it on my bill, Jeff," he said, and there was bewilderment but no anger in his voice.

22

Vanover Closes Up

F red Vanover was tired, strangely so, for he was a rugged man, and what he had accomplished tonight should have put new strength in him. It hadn't. Not until it was over had he come to the full realization of what might have happened if the meeting had resulted in a deadlock. The half hundred men who had just left town so peaceably had come here ready to turn their guns on each other. That he had been even partly responsible for a situation that might have cost many lives still filled Vanover with awe and misgivings. Middle Arizona had placed too much power in his hands. It wasn't right that he should be so able to control men's destinies. He wasn't deceiving himself. Luck had been with him tonight, just plain fool luck. And that same brand of luck had been with him in his talk with Neal Harper afterward. He'd bluntly told the Texan how things stood, that Middle Arizona no longer needed gunfighters. His surprise at Harper's ready agreement overshadowed even the earlier one of the meeting's outcome. He had been expecting trouble with Harper and none came.

"We're goin' stale anyway," Harper had said. "Nothin' ever happens here."

No, nothing had happened, fortunately. Vanover's feeling of relief was now so acute that he felt weak, hollow inside, as he looked across the office at the chestnut-haired girl working over the ledger at the side table. Sight of her brought a flash of tenderness that drove the severity out of his lined face.

"Time to quit, Jean," he said, and emphasized his words by pulling down the shutter on his roll-top desk. "We move out in the morning. Glad?"

"As glad as you are." Jean Vanover laid her pen aside, closed the heavy account book, and reached up with her arms to stretch in a very unwoman-like way. When she turned and looked across at her father, her face was lighted by a smile backed by the understanding of his long struggle, now ended. Fred Vanover had tried so hard to keep this office from becoming what it was intended to be, a loan bank set up for the sole purpose of impoverishing the ranchers of the country. He had even turned over the management of the ranch to another man and moved to town to be close to things. Tonight he had won his long battle.

"One day they'll know what you did for them, Dad," she said, coming across and leaning down to kiss his high forehead.

"I doubt it." It didn't matter to Fred Vanover whether anyone knew or not. The only thing that did was his conscience, and that was now at ease.

Jean set about the routine of closing the office, pulling down the blind at the front plate-glass window, blowing out the big bracket lamp, turning down the smaller one, seeing that the alley door was locked, and finally that the big safe was closed. Fred Vanover purposely didn't help her in these tasks, preferring instead to tilt back in his chair and use the brief moment of leisure in watching her.

It wasn't often he had the chance really to look at her, or thought to. He was inordinately proud of this girl, of the easy grace with which she moved, of that boyish look that made her shoulders more prominent than her slim hips. Years ago he'd had his moments of wishing she had been a boy, but that feeling was long gone. He noticed now the way she carried her head at a tilt that was almost proud. It was the one thing in her that reminded him of her mother. Aside from that, she might have been another woman's daughter. Martha hadn't been pretty and Jean was definitely so. Jean's hair was a deep rich chestnut; her mother's had been blonde. Jean's eyes were his own, hazel, and had a direct way of looking at a person that met with his approval. There was no guile, not even shyness in Jean Vanover. He had to admit that she was a powerfully appealing woman. "To me, at least," he said half aloud.

"What's that, Dad?"

"Nothing, nothing. Talking to myself." Vanover rose from the chair and took his narrow-brimmed Stetson from the peg on the wall by the desk. "Ready?"

"Ready," she said, and went through the street door ahead of him.

From obliquely down the wide aisle of buildings came sounds of a scuffle, the scraping of boots, the grunting intake of breath of a man being hit. Jean heard it and, a moment later, her father.

"Sounds like someone's workin' off some steam across there," he remarked as he reached around to close the door.

Vanover was inserting the key in the lock when the Mile High's window shattered under the weight of Ed Merrill's body. He wheeled around and was in time to see the curtain pulled down, the man falling through the window, the one on the walk. And he watched as Joe Bonnyman picked up his hat, stepped in through the shattered opening, and out of sight.

Vanover whistled softly. "Did pack a wallop," he drawled.

"Who could it be?"

It came to him then, recognition of that wide shape. "Joe Bonnyman," he answered. "I forgot to tell you . . . he came in on the train tonight."

"Who was he fighting?"

"Couldn't tell." Vanover took Jean's arm and gently drew her to his side as he started down the walk in the direction opposite the hotel, toward the small frame house they had rented since Vanover had left the ranch to work in the land company office.

Jean's glance was still on the saloon and the broken window. "Is he really as bad as they make him out to be?" she queried, matching her father's stride.

He shrugged. "It wasn't exactly what I'd have done . . . to sell out on my father."

"That old . . ." Jean couldn't find the word to express her feeling for Yace Bonnyman. "I'd have done the same."

"You probably would," her father agreed, chuckling over her rejoinder. "But would you also knock a man through a saloon window and . . . ?" His words ended abruptly as three men emerged from the Mile High's doors. He recognized them and added dryly: "At least he's in good company now."

"Do you call Clark Dunne good company?" asked Jean.

"Yes," he said, surprised by her vehemence. "Don't you?"

"I suppose so."

Something in her tone made him query sharply: "Hasn't he been a gentleman with you, Jean?"

Her easy laugh, striking into the stillness and sending back a small echo from across the street, reassured him. "Quite," she said. "But I don't like him to keep on seeing me when he's practically engaged to Ruth Merrill. It makes me sort of . . . sort of playing second fiddle. Not that it matters. But there are things about him I don't understand. I'm not sure I like him very much."

"Then don't see him any more." Vanover hadn't thought of the matter in this light before, but now that it was called to his attention, it did seem a little queer that Clark Dunne should be seeing his daughter so often when he was chiefly interested in Ruth Merrill.

"I don't believe I will, Dad," Jean said, pressing his arm affectionately. "Thanks for helping me make up my mind."

Mike Saygar

The sound of a woman's laughter striking across the quiet street took Joe Bonnyman's glance across there. He saw a man and a woman pass before the night-lighted window of a store almost opposite, and in a moment recognized Fred Vanover.

"Vanover married again?" he asked curiously.

"That's his daughter," Blaze said, immediately thinking of something else and adding truculently: "You've made a fine start at healin' up the old sore, friend."

"His daughter?" Joe still peered across the wide street. "You mean the kid that used to run around in short skirts and pigtails?"

Alongside, Clark Dunne's voice had an edge to it: "What's so strange about a girl growing up?"

"Nothing, only . . ." Joe didn't finish what he'd started to say, which in essence was that Jean Vanover's voice had sounded exceedingly pleasant and womanly.

"How you goin' to make it up to Merrill?" Blaze was insistent on getting an answer to his worry. "He's growed up, too. Casts a mighty wide shadow lately."

"It won't need makin' up," Joe told him. He decided not to mention Merrill's coupling of Clark's and Ruth's names. Anyway, it didn't matter. "I'm headed out."

"Out? Away from here?" Blaze was incredulous and added a ripe oath.

Joe nodded. "In an hour, unless they've stopped runnin' that late freight."

"But you can't drift again," Blaze insisted. "Take it from a man crowdin' middle age, mister. You'll never lick anything by runnin' from it."

Clark saw the angry turn of Joe's head and knew at once that Blaze's remark had touched on a sore spot. "Joe's not runnin'," he said quickly. "But there's something to what you say. Joe, I've got an idea."

"The answer's no," Joe drawled.

He was abruptly sobered by the thought that these two old friends, really the only two he cared anything about, would now urge him to stay on. Their attitude was natural; what sobered him was knowing that from now on he'd be living among strangers, not among men like this pair with whom he could forget the ingrained wariness and suspicion that were the unwanted fruits of his absence.

"Wait'll you hear what I have to say," Clark insisted. "I'm in this land company now and I need help. Vanover's to be trusted, but, after all, he works for Middle Arizona. So long as I'm goin' at this thing at all, it'll be whole hog. I'll need a man to help me with the saddle work. Shippin' time is close, and we could divide the county, you workin' the south half, me the north, keepin' check on the gather. That way we could . . ."

"I said no, Clark."

"But listen, man. You get, say, twice the wages you can draw on a ridin' job. You're fifty miles from your old man, sixty from Merrill. What . . . ?"

"I told you I was leavin'!" Joe said sharply.

Clark thought he saw then how to carry his point. He wanted Joe to stay, wanted him badly enough to run the risk of his anger. "Then what are your reasons?" he asked bluntly, not denying the inference Joe had put to his mention of Ed Merrill. "Name me a good one."

"I'm fed up with the whole mess. If Merrill doesn't try and knock the chip off my shoulder, someone else will."

"Don't put one there to get knocked off," advised Blaze. "Stick it out here and make these jaspers admit you ain't the sidewinder they've pegged you for."

"No." Joe's refusal was as positive as it had been the first time.

* * * * *

And so it was an hour later, when Joe tossed war bag and saddle up onto the caboose platform of the freight. He gave his two friends a look that showed them none of his regret, no emotion whatsoever, as he drawled: "Give Yace my apologies for bein' in too much of a hurry to say good bye."

"Yeah, he'll be touched." Blaze's blocky face was cracked by a set smile that didn't quite hide his disappointment.

"No use tryin' to argue you out of it?" Clark was serious, sober.

"No use."

Far up beyond the station, by the water tank, the locomotive's whistle gave two sharp blasts to call in the brakeman. The waiting interval it took his lantern to crawl in along the tracks to the caboose was awkward for all three. But finally Joe was stepping up onto the platform after the brakeman and the conductor's lantern was arching the highball to the engineer. The long line of cars shuddered as slack went out of the couplings. The caboose finally lurched into motion. It was twenty yards down the track when Joe, lifting a hand in a gesture of farewell, turned and the orange-lighted caboose door swallowed his wide shape.

"Devil of a note," Blaze growled.

Clark Dunne didn't speak until the two lights of the caboose had almost gone out of sight in the darkness. Then he gave a gusty sigh. "Too bad," he said.

They were silent as they went back up the street as far as the Mile High, where Blaze's horse was tied, each too engrossed in his thinking to bother with talk. As Blaze jerked the knot of his reins, Clark said: "Sure you won't stay over? I can put you up."

Blaze shook his head, stepping into the saddle. A bleak look touched his eyes as he glanced toward the saloon's window, now covered with a tarpaulin nailed to the outside facing.

"He sure was a wild man, eh?"

"You talk like we weren't going to see him again."

"I got that feelin', friend."

Clark could think of no argument to use against this reasoning, and, when he remained silent, Blaze lifted his reins and turned the Anchor-branded gelding out into the street with a—"Be seein' you."

Clark watched him ride out of sight, feeling a strange and restless sense of unfulfillment. He was at a loose end, half angry without knowing why. The hour was late, yet he wasn't sleepy. His look went the way Blaze's had a moment ago, toward the Mile High's doors, and he regretfully ruled out the idea of going in there for a nightcap in the knowledge that Olander and his late customers would be talking about the fight and wanting his views on it. It occurred to him only then that neither he nor Blaze had asked Joe for any particulars on his argument with Ed Merrill. He wondered what had led to the fight. He had a hunch it had started over Ruth, over Ed's seeing Joe talking with her.

"Got a minute, Clark?"

The low-drawled words coming from beyond the walk startled Clark momentarily. He looked across to the head of the narrow alleyway running between the saloon and the adjoining building, and made out Neal Harper's indistinct shape. He glanced warily both ways along the walk before he stepped over there.

"You don't need to creep up on a man," he said curtly. "What is it?"

"Thought you'd like to know Vanover's lettin' us go." Harper's drawl bore a faint edge of insolence, of demanding an answer.

Clark was nervous under the implication lying behind those words. When he made no immediate reply, Harper went on: "We ain't exactly built a stake we could retire on."

Here was a reminder of an old promise. Clark was edgy under that reminder and said dryly: "Can I help it if they bury the hatchet?"

Harper's shoulders lifted meagerly. "I'm only tellin' you what happened."

"I'll see what I can do about it. When are you due to pull out?"

"Vanover didn't say exactly when."

"Then keep in touch with me. Something may come up."

"Such as?"

"How do I know?" Clark said sharply. He nodded back along the passageway. "Get goin'. Someone might spot me standin' here, and begin to wonder."

Harper said—"Yeah."—and faded soundlessly back into the deeper shadows.

Back out at the edge of the walk, Clark put the Middle Arizona man from his mind and thought back on the matter that had occupied his attention when Harper interrupted him. It had been Joe and Ruth, his hunch that Ed Merrill had said something to Joe about his sister that had started the fight. This first insistent awareness of envy for Joe stung irritatingly, like the bite of a small insect. Clark tried to ignore it, couldn't. It was related to another sobering fact, one he had put off facing, and that fact concerned himself in relation to Ruth Merrill. Talking to Ruth this afternoon, he had learned that she was in town primarily to see Joe, as she put it, "to prove to myself how lucky I am in having you, Clark."

Ruth's bland statement now only heightened a growing distrust of her real feeling toward him. He thought he knew Ruth better than most men; he told himself he understood the guileful urgings that had left her unsatisfied with each conquest as a girl and pushed her on to the next. A year ago she had begun to favor him, but lately her interest seemed to be lagging. Clark wanted to believe it was because she had become so used to him that she had dropped the pretense of coquetry and flirtation for the more serious and deeper emotion that should eventually draw them together as man and wife. Yet, wanting to believe these things didn't rule out the suspicion that, had Joe stayed, Ruth might have switched her favors once again.

He rolled a smoke and forgot to light it, so somber were his thoughts. Yes, he would marry Ruth regardless of any doubt in his mind. It might turn out to be nothing but a marriage of mutual advantage, one in which there was respect, but no love. But, regardless of what the future held for him and Ruth, being taken into the Merrill family would strengthen his weak hold on the top-most rung of the ladder of this range's society. That, bluntly, was the thing Clark Dunne was after.

He had come to Anchor as the lowliest rider in a big crew twelve years ago, a gangling overgrown kid with a strong back and the guts to use it. He could admit now that he had been kept on because he and Joe got along so well together, not because Yace Bonnyman, or Blaze, found him indispensable as a rider. That had been his first toehold, and he had played it for all it was worth, ingratiating himself to old Yace to the point where he was allowed to run his own small herd along with Anchor's, and thus get his start.

Clark didn't like to look back on the first year he was on his own, after he'd cut loose from Anchor to homestead high along the Troublesome in the hills above the mesa. The temptation to comb the hills for strays and work over their brands had been too strong to resist. It had been plain rustling, with not much risk involved. For Mike Saygar had also made his start in this country that same year, and Clark's petty thievery had been obscured by the outlaw's, which was on a wholesale scale.

The sharp rise in Clark's cattle count had passed unnoticed by everyone but Saygar himself. It hadn't taken the wily outlaw long to trace the small bunches of Anchor- and Brush-branded beeves he was blamed for stealing, but hadn't taken. And it was typical of him not to expose Clark. Rather, he had asked a favor in return for his silence.

Clark, accepted as an up-and-coming young rancher, was on the inside as far as the law was concerned. All Saygar wanted was advance notice from Clark of any moves the sheriff's office proposed making against him. Thus it was that a posse of forty men, that first spring after Mike Saygar's coming, found his hill cabin deserted when they thought to surprise him and his wild bunch at dawn one morning. And in these last years of trouble with Middle Arizona, the partnership of rancher and outlaw had profited handsomely, dividing the blame for continued rustling equally between the cattle company and the Mesa Grande outfits. Clark's Troublesome Creek layout had assumed mushrooming proportions, due, according to Yace Bonnyman's own statement, to a mighty fine mixture of brains and muscle.

To all appearances, Clark had worked hard. He'd had a little luck, too, in the form of a publicly proclaimed legacy of some $4,000, left him by an uncle back East. That uncle had in reality been Mike Saygar, who was willing to loan the money when Clark had the chance to buy out a neighbor's ten sections. Clark had also increased his indebtedness by added borrowing from Middle Arizona's land company. With the money he had thrown up an earth dam to catch spring flood water, and thereby increased the potential value of his newly acquired land. Lately Saygar had become a little impatient over the repayment of his loan. Clark had no idea how he was going to take care of it.

This unwanted inspection of his past, prompted by his brief meeting with Joe, now increased Clark's feeling of uneasiness. He was angry without that anger being directed at any one thing or person, unless possibly he blamed Joe for leaving. His way of life had lately left a bad taste in his mouth, and he had looked for Joe's return to bring back the carefree feeling of the old days, when he and Joe and Blaze traveled together and horsed around at any deviltry Joe could think up.

Then, abruptly, Clark saw something he hadn't taken into account before. Joe's staying wouldn't have helped beyond the diversion of erasing a little of the sense of guilt that had lately begun crowding him. They might have had some good times together, but, all in all, his friendship with Joe would have been held against him. Yace's putting him up to head the land company, along with the ready compliance of the men he had once envied, the big augurs of this country, opened before Clark a vista of influence he hadn't realized until just now. He had suddenly become an important person. In years to come he might even gain the prominence and influence Yace Bonnyman now held in the affairs of this country. His prospective marriage would see him topping the last long rise that blocked the wide vista of his future. And, come to think about it, friendship with a man who had betrayed his father and his friends would have counted against him in the end. Joe had served him well in the beginning, but that service was no longer important. He was on his way, and he didn't need Joe.

Clark felt better immediately after taking this line of reasoning. He dragged in a deep breath of the chill night air that still bore the taint of the freight's coal smoke, remembering only then the unlighted cigarette between his lips. The flare of the match broke the solemn run of his thoughts as they dwelt briefly on Neal Harper. As he sucked the smoke alight, he abruptly felt good, better than in a long time.

His downward stare as he flicked the match away showed him something in its waning light, something that lay on the walk almost at his feet. He stooped and picked it up. It was a black-and-white braided horsehair hatband. He studied its woven design in the faint light, admiring it, trying to remember where he'd seen it before.

All at once he knew. This was the hatband that a Texas rawhider had years ago traded Joe for a cheap clasp knife. It was so long ago that Clark couldn't remember the Texan's looks. Joe would miss this, for he had worn it all these years when he could have afforded a better one. Trying to think how Joe could have lost it, Clark remembered his friend bending over to pick up his Stetson after the fight with Merrill, and knew then how it had happened.

He folded the circle of horsehair and thrust it into a pants pocket. Then, still reluctant to turn, but unable to think of anything better to do, he sauntered over to the hotel and into the lobby. Snores sounded from the clerk's cubbyhole room under the stairway behind the counter. Clark tiptoed over there, reached down the key to his room from the board over the desk, and climbed the stairs.

A few strides from the door to his room he stopped at sight of a sliver of light shining through at the sill. He frowned, and the automatic gesture of hand to gun was as swift as the change of expression on his face. He approached the door and opened it. As it swung wide, he looked across to where Mike Saygar sat tilted back in a chair, boots cocked on the foot of the bed, and smudging its clean, gray-blanketed surface.

Clark took his hand away from holster, but something tightened in him as he stepped in, closed the door, and said flatly: "I thought we didn't know each other, Mike."

"We don't." Saygar's full round face tilted up and he regarded Clark directly, his squat frame relaxing from the cocked attitude it had assumed at sound of the door latch *clicking*. His expression was his habitual one, a faint meaningless smile, as he added: "Don't worry. I come in the back way."

Clark tossed his Stetson toward the row of pegs on the back of the door. The hat missed and fell to the floor. He ignored it. "Well?"

"Can't a man drop by to offer congratulations?"

"For what?"

"Your new job. Brother, you're in."

Clark was irritated at what he made out as a certain note of disdain in Saygar's voice. He was about to speak, when Saygar added: "And I'm out."

The puzzled frown that crossed Clark's face was intended to mask his foreknowledge of what was coming. "How come?"

Saygar shrugged his thick sloping shoulders and deliberately lowered his boots to the floor. He carefully dusted a peppering of dried mud from the blanket, and only then said: "Sort o' dried up our well, didn't it? This scrap bein' settled so lady-like."

"Did it?" Clark queried cautiously.

"That's the way I figure it. They been layin' off me lately and I've kind o' got used to it. Now all that'll change."

"You can work something out, you and Harper together."

"Sure. But it'll be penny-ante stuff. No one to blame it on now. Maybe I ought to be pullin' out."

Here it is, Clark was thinking, and said aloud: "You'll travel plenty far to beat this set-up."

Saygar shook his head, his look mock sober. He came up out of the chair with surprising ease, a slight forward motion of his thick torso giving him all the momentum needed. Erect, he was a brute of a man, barrel-chested, long-armed.

"Nope," he drawled, "I'm about washed up here. The boys won't stick if the goin' gets hot again."

The suspense was grating on Clark's nerves. Before he realized it, he had worded his worry. "Then you'll be wantin' the four thousand?"

Saygar's two big hands made an outspread gesture of helplessness. "I reckon there ain't no choice."

Clark paced the width of the room to the window, turned there, and said querulously: "You'll have to give me time."

"How much?" Now that the formalities were over, Saygar wasn't wasting words.

"That's something I can't tell. A month, maybe longer. The crew finishes gatherin' week after next. It takes a week to ship and collect my money. What happens in between depends on the weather and how our luck holds. This means I'll have to comb my range pretty clean."

"It'll sure clean it out, brother. What if your friends wise up?"

"It's none o' their blasted business!" Clark flared.

"But it'd be nice if you didn't have to ship all that stuff."

Clark eyed the outlaw coldly, reading something behind the remark without quite knowing what it was. "Meanin' what?" he asked tonelessly.

"Meanin' there are other ways of layin' hands on money. After all, you're president of a bank, or somethin' awful close to one."

"They wouldn't carry me to the tune of another four thousand. You know I already carry a loan with them."

"Did I mention askin' for it?"

The shock of Saygar's words had a visible effect on Clark. The belligerency that had been gathering on his face faded before a look of studied calculation. He appeared to be about to say something, then changed his mind. Saygar sauntered to the door, his hand reaching out for the knob.

"Say a week from now, in Hoelseker's cabin above the basin, Clark," he said.

When Clark appeared not to have heard him, Saygar let himself quietly out into the hall, glancing both ways along it before he closed the door and made for the back stairs.

The Man at the Safe

Bill Lyans had been pulling on his coat as he came out the door of his house and followed Ernie Baker, the Mile High swamper, down off the porch and out onto the dark street.

"How'd it happen?" he asked.

Baker shrugged. "No one knew a thing until Merrill come backward through the window. There ain't a mule alive could have kicked him any harder."

"He's still out?"

"Cold. They carried him across to a room at The Antlers."

Lyans's smile passed unnoticed in the darkness. By rights he should have been angry about being dragged out of a hot midweek bath to officiate at the outcome of a brawl. He wasn't. Half an hour ago he had hurried home to give his wife the news of the settlement made at the Middle Arizona ranchers' meeting.

Her relief had been as keen as his, for the past few weeks had been a waking nightmare to both of them, with the threatened violence between the cattle company and the Mesa Grande outfits a constant worry. As deputy sheriff, responsible for law enforcement in this remote corner of the county, Bill Lyans considered himself a lucky man at the way things had turned out. Now he could concentrate on his job at Olson's feed mill, meanwhile dealing with such petty duties as arose, like this trouble between Merrill and young Bonnyman.

"He'll probably hop that late freight," Baker said as they came abreast of the first darkened stores.

Lyans had been thinking of something else. "Who?" he asked, half absently.

"Joe Bonnyman."

"Here's hopin'." Lyans breathed the words prayerfully, knowing Joe Bonnyman's capacity for making trouble. He considered his natural liking for Yace Bonnyman's wild son as something alien in his make-up, like his taste for whiskey, and now conscientiously tried to bridle his regret at not having seen Joe or had a drink with him during his brief return to Lodgepole. He was sure that Baker's hunch on Joe's leaving was correct.

* * * * *

Ed Merrill was lying on the bed of an upstairs room, head and shoulders propped on pillows. Doc Nesbit was offering him a bottle of smelling salts, which he pushed roughly aside as Baker and the lawman entered. Ruth Merrill was there, holding a lamp Nesbit had needed in applying antiseptic to the cuts and bruises on her brother's face. When Lyans stepped in, she returned the lamp to the table and moved quietly into the background, anticipating an immediate outburst from Ed.

That outburst didn't come. Ed's look turned sullen at sight of the deputy. He seemed about to say something, then evidently changed his mind.

Seeing that Merrill wasn't going to speak, Lyans queried: "Everything all right, Doc?"

"He needs rest. No bones broken." The medico came up off the bed and began packing his black kit bag.

Lyans looked at Merrill and waited, giving the man a second opportunity to speak. But again Merrill chose to retire behind the shell of his sullenness.

"Goin' to bring charges?" Lyans asked at length.

Merrill shook his head.

The deputy lifted his shoulders in a meager gesture of dismissal. Then, seeing the doctor heading for the door and Baker already gone, he felt that his presence here was unwanted, and said: "I'll walk along with you, Doc."

The steps of the two men had receded down the corridor toward the stair head before Ed said querulously: "A sawbones and the law! Where's the coroner? They act like I'd been murdered."

The perfect oval of Ruth Merrill's face took on a smile. "You nearly were," she said, a dry edge to her voice. Abruptly her look changed, robbing her of some of her composure. "What did you say to Joe?"

Ed glowered up at her a moment before answering. "Told him to stay away from you."

She nodded. "And what else?"

"Did there have to be anything else?"

"Yes. If you remember, staying away from me is an old story to Joe. You must have said something else."

Merrill swore softly, adding the weight of a mocking laugh to his words. "Dog-gone it, you're a little flirt! First you wouldn't have anything to do with Joe because he wanted you. Now you've . . ."

The girl's face flamed hotly in anger. All at once she stepped up to the bed, drew back her hand, and slapped her brother hard across his cut and swollen mouth. There was no pity in her as he groaned in pain. She stepped quickly out of the way as his hand snatched out, trying for a hold on her skirt. At the door, turning to give him a last loathing look, she said scathingly: "You're still the same spoiled brat that rubbed burrs in that tame little Shetland's saddle blanket to make him buck. I wish I could hope Joe was staying to finish what he started."

The dark look that came to Ed Merrill's face didn't pass until minutes after she had closed the door and gone to her room. At this moment, he was a man half insane with rage and shame, rage at his sister's reminder of a bullying childhood, shame at having suffered another defeat at the hands of a lifelong enemy. Never before tonight had he been really afraid of Joe Bonnyman. But now, remembering the ease with which Joe had licked him, the studied viciousness of those last blows driving him back through the window, he was afraid, and that fear fed the flames of his impotent hate.

Although he didn't will it, Ed's mind incessantly brought up pictures of the past, mostly of his relations with Joe Bonnyman. In the next couple of hours that he should have spent asleep, he took a better look at himself than ever before in his life, and what he saw didn't please him. He was plagued by the certainty that he had been in the wrong tonight, shamed at having let a smaller man whip him, and finally his fury was directed at the doctor and Bill Lyans for their offers to be helpful. He couldn't put down the idea that they had been making fun of him, gloating over his helplessness in a smug and mock-serious derision. Well, he wasn't going to give anyone else that chance. As he decided that, he was swinging his legs down off the bed and stepping into his boots.

A spell of dizziness, quickly passing, hit Merrill as he stood erect. He looked at his watch and was surprised to find the hour close to 1:00. He went to the window, cupped his hands to his face, and peered out and down along the dark street. There was a light on in the window of a bakery, the semaphore at the station winked greenly, and out beyond that, in the distance, the bright myriad of stars dimmed before the darker shadow of a cloud bank.

Ed crossed the room unsteadily to stand with feet spread widely, peering at his reflection in the cracked mirror over the washstand. His right eye was swollen shut; no matter how hard he tried, he couldn't even slit it open. Both it and the left were purpling under deep bruises. The cheek bone below the shut eye was gashed and a livid red. Merrill had refused to let the doctor put sticking plaster over it. His upper body and arms were sore to the touch in a dozen places, and he couldn't close his left hand because of the intolerable ache in a bone of the palm. He knew that his impulse to ride out home tonight, to avoid the looks and questions of friends and acquaintances on the street tomorrow, was a rash one, yet any amount of torture was worth the saving of his injured pride, and, when he walked back soundlessly along the corridor to the back stairs, he knew that he would get out to Brush tonight if it half killed him.

In the alley, Merrill turned left toward the feed barn lot, hoping the stableman had left his horse in a stall. He had taken perhaps thirty steps, and the outline of the big pole corral was coming up out of the darkness, when a sound from a building close at hand abruptly stopped him.

That building he identified as the Acme Land Company's. The sound he couldn't define; it was a muffled tapping, sharp yet indistinct, the ring of metal on metal. Then, suddenly, Ed was seeing the big safe that sat behind Fred Vanover's desk in the Acme office, and as suddenly knew that someone was trying to break into that safe.

He stood there uncertainly, ruling out at once the idea of calling help because he was in no shape to be seen. His gun was in a pouch of his saddle, down at the barn, but to find the saddle and get back here might mean he'd be too late. Still hesitating, he peered hard into the thick shadow at the building's rear. Something he saw sent him tiptoeing in toward the door, aware that the sounds inside had ceased.

He was reaching out for the broken handle of a broom that leaned against the wall when the door close beside him grated open. Snatching up the rounded three-foot stick, Ed whirled to face the door, and the man who lunged through it. He swung the stick viciously, yet the blow that took his assailant across the forearm only increased the power behind the gun arcing down at Ed's head. Its sharp heel caught him high on the forehead, and made a pulpy sound as it drove deeply in his skull. His big frame went loose all over, and he melted down into the darkness. A moment later a dull heavy *thud* rode across the stillness.

PETER DAWSON

The man who had hit Merrill wheeled in through the doorway quickly on the heel of that muffled explosion. He choked as the stinging stench of burned nitroglycerin bit into his lungs. Coughing, his eyes filled with tears, he crossed the dust-filled room, kicked aside an overturned swivel chair, and pushed open the sprung door to the safe.

By the brief flare of a match the man located a strong box and two filled money sacks. He was out the alley door and running in toward the hotel's high outline by the time the first shout sounded on the street. Presently he disappeared into the shadow at the rear of the hotel. The faint *squeak* of a door hinge deep in that shadow was the only sound that betrayed his entrance into the building.

43

Homeward Bound

Joe Bonnyman was disappointed and angry. Barely a mile out of Lodgepole, he had left the dry, smelly warmth of the stove-heated caboose to stand on its rear platform, his frame wedged against the wall by a boot braced on the sooted railing. There, tense under the violent lurching of the long line of cars gathering speed under two locomotives for the stiff grade leading to the pass, he watched the lights of the town recede into the distance. He could no more define his regret at leaving Lodgepole than he could the impulse that had brought him down here from Wyoming after vowing never to lay eyes on his father again.

The twin ribbons of steel unwound beyond the platform's edge into the night. For a time they held Joe's glance fascinated, two bright spots reflecting the gleam of the caboose's warning lanterns glowing rosily. Finally he let his glance stray to either side and out into the country flanking the railroad's line. To the south the flats stretched mile upon mile, dropping ultimately to the desert, he knew. Northward, he could picture the climbing folds of the sage country that would eventually put a man at the edge of the broad mountain-backed mesa on which Anchor and the other big ranches were lost in the vastness of a rich and grassy land.

Joe tried to put down a small run of excitement as he saw a pinpoint of light shining down from that high country. That light might well be coming from a window of Anchor's sprawling stone house, his home, or it might be the lantern hung outside the bunkhouse door to guide in a late rider, his father, or Blaze.

Joe eyed it long and fixedly, hardly aware of the train's labored jerking as it took the long grade into the low tangle of foothills that was an offshoot of those northward peaks backing Anchor.

Now that Joe was alone and could look back sanely upon the night's happenings, his mind gradually built a web of thinking that was logical and dispassionate. Back there his judgment had been a little warped by the unexpectedness of once more clashing with his father's will. But little of his anger remained when he remembered Yace's look, how much he had visibly aged. He knew his father must feel himself on the downgrade of life. Soon, five years from now, ten at the outside, Yace would be but a shell of the man whose brute strength and iron will had carved a cattle empire from this far frontier. Then, his family gone, the fruits of his life's struggle would seem barren and valueless in his loneliness. Yes, even Yace Bonnyman would one day find his world meaningless.

A slow rebellion built up in Joe as this picture flashed before his mind's eye. He could even feel sympathy for Yace, see him as a pathetic, lost figure whose only solace would come in memories of days long gone. He considered his reasons for leaving—his inability to get on with Yace, his reluctance to face the blame for his original foolhardy act of selling out to Middle Arizona. And he knew now that, wherever he went, whatever he did, the memory of having backed down before these two obstacles would always rankle.

It naturally followed that Joe began considering ways to make amends, supposing for the moment that he stayed on in this country. He could avoid Yace, get a job that would never take him to Anchor; the job Clark had offered was such a one. He could pull in his horns, mind his own business, and maybe one day prove to the others that he wasn't all bad. Blaze had been right; he should take the chip off his shoulder. People would gradually forget, so would Yace, and in the end, when time had glossed over the past, he could one day go back to Anchor.

Suddenly Joe awoke to the fact that his problem was already half solved. In his experience, the actual doing of a thing was, more often than not, less difficult than deciding to do it. Now that he had decided there was no logical reason for not remaining here, the thing to do was act on that decision.

He did, turning at once in through the door into the caboose's now dark interior. The conductor had undoubtedly turned into his bunk for a couple of hours' sleep before the train reached Junction. The brakeman was up in the cupola, at his solitary vigil of watching the top of the long line of freight cars.

Joe lugged saddle and war bag out onto the platform, and then down the steps. He tossed the saddle down the embankment, and then, war bag in hand, swung out with a tight hold on the hand rail. He hung there for a moment, judging the train's speed. When he did let go and jump, he found the shadows deceptive.

Misjudging the depth of his fall, he landed with knees rigid. His weight overbalanced and he fell inward, barely avoiding the iron steps. His war bag was torn from his grasp and his left arm whipped down across the near rail with such force that it set up an ache that traveled to his shoulder. Then, the pain quickly passing, he lugged the war bag back to where the saddle lay, and stood peering out across the night-shrouded reach of land close by.

Off there some place, no farther than a mile, he judged, lay Ernie Baker's ranch house. Ernie was good for the loan of a horse.

Joe cached the war bag under a piñon close to the embankment, and, slinging the saddle over his shoulder, set off diagonally northwest from the line of the rails. He didn't mind the long walk that lay ahead, for his mind was at ease and a world that had minutes ago seemed gloomy and depressing was now to his liking.

It was less to his liking some forty minutes later, as he threw his saddle on the back of a scrubby big-headed bronco alongside

Ernie Baker's corral. His only greeting had been the persistent yapping of a cur dog that had heard his approach and signaled it long and loudly.

The weathered frame house was deserted, and Joe had found the corral gate open. It was only by accident that this pony had been inside the enclosure, licking at a salt block. There was every evidence of Baker's having been away for several days.

As he reined the tough-mouthed horse out across the barn lot, Joe remembered that Baker usually worked for one of the mesa outfits each fall on roundup. Doubtless the man now lay asleep in his blankets close to one of the chuck wagons working the higher hills.

Within 100 yards of the corral, Joe realized that his luck had been bad on the horse. The animal was lamed in the right foreleg. Dismounting, Joe inspected the leg and found a swelling above the hoof. It wasn't sore to the touch, but neither was it sound. Anchor lay a good twenty miles away, and Joe doubted that the animal was good for that distance. But he would use him until he lamed badly.

He rode back and found his war bag. When he had tied it to the cantle and had pointed the pony's head toward the peaks, he was whistling. It was good to be on his way home.

The Horsehair Hatband

Fred Vanover's face as he looked in upon the lantern-lighted ruin of Acme's office showed as bleak an expression as Lyans or any other of the half dozen men inside had ever seen it wear. The Middle Arizona man had been informed of the main fact on his way down with Roy Keech, the hotel clerk, who had been sent to get him. He knew that the safe had been robbed, and he knew that Ed Merrill lay dead in the alley, the front of his skull crushed in from the blow of a gun butt.

He now looked at Lyans and at Clark Dunne, standing alongside the deputy, as he came in the door, and Lyans said courteously: "We didn't touch a thing, Mister Vanover."

The Middle Arizona man nodded briefly and surveyed the room. The safe's flimsy door was buckled outward, torn from its lower nickeled hinge. The roll-top desk had been pushed away by the concussion, three of its slats broken in by a piece of flying metal. The swivel chair lay on its side on the floor. Both lamps had fallen and were broken, ringed by their puddles of coal oil. The big window at the front was now glassless. Vanover had noticed that someone had swept the walk outside clear.

The extent of the wreckage left Vanover with a helpless, muddled feeling. Because he didn't know Lyans well, his look went to Clark Dunne as he asked: "Any ideas?"

"Not many, Fred," Clark told him. "The safe door was pried open above the lock, and nitroglycerin poured down the slot. Whoever did it broke into the powder shed behind the hardware store and stole what he needed. That safe wasn't any too strong."

48

"I've been trying to get them to send me a new one," Vanover said ruefully.

"You'll have to tell us what's missin'," Lyans put in, and stepped over to hold his lantern so that its light illuminated the safe's interior.

Vanover knelt in front of the deputy. His brief glance showed him the strongbox and the two money bags missing. He said tonelessly, speaking more to himself than to them: "This is out of my hands now. They'll send their own crew up here to recover the money."

"Was there much?" Clark asked.

Vanover looked back over his shoulder at him. "Close to nine thousand. My instructions were to have it on hand to make a cash payment on any outfit that came up for sale."

Lyans whistled softly, eloquently. "That much?"

Vanover nodded and came erect, his face looking tired and worn. "Have you moved him?" he asked quietly.

"No. He's out there." Lyans led the way to the alley door and, through it, stepped aside and held his lantern extended so that the canvas-covered mound lying close to the door was fully lighted. He motioned to a man standing beyond, and the canvas was pulled back to reveal Ed Merrill's body lying huddled, face down, one arm out of sight. It was as though Merrill had gone to sleep under a light covering, and had hunched his big frame together against the night's bitter chill.

Vanover took a hasty look. "Where was he hit?"

"Stoop down and you can see," Lyans said. "We ain't touched him yet. Wanted you to be here before we did."

The pallor of Vanover's face clearly indicated his reluctance to be a witness to this. Without bothering to inspect the body further, he said: "Go ahead with what you have to do."

Lyans set his lantern on the ground, nodded to the man who had been standing guard, and together they knelt and gently rolled the body on its back. Vanover looked away quickly as the gaping hole in the forehead came into sight. Because he looked away, he didn't know the reason for the deputy's quick intake of breath.

It was Clark Dunne, behind Vanover, who asked: "What is it, Bill?"

"Have a look for yourself."

Only then, when he realized that something unusual was happening, did Vanover force himself to look again. When he did, it was to see a braided band of black-and-white horsehair clenched tightly in Merrill's hand, the hand that had been out of sight beneath his body.

"You're a witness to this, Mister Vanover," Lyans said tonelessly. "He must've grabbed it just as he was hit. Who knows where it came from?"

There were seven men crowded around the body now, those who had been in the office plus one or two more who had been waiting out here. One of them spoke up immediately: "I wouldn't swear it was his, but Joe Bonnyman used to own a hatband a lot like that."

"Don't be a fool, Corwine," Clark Dunne said softly, yet explosively. "Joe couldn't have done this . . . wouldn't. He's not the kind to club a man with the butt end of a gun. Besides, Blaze and I were with him when he climbed onto that late freight. He's fifty miles from here by now."

"Let's get this straight," Lyans said quickly, eying the man who had identified the hatband. "You're sure about this, Corwine? It's Bonnyman's?"

"Holy mackerel, no, I ain't sure. I said it could be."

"And them two had a scrap tonight," Lyans breathed, thinking aloud. Sudden determination showed on his face as he wheeled on the nearest man. "Al, go get Johns out of bed and down to the station to wire the agent at Junction. He's to find out if Bonnyman's on that train. She's due at Junction at two-ten. If Bonnyman ain't on the train, tell Johns to get a report from the conductor on when he got off." He nodded to the man who had been watching the body. "You and Bates carry him on down to Hill's, Ned. The rest of you hang around until I get the report. We may have some ridin' to do before mornin'."

Ned and two others were lifting the body, slung in the canvas, ready to carry it on down the alley to the undertaker's, before anyone spoke.

It was Clark Dunne who said gravely: "I'd go easy on this angle, Bill. Joe isn't a killer. He's on that train, I tell you. If that's Joe's hatband, there's a good reason for its being here."

"Sure, sure," Lyans drawled easily. "Only you don't expect me to just forget about it, do you?"

* * * * *

Jean Vanover had been wakened by the strident knocking on the front door, and was about to answer it when she heard her father cross the living room. A moment later she recognized Roy Keech's excited voice and, standing at the head of the back hallway, caught most of what he said. A strong foreboding took her as he told of the robbery, an intuitive feeling that the suspicions and hatreds eased by tonight's agreement between the ranchers and Middle Arizona might come alive again. But, more immediately important, was the tragedy of Ed Merrill's death.

As Lyans's messenger finished giving Fred Vanover the brief but grisly facts on the killing, Jean called: "Dad, what's being done about Ruth? She's there alone at the hotel, isn't she? Could I go stay with her?"

Keech answered out of the darkness: "That'd sure be a help, ma'am. Far as I know, Lyans ain't thought of any way to tell her yet. She's in room Number Fourteen."

Jean dressed hurriedly, hearing her father and Keech leave before she had quite finished. Out on the street, she gathered her coat tightly about her against the bite of the cold night air. She took the dogleg bend in the street, and, seeing the crowd and the lights at the Land Office close ahead, she purposely avoided going over there by keeping to the opposite walk. She wished she could be with her father now, to help him take this bitter defeat that might undo all the fruits of his long struggle to settle things peaceably with the ranchers. But this other was more important. Ruth Merrill's manner was always proud and distant, not only toward her alone; Jean knew that at such a time as this the girl would be alone and friendless, and the stubborn streak in her wouldn't let her side with others when it came to gloating over Ruth's misery.

The upper hallway of The Antlers was empty and so dark that Jean had a hard time finding the Number 14 on a door far back along it. Her knock remained unanswered for a long interval, so that she had to repeat it, much louder the second time.

Finally Ruth Merrill's voice called sleepily: "Who is it?"

"Jean Vanover, Ruth. May I come in?"

Ruth made some unintelligible response and Jean tried the door. It was locked. She waited as sounds of movement came from inside. Finally lamplight glowed beneath the sill, and a moment later the door opened on Ruth. She was pulling a robe about her, tying its cord. Her silvery blonde hair was mussed, the braids hanging down her back loosened to give her a slightly disheveled look. Typically she smoothed down the robe at her slender waist and reached up to run a high-backed comb through her hair; her two hands came down to rub color into her cheeks, and at once she was her usual beautiful self, calm, assured, her look a trifle aloof as she said: "Isn't it rather late?"

"Yes, Ruth. But something has happened. It . . ."

"To Ed?" Ruth asked with surprising intuition. She stepped aside and Jean moved past her into the room.

"Yes, to Ed. There's been an accident."

Jean was trying to think of words to add, words that would ease the shock of the message she was bringing, when Ruth breathed softly: "He's dead. I know it. You don't need to tell me."

All Jean could do was give a brief nod of her dark head and watch the change that came over the other girl. Ruth seemed to shrink visibly, to lose her proud bearing as her shoulders sagged lifelessly. Her bright-blue eyes became moist, then tear-filled, and she was no longer quite so beautiful. Jean held out her arms. The other girl, stripped of her cloak of pride, came to her, trying to stifle a sob.

"It'll do you good to cry, Ruth," Jean said softly.

In the following minutes she was humble before the knowledge that Ruth Merrill wasn't the cold and unapproachable woman she had always appeared to be. She was but a girl, tragically lost in a maëlstrom of grief, bewildered and afraid. And, when that spasm of grief had worn itself out, Ruth Merrill showed the tough fiber of her make-up. Gently she pulled away from Jean, dried her eyes, and said: "You are kind, Jean. Now tell me how it happened, all of it."

Jean told what she knew, of the robbery, what Keech had told her father, omitting only the hotel clerk's lurid details of Ed's death. Ruth listened without once interrupting, dispassionately now, as though the well of emotion within her had been drained dry.

As Jean finished, an enigmatic smile touched the other girl's face. Catching Jean's puzzled look, she said in a tense and low voice: "I'm only thinking how typical this is of everything that's ever happened to Ed. In a way I can be sorry for him. In another way I can't. Tonight I hated him, loathed him for what he tried to do to Joe. Is it cruel of me to say that? I was glad he got that beating."

"I don't know, Ruth."

"He's always hated Joe. Tonight he must have heard that Joe's father had turned him out again. He must have decided to kick the man while he was down. Well, it didn't turn out that way. Ed must have been thinking of that, of the beating he took, when he died." In the silence that followed, Ruth seemed to be staring through Jean, not seeing her, as an imaginary picture blocked out of the real one. "Ed could never understand that I loved Joe, that I still do love him."

"You love Joe Bonnyman?" Jean breathed incredulously. "I thought you and Clark . . ."

Ruth laughed uneasily and turned to walk to the bed and sit on it. She clasped her hands tightly in her lap, so tightly that her slender fingers were white at the knuckles. She eyed Jean squarely, intently, as she said: "It shouldn't matter to me that you understand how I feel. But it does. Someone must understand. Ever since I can remember, Joe Bonnyman has stirred up a feeling in me that's like the run of a grass fire before the wind. He's the only man who ever affected me that way. He's everything Ed wasn't. Perhaps that's why I liked him so much. He's kind and impulsive, and maybe a little wild. But he was never cruel, even in what he did to his father. Ed was cruel. He was calculating. All his life he hated Joe. And because we were so opposite, I suppose he drove me toward Joe."

Jean caught the touch of hysteria in Ruth's voice. "You'd better lie down," she said. "I'll see if the doctor won't let you have some sleeping tablets."

"I don't want to sleep." Ruth said. "I want to think, to get things straight. Seeing Joe tonight has changed things as much as Ed's not being here to hound me any longer will change them." There came again that strange smile of a moment ago, one that did little to heighten Ruth's good looks. "You wonder how I can talk of Joe in the face of things as they stand between Clark and me? Jean, I have a little of the devil in me. Joe was mine once, and I wouldn't have him. Now that I have Clark, I'm not the least surprised that it's Joe I'm thinking of. But can't you see, it always has been Joe? There was never anyone . . ."

They both turned at a knock on the door. A quick change came over Ruth, and once more she gave momentary attention to her appearance, lifting her hands to smooth her hair, to gather the robe closer at her neck. Then she called: "Come in!"

It was Bill Lyans who stood in the doorway as the panel swung open. His hat was in his hand, and there was an uncomfortable look on his face at having invaded the privacy of a woman's bed-room. He gave Ruth a quick glance, and his eye went to the floor, defensive in his embarrassment.

"I wanted to stop in and tell you how sorry I am this happened," he said tonelessly. "We'll all miss Ed."

"It's nice of you to say that, Bill. Yes, we'll miss him."

"We found something that may help us," the deputy went on hastily. He dipped a hand in a coat pocket and brought out the horsehair hatband. Before he had a chance to continue, Ruth gave an audible gasp and his eyes went to hers, intercepting their startled expression. For a moment he was puzzled, then he asked: "Know whose it is?"

"Joe's," Ruth breathed. "Where did you find it?"

"In Ed's hand." he told her. "It looks like pretty clear proof that Bonnyman killed him."

"No!" Ruth was up off the bed, fists clenched, eyes blazing defiance. "It couldn't be! Joe wouldn't kill that way. Ed wasn't that important to him."

"He knocked Ed through a saloon window not three hours ago," Lyans reminded her.

"That!" Ruth was breathing deeply, as though from violent exertion. "It was some silly argument they had."

"Did Ed tell you what it was?"

Jean Vanover's glance was fully on the other girl, waiting for her answer. Strangely enough, she hoped that Ruth would have that answer, one that would clear Joe Bonnyman of guilt in this murder. She didn't know why that hope struck her, but it was there.

But Lyans's question brought a look of uncertainty to Ruth's face. "Of course he did," she answered evasively.

"What was it?"

Ruth hesitated a moment, as though deciding something. Then: "Ed had once warned Joe to stay away from me. He warned him again tonight. Joe wouldn't take it, so they fought."

Lyans shrugged and put the hatband back in his pocket. "It won't hurt to check up," he said. "Johns is wirin' the agent at Junction to find out if Joe's on that late freight. If he is, he's cleared." The deputy paused a moment before adding: "And I'm hopin' he is on it." He looked again at the two girls in the same embarrassed way he had at first entering the room and muttered: "I'd better be goin'."

"Wait." Ruth's word stopped him. "What if Joe isn't on the train?"

"Then we'll have to get out and hunt him."

"But you can't believe he would murder a man!"

"If it was him, he not only committed murder, but robbery as well. Whoever did it got close to nine thousand from Acme's safe."

Peculiarly enough, Jean felt little emotion beyond a curious anger as her fear of Acme's loss was substantiated. She was too engrossed in Ruth Merrill's strange determination to defend the man who might be her brother's murderer, too wrapped in her own odd wish to see Joe cleared, to take in the full significance of what the robbery might mean to her father.

"So you've already found a victim?" Ruth gave a laugh edged with hysteria. "Why would Joe steal?"

"A lot can happen to a man in five years," Lyans said mildly but pointedly. "Maybe he figured Middle Arizona got his layout for a song. Fact is, they did."

There was loathing and contempt in the look Ruth gave the lawman. But she had herself well under control now, and, when she spoke, her voice was firmer. "Will you promise me one thing? To let me know before you go ahead on this?"

"That's fair enough," he agreed. "After all, you got the right to know before we . . ."

He broke off in mid-sentence as steps sounded on the stairs coming up out of the lobby. He turned into the doorway and looked along the hall.

"Clark . . . and Johns," he said shortly. "Johns has probably talked with Junction."

Jean could see the tension that ripped Ruth as they waited for the approach of Clark Dunne and the station agent along the hallway. Although her instinct was to side with this girl, she was disturbed by the contradiction in Ruth's reasons for wanting to prove Joe Bonnyman innocent. Here was a girl who, on the surface at least, had everything she wanted. Yet she was pushing aside all the ethics of convention to protect the man who might be her brother's murderer. It was bewildering to Jean to understand Ruth's real feelings in the face of everything she knew about her, of her feeling for Clark Dunne, for instance. It was even more bewildering to understand her own feelings at this moment.

Clark was first in the door. He came over at once to Ruth, taking her in his arms. But in the moment she should have answered his embrace, she pushed away and looked at Johns.

"What did you find out?" she asked.

"Looks like it was Bonnyman," Johns answered respectfully. What he next said was directed to the deputy. "They don't know where he left the train, or when. The conductor hit the blankets right after he left here, and the brakeman was sittin' look-out."

Lyans looked at Clark, and the rancher said: "That's still not proof."

"We'll see." The deputy started out the door.

"Where are you going?" Ruth spoke so sharply that Lyans stopped in mid-stride.

When he faced her again, his face bore a harassed look. "To look for him, I reckon. It ain't that I want to do this, Miss Merrill. But a man's been murdered, your brother. Bonnyman could've left that train close to a dozen places where he could find a horse and get back here. The time checks pretty close. What I'm scared of is that he's got away."

Ruth gave no answer to that, and Lyans, sensing her antagonism toward his line of reasoning, went out into the hallway and along it, followed by Johns. They heard Johns ask—"You want me any more, Bill?"—and the deputy answered: "Yeah. You're to wire Gap and Junction and tell 'em to be on the look out for . . ." There his words became lost in an unintelligible mutter as he went down the stairs.

Jean was feeling uncomfortable at having witnessed the contradictions of these past twenty minutes. She felt sorry for Ruth, and at the same time angry at her for having so openly defied all the conventions that should govern her action and thought at a moment like this.

"I mustn't stay, Ruth," she said now. "We'd like to have you come to the house if it would be any more comfortable for you."

"Don't go yet, please." Ruth turned to Clark. "Will you do something for me, Clark?"

"Name it," he said.

"They'll send out a posse, won't they?"

He nodded soberly, frowning in his effort to see what she was leading up to.

"And Joe would naturally head for Anchor, wouldn't he? To see Blaze and get an outfit for the ride out across the hills."

Clark's look sharpened. "Joe didn't do this, Ruth. He couldn't have . . ."

Jean wondered why he didn't complete his thought.

"But Bill Lyans thinks he did. So will the others," Ruth insisted. "It's up to you to get out there and warn him, warn him to keep out of sight, to get out of the country, anything to avoid arrest."

"I tell you Joe didn't do it."

"Of course he didn't." The perfunctory way Ruth gave her denial made it plain to Clark that she didn't believe what she was saying, and Jean caught his look of astonished bewilderment. "You must tell Lyans you're riding out to break the news to Father. You might even start with the posse. But you're to get to Anchor before them. Do you understand, Clark? You mustn't let them take Joe."

His look underwent a slow change, one Jean couldn't understand. It hardened out of perplexity into a cool restraint. "You still care for him, don't you, Ruth?" he asked tonelessly.

"Of course I do. He's an old friend. I don't want to see him made a victim by all these people who hate him."

"But supposing he really killed Ed?" Clark's question demanded an answer.

"Then he must have had a good reason."

Clark let a moment's silence run out before he said: "You're defending him, even if he's guilty?"

"But he isn't. You say so yourself." Ruth laid her hand on his arm and gave him a warm smile as she gently turned him toward the door. "Come back as soon as you can, Clark. I'll want to know."

He hesitated, seeming about to protest. But in the end he left without a word.

Jean was trying to think of a way to excuse herself when Ruth gave her a look that was relieved, almost happy. "You really wouldn't mind staying with me tonight?" she asked. "You can get your things and come back. I don't think I could bear it to stay here alone. They'll think they have to come and sit with me, talk with me . . . all these women who hate me. You're very kind, Jean." Having thus put Jean to an inconvenience, rather than herself, Ruth put her arm around the other girl, ushered her to the door, and said: "Don't be long, will you?"

* * * * *

Down on the street, walking toward the jail where a dozen riders were already gathered, Clark Dunne faced the sober fact that his guess of earlier tonight had been proved correct. Excitement and nerve strain had robbed Ruth of a measure of her subtlety; otherwise, she would have sent him on this errand without betraying the fact that tonight had seen a revival of her former feeling for Joe. The realization of how exactly the facts were matching with the somber picture of his earlier imagining did nothing to improve Clark's frame of mind.

A loose board on the high-galleried front of a store across the way banged before a gust of wind. Dust was lifted from the street and swirled across to fog the light of the posse lanterns. The wind cut through Clark's coat, laying a cold touch along his back. Glancing skyward, he couldn't see the stars, and judged that it would be snowing before long. He would have to get his sheepskin before he started out.

As Clark approached, Bill Lyans came onto the walk, four rifles under his arm. He handed them out to the waiting men, saying brusquely: "We'll stick together as far as Bonnyman's, and then split up in twos. Sparling leave?"

One of the men gave an affirmative. Clark saw his chance to speak, and said casually: "Someone ought to swing off to Merrill's. Reckon that's my job. Wait for me at Anchor, Bill."

Lyans gave him a brief look that held a meaning Clark didn't grasp until the deputy said: "Sparling's already left for Brush. It'll save you the trip."

Thus, offhandedly, did Bill Lyans let Clark know where he stood. The deputy had delegated another man to a task that was logically Clark's. Clark was a friend of Joe's, and was therefore to be watched until the hunt was well organized.

"As you say, Bill," Clark answered, only faintly irritated by the studied unconcern of the others, who understood well enough what was going on. He found satisfaction in not being able to follow Ruth's wishes. What he didn't like, though, was the prospect of having to be under Lyans's orders during the hunt for Joe. Certain private matters needed his urgent attention, and this misdirected manhunt might prove a costly waste of time. However, there was nothing he could do about it.

Manhunt

The wind came out of the east, its first fitful gusts bringing snow. It whipped down the washes below the mesa rim, kicking up a scud of dust so thick that Joe Bonnyman tilted his head against it, eyes squinted. But that wind bore a sweet smell of grass, and drove out the tang of sage that had been in his nostrils these past two hours. He welcomed it. He would always associate that fresh sweet odor with home.

He had quit the roan two miles back, not wanting to lame the animal too badly. He'd left his saddle and war bag back there, pausing only long enough to get his gun and strap it about his waist. He had chosen to wear the weapon out of habit that had lately become too strong to ignore, an instinct that warned him never to travel a strange country without it.

He was, he judged, still some seven miles short of Anchor. Somewhere east of him, into the wind and close, lay the trail that climbed gradually toward Tom Sommers's place and, beyond that, led to Anchor. He could get a horse at Sommers's.

He heard the faint drum of hoofs at almost the exact moment that he saw the faint ribbons of the road's wheel marks directly ahead and downward over the rim of a high bank. Then a gust of wind brought the sound of voices. They came from downward and to his right. Someone was coming up the trail.

Joe's first inclination was to call out. His second, the stronger, was to step back into the tree shadows and wait, trusting to luck to identify the riders, for the increasing volume of sound had by now told him that there were several, and he knew that wherever several men gathered there would be at least one or two who wasted no love on him.

A pair of moving shapes came into sight suddenly, almost directly below him, so dense was the darkness. One he made out as a gray horse and its rider; the second man was astride a darker animal. Close behind came three more, then another pair, then a single horseman. As this last lone rider came abreast him, Joe decided to call out.

But at the moment he was about to hail the man, one of the pair directly ahead said distinctly: "How'll we know this gent Bonnyman after we split up, Sid? You 'n' me have never set eyes on him."

The single rider answered that question, and, when he spoke, Joe recognized Al Corwine's voice. "He's about your size, Mel, only bigger through. But don't worry. You ain't goin' to see him. If it was him, he's hightailed."

"You reckon it really was him?" the man who had spoken first queried.

"Search me," Corwine replied. "He's sure changed a lot if it was. Time was when me and him . . ." A gust of wind whipped away his further words and shortly he was swallowed by the darkness.

The words he had heard had turned Joe rigid, so that he stood for a long moment in the shocked paralysis of complete surprise. And now he remembered the gray colt Bill Lyans had bought shortly before his leaving, five years ago. This was a posse. These men were out looking for him. Lyans was in the lead.

Joe had but a brief moment to weigh the implications behind this realization when other riders passed below, many of them. He stopped counting when their number totaled fifteen, knowing that something momentous and awful had taken place to put so many men on the trail in the beginnings of this unseasonable storm. Then they were gone, and he was left standing there in a futile attempt to fathom the reason for their search. He'd fought

Ed Merrill, given him a bad licking. But was that any reason for men to be out searching the country for him? It could be a reason if Ed had died without regaining consciousness. But if that had happened, how could they know he wasn't on that freight, somewhere far west of Junction by now?

The moan of the wind abruptly eased off, leaving a stillness so complete and empty as to give him an uneasy feeling. It was as though that wild rush of wind had formed the background for a violent upheaval of his very foundations and, now that he was thoroughly shaken, was giving him a brief respite in which to gather strength. He couldn't think in this strange stillness, couldn't decide what to do, even to move on down into the trail. He knew that he would have to plan carefully, to find his way out of the country somehow. Or he might yet get to Anchor and to Blaze. Blaze would know what was wrong.

Into the jumble of his thoughts came a sound, the nervous stomping of a horse close below, the irritated expelling of a man's breath as he muttered: "Whoa, you loco Jughead!" Someone was down there, downtrail, beyond the limits of Joe's vision. And because there were no other voices, he concluded that the rider was alone.

He started down the steep incline to the trail, digging boot heels into the sandy clay to keep from slipping. At the foot of the slope he wheeled sharply to the right. Within five paces he came within sight of two vague shapes, a horse and a rider out of the saddle. The man was hunched down alongside the horse.

Sensing Joe's stealthy approach, the animal shied nervously, and the man said irritably: "Stand, blast you!"

Joe could see now that the man was working at a broken stirrup leather. He lifted his gun clear of holster when he was two paces away. Peering hard into the darkness, he tried to be sure of the exact outline of the man's head against the dark background of the horse. He was reassured at seeing the reins looped over the rider's arm as he took the final step in.

He struck sharply downward with the .38's long barrel. The man's Stetson cushioned the shock nicely. Joe could feel that the blow was expertly struck even before his victim's outline melted into the shadows toward the ground. The horse reared, but was checked by the taut reins. Joe knelt and unwound the reins from the arm of the unconscious man. He found himself looking down into the face of a man he knew, Sam Thrall, owner of the Emporium in Lodgepole.

An unamused smile was on Joe's face as he straightened after his brief inspection of Thrall to finish the task the man had nearly completed, the repairing of a broken latigo. The horse was a big black animal with good legs and a light mouth. That much Joe discovered before the horse had taken a dozen prancing steps. This was the kind of horseflesh Joe would have expected Sam Thrall to travel on, high-spirited, probably a good part thorough-bred, the kind of animal the average cowpuncher would give his right arm to own, but rarely did.

A scabbard was laced to the saddle and held a .30-30 carbine. A canvas bag filled with light provisions was tied to the cantle; there was also a poncho, and, as the wind resumed its fitful whine, bringing a stronger spitting of snow now, Joe unlaced the poncho and pulled it on. Reining the black left out of the trail, he headed into the southwest at a steady trot.

He had gone less than fifty rods when he pulled the animal in sharply, only then fully aware that his instinct for self-preservation had automatically started him on a line that would take him around the southward spur of hills and out of this country. He was running again. From what, he had no way of knowing. It was the very thing he had rebelled against when he jumped the train. No, this was even worse, for now he didn't know what he was running from. And for the second time tonight a strong rebellion and anger was in him. In the next few minutes there was a stiffening of his pride, an unconscious realization that, if he was ever to fight this hang-dog instinct, he would have to fight it now. Just as quickly as he had stopped, he had seen the fallacy of his move and was reining the pony around, heading him north.

He knew this country well, even in pitch-black darkness. Topping the low hill to the west of Sommers's place, he angled obliquely to the left, farther west, knowing the trail lay half a mile to his right. He put the black into an easy lope, judging that the posse would hold its steady pace and that shortly he could angle back into the trail and ahead of it.

* * * * *

Blaze couldn't be quite sure of the exact moment the change came over Yace, but it was there, a fading of his first helpless bewilderment and the gathering of a fury that put a cold gleam of defiance in his pale-gray eyes. Had the light been better, had Bill Lyans and these others concentrated more on Yace and less on giving the last gruesome detail of their story, they would have been less emphatic.

Finally the outburst came. Lyans was speaking when Yace cut in on him with an explosive: "Hang it, watch your tongue! Leave Joe out of this!"

"We're only tellin' you what happened," Lyans said defensively.

"You accuse Joe of clubbin' a man to death with an iron. It's a lie. Much as I hate his guts, I won't believe that of him."

Lyans glanced around at the others for support. None came.

Blaze gave only half his attention to what was said after that, for he was puzzled by this change in Yace, in the cowman's defending his son now, where four hours ago he had driven him from home a second time. Trying to see what lay behind the old man's stubbornly defiant attitude, Blaze came to the gradual realization of a truth that had escaped him all these years.

That other time it had been the same, Yace publicly defending his wild and reckless offspring, while privately making Joe's life unbearable. Then, having driven Joe into committing a foolhardy act, having forced him to make that attempt at independence,

Yace had turned on his son with an awesome intensity. The reason, Blaze knew now for the first time, was that Yace Bonnyman put a higher value on public opinion than he did on understanding. Just now he was confused, hiding behind his natural belligerence until he made up his mind which way the wind blew. Perhaps he really believed what he claimed, that Joe wasn't capable of cold-blooded murder. But stronger than that belief, Blaze knew, was anger at these men for having branded his own flesh and blood with the mark of suspected murder. Yace was being prodded at his most tender spot, his pride, and he rebelled. And Blaze now saw in him not the massive symbol of brute strength and power he had always seemed, but simply an old man, harried and uncertain, more to be pitied than admired.

The foreman's glance strayed around the big cavernous living room. Even the dozen men grouped here at its far end were lost in its immensity. It was a dreary room where once it had been gay and cheerful. Most of its feminine touches were gone; its high-beamed ceiling sent back hollow echoes of the subdued voices; its somber emptiness was a far cry from those days when Caroline Bonnyman had filled it with countless guests and parties and good times. *Like the night we celebrated their twentieth anniversary*, Blaze was thinking. *Seven cases of champagne and the table saggin' under all that food. Yace with his arm across Joe's shoulders, both of them bellowin' like a pair of tomcats over there by the piano. Couldn't hear yourself talk for the laughin' and the music.* These days the room, always closed, was a striking symbol of Yace Bonnyman's last few barren years.

Yet for a brief moment now, as Yace countered a statement of Lyans's with—"Blast it, he had money! Why would he bust open a safe?"—Blaze had the feeling that the room might once again come awake before a revival of the old carefree days. He was momentarily inclined to think that he had been mistaken, that maybe this time Yace meant what he was saying, that he was with his son once more. They would make an unbeatable pair, come what might. Then, dully, he realized that this was wishful thinking, that Yace was merely keeping a hold on his pride by this defense of Joe, that there could never be a reconciliation between father and son. And it would take that, nothing short of it, to bring alive the haunting memories Blaze always associated with this room.

With an effort, Blaze brought his attention around to what Lyans was saying, hearing: "All right, I'll go along with you in hopin' it wasn't Joe. But who was it?"

Blaze himself was speaking before he quite realized it, wording the first idea that struck him: "Why not check on where Neal Harper was tonight?"

The deputy's glance narrowed as it came around to Blaze. "What's Harper got to do with this?" he queried tonelessly.

"He's out of a job, him and his gun-slick crew, now that Middle Arizona's saved itself a scrap."

"So he's out of a job," Lyans agreed warily.

"Supposin' he figured it this way." Blaze paused a moment to think the thing through. He looked at the others before continuing. "Winter's on the way and him and his hardcases will be ridin' the grubline. He's sore because Vanover can't pay him fightin' wages any longer, so he decides to collect what he figures the outfit owes him. He blows open the Acme safe. As he hightails, he runs into Merrill."

A weighty silence followed his words. It was Yace who finally said: "Now we're gettin' somewhere. It'd take a cold-blooded devil like Harper to kill that way. When you do find your man, it'll turn out to be something like Blaze says, some . . ."

"Hold on!" Lyans cut in. "What about that hatband of Joe's? We can't just settle on a man we'd like to see guilty and say he done it."

"No," agreed Blaze, "but that hatband don't prove anything. Joe could have lost it. I'm only tryin' to point out that there are other angles to look into. You'll admit Harper's a possibility. He's

proddy, dangerous as a sidewinder, and probably riled over bein'
fired. He might've found the hatband and worked a frame-up
around it. All I say is . . . check up on a few like him."

The eyes of the gathered men left Blaze as the massive door
leading out to the *portal* opened and Shorty Adams, an Anchor
crewman, gaunt even in the shapeless loose hang of his poncho,
came through it and closed it in a hard *slam* against the rush of
wind. His glance drifted over the group, and then swung to the
room's far end.

"Where's Sam Thrall?" he queried, frowning.

"Not here," answered Clark Dunne.

"Then Quinn's right," Shorty breathed, and their attention
came more sharply to him. "Somethin' mighty queer's happened,
Lyans. Quinn says Sam dropped back to fix his cinch a mile or
so below Sommers's place. He hadn't caught up by the time you
pulled in here. Couple of minutes ago, Quinn says, he wondered
what was slowin' Sam, so he took a look out the cook shack door
to the head of the lane, to see if he was on the way in. Then he
seen somethin' movin' over by the wagon barn, a rider. He swears
it was Sam's black, the one with the two white stockings. So he
calls out. Instead of answerin', this jasper fades out of sight down
by the big corral."

"Quinn's spooked over nothin'," Lyans said. "How's breakfast
comin'?" He had delegated Adams and Quinn to cook a meal
for the posse in the absence of the cook, who was somewhere up
Porcupine Cañon with the Anchor chuck wagon and crew.

"It'll be ready in a minute." Shorty's face didn't lose its look
of gravity. "You'd better come have a look, Bill. We went over to
the shed and found a lot o' gear and harness layin' around, and
maybe half a bushel of oats scattered on the floor by the bin. That
ain't the way we keep the place, is it, Blaze?"

"Shucks, no," Yace answered for his foreman. Although he
wore only underwear, Levi's, and boots, having been roused from
bed by the posse's arrival, he was the first to start toward the door.

Following Yace out across the broad *portal,* Blaze took down the lantern that was hanging on a roof post to light the house's main entrance. He tilted his head against the frigid bite of the wind and buckled his windbreaker tightly at the neck as he and the others started over to the wagon shed. Beyond the far corner of the house he found it hard to walk against the wind and keep up with Anchor's shirtless owner, for there it blew in off the mesa with full force. A foot-deep drift of snow had already piled up at the lee corner of the wagon shed, and Blaze was thankful for the relief of stepping in behind that building's protection. He grunted—"Here, let me."—when Yace fumbled awkwardly with cold-numbed fingers at the door hasp.

As Shorty Adams had said, the floor below the front rack was strewn with a disorderly array of harness. Across the way, by the grain bin, a couple of scoops of oats lay scattered across the worn planks. But Blaze saw something else, something Shorty hadn't noticed, before the others came over to the bin, Yace now carrying the lantern. On a high broad shelf over the door to a side lean-to close by were stored an assortment of odds and ends, boxes, trunks, two old battered suitcases, and a few tools. As Yace's step sounded behind him, Blaze was seeing a chisel handle projecting beyond the shelf's edge and, directly above it in the shadow along the wall, a freshly gouged mark in the wood. That mark was an arrow pointing upward.

Sight of it made Blaze quickly lower his glance and peer at the spilled oats at his feet. His fervent hope was that no one had seen him staring toward the shelf. Mentally cataloguing what should be up there, he knew instantly that at least one item was missing—Joe's canvas-jacketed bedroll, stored there since he had left five years ago, was gone.

"Now who in tarnation could have been that sloppy?" he growled. "It wasn't this way at noon, when I grained our horses, Yace."

The face of Anchor's owner was a study in perplexity as the others gathered behind him. "Then Quinn wasn't seein' things," he drawled. "Who could it have been?" He had lost some of his certainty, and was as mystified as the others. He seemed to feel Bill Lyans's glance on him and turned. When he caught the studied severity of the deputy's stare, he asked querulously: "Well, who was it?"

Lyans didn't answer that, but turned to the others. He spoke quietly, his voice barely audible over the moan of the wind. "A couple of you make a fast circle south. Shorty, you're good at sign. You and I will swing north. There's enough snow so that we may be in time to spot his tracks showin' through to the ground."

"Whose tracks?" Yace asked, irritable under the deputy's ignoring of him and his ordering around an Anchor man.

Lyans gave a grunt of disgust. "Joe's, of course. He's been here all the time. I'd arrest anyone else who tried to run this kind of a sandy on me, Bonnyman."

"What kind?" Yace bridled.

"Stallin' us while Joe made his getaway."

"Why, you . . ." Yace checked his outburst as the deputy turned his back and headed for the shed's wide door. The others filed out after him, all but Yace and Blaze.

When they were gone, Blaze drawled: "I'd give my right arm if what he said was true about your helpin' Joe make a getaway. Only it ain't."

"How could it be? I didn't know he was here."

"No. If you had, you'd have turned him in."

Yace's jaw muscles corded in sullen anger, but he made no reply. He was plainly too baffled to rise to Blaze's baiting.

"So you're as sure as they are, eh?" Blaze queried dryly.

"Did I say so? Sure of what?"

"About Joe beefin' Merrill."

"He wasn't on that train, was he?"

Here, indirectly, came the admission Blaze had been after, the admission that Yace Bonnyman thought his son a murderer, that his blustering back there at the house had been only a device to gain him time to make up his mind. Now it was made up. Blaze was suddenly angry, so full of emotion that the lantern's light wavered before his eyes.

"Yace," he drawled, "there are times when I wonder why I stay on here lookin' after a bull-headed old fool like you. Them times I wonder what I ever saw in you in the first place. By Satan, I don't know, now that I think of it."

He had wanted to hurt Yace. But now a strange tranquility seemed to be settling over the old rancher's face, and he breathed: "He'll shake 'em, if it was him. They won't lay a hand on him. But why didn't he come to me for help?"

"To you? After the glad-handin' you gave him at the depot tonight?" Blaze laughed. He didn't know what to think. First Yace hinted one thing, the next moment another.

Yace's expression sobered. He shook his head. "No tellin' why I did that," he said in a surprising admission.

Blaze was puzzled, sore. He had an impulse to tell Yace about the mark over the shelf, about Joe's being headed for Hoelseker's abandoned Broad Arrow cabin high along the Troublesome, but he checked it. There was no trusting Yace's hair-trigger moods. A minute ago he had been halfway convinced of his son's guilt; now he was trying to persuade himself that he would have helped Joe had he had the chance, that he didn't believe him guilty. No, Blaze decided, he wasn't going to let Yace in on this, wasn't going to trust him with the safety of a man's life. And he knew it amounted to exactly that. Joe Bonnyman was in a tight spot. So he drawled: "Well, you goin' to let Lyans ride up Porcupine this mornin' and deputize your crew to hunt Joe down?"

Yace's lips drew out to a hard thin line. "No, by Jehoshaphat," he said curtly, and stomped out the door bawling Lyans's name.

Blaze followed more leisurely, letting the wind push him along. As he crossed the barn lot, he turned down toward the cook shack, seeing Clark's shape briefly outlined in the lighted door there. He would take Clark aside and tell him where Joe was headed. It eased his troubled run of thinking when he saw Clark. He had almost forgotten that he wasn't Joe's only friend.

A Warning

The storm unleashed its full fury as the darkness gave way to the first hint of dawn's opaque dead-gray light. The wind, strong in the before-dawn hours, took on the proportions of a howling gale. And snow came with it, snow so fine that it sifted in around the tightly drawn tarps of the chuck wagons that fed the crews working the roundups, so hard that it made raw the faces of the luckless cowpunchers who had night-herded the bunches of miserable, bawling cattle, holding them in what scant shelter they could find.

The Sierra & Western tracks at the foot of Crooked Gulch were drifted eight feet under so that the through express, due in Junction at six, had to back the twenty miles to Lodgepole to wait out the blow. Anchor's water mason scraped the frost from his shack window and could see enough through the easing gloom to wonder if the brimming pond's new spillway would be able to handle the overflow when the melt came. For a melt would come, this being early November.

In Lodgepole, Jim Swift, the day hostler, made his solitary way along the darkened street toward the feed barn, the moan of the wind against the galleried false fronts of the stores heightening his unnaturally lonesome feeling that was little relieved by the knowledge that the town would be astir in another forty minutes. Breasting the narrow alleyway between The Antlers and Sayler's Bakery. He heard a horse stomping and guessed that some rider, caught by the storm, had left the animal there to save a 30¢ board bill at the livery. Shortly he was glad to step in out of the wind's bite through the walk entrance of the barn's tightly closed doors. He set at once about pitching hay down from the loft.

The horse Swift had heard stomping in the passageway alongside the hotel was Sam Thrall's. Joe Bonnyman had briefly glimpsed the hostler approaching through the fog of snow and had thanked a momentary lull in the wind's intensity that had let him soundlessly enter the lobby of The Antlers. Once in there, his chilled body soaking in the room's comparative warmth, he had hesitated to set about the thing that had brought him here.

Out there at Anchor an hour ago, Joe had had a bad few minutes, circling the posse men Lyans had put out to look for him in an attempt to spot either Blaze or Clark and have a word with them. He'd missed his chance with Blaze, not recognizing him until he was too close to the cook shack, and after that had put distance between himself and the house. Common sense had told him that the thing to do was to ride for the Broad Arrow cabin and wait for Blaze, for certainly Blaze already knew where to find him. But that might mean a day, possibly two, of prolonged curiosity as to why the posse was hunting him. Blaze might not be able to get away. Joe couldn't wait that long.

In that moment he had thought of Ruth Merrill, remembering Clark's mention of her staying in town overnight. And, as the thought struck him, he was putting the black over toward the Lodgepole trail, judging that he had better than an hour until daylight.

Now he was held tense by acute nervousness, not so much before the threat of discovery as before the prospect of seeing Ruth Merrill again. She would be asleep in one of the rooms upstairs. The thought of seeing her again threw him into a near panic of anticipation.

He cat-footed across to the counter, hearing Roy Keech's snores issuing from the cubbyhole room under the stairway. The counter *creaked* loudly as he leaned on it, reaching across for the register on the desk behind. He breathed shallowly, and his hand dropped to the handle of his Colt as he waited out a brief interval, listening for a break in the clerk's heavy breathing. Then, reassured, he opened the register and scanned it by the feeble light of the turned-down lamp over the counter. Shortly he found Ruth's name with the number **14** after it.

Halfway up the stairs, he paused as the sound of Keech's breathing suddenly let off. Then, quickly, he climbed up out of the far margin of light into the total obscurity of the upper landing. He judged that room Number 14 lay back along the hall rather than toward the street, and started toward there. He stopped when his groping hand felt the third break in the flanking partition. He struck a match, snuffing it out at once. He stood before the door numbered **14**.

He rapped twice, lightly, and waited. No sound from inside the room came to him. He tapped again, just as softly, but half a dozen times. Then he heard the *creaking* of a bedspring, the slur of a light step on the floor. A faint glow of lamplight showed from under the door. Then, before he was quite aware that anyone was close, the door swung open abruptly.

A tall graceful girl stood holding the lamp. Her wavy chestnut hair fell about her shoulders, a light robe was gathered tightly at her slender waist. She looked frightened as the lamplight fell across his high shape and she took a step back away from him.

Joe misread her move and thought she was about to scream. Stepping swiftly over to her, he put a hand across her mouth, the other tightly about her waist so that she couldn't draw away from him. He said urgently, low-voiced: "Don't yell. I thought I had Ruth Merrill's room. Just let me get out o' here."

The alarm died out of her eyes. He said—"Goin' to be good?"—and, when she nodded, he took the hand from her mouth.

"I remember you now," she said in a whisper. "You're Joe Bonnyman."

Still he wasn't sure of her. He nodded. "Correct. Ruth's registered for this room. How come she isn't here?"

"She is, asleep," the girl said, and looked down pointedly at his arm without trying to draw away from it.

Joe was keenly aware of her closeness, of the way her willowy body yielded to the pressure of his arm. Yet he couldn't afford to let her go until he knew exactly how far to trust her. "You're a friend of Ruth's?" he asked.

"Yes. I'm Jean Vanover."

"You won't yelp if I let you go?"

"I might." Her look was faintly provocative. When she caught the color mounting to his face, the trace of smile touched her eyes, and she said: "No. I'll be good. You needn't keep your arm there. Now what about Ruth?"

"I want to talk to her." His arm came away.

"She's had a pretty bad time of it. She needs her sleep." Jean looked over toward the bed, only a faint gray shadow in the lamp's edge of light.

"There's something I've got to know," Joe said. "I think she can tell me."

They still stood close to the door, practically in it, and Joe should have attached some significance to her glance going momentarily beyond him and out along the hallway. But he didn't, for he was impatient to have her answer.

"Couldn't I tell you whatever it is?" she asked.

"You might." He hesitated only a moment before coming out with it. "There's a posse out after me. Why?"

Her wonderment was quite genuine. "You don't know?"

"Should I?"

"Better than anyone else, if what they're saying is true."

Again her glance strayed beyond him, and now her hazel eyes showed quick alarm. Wariness flooded through him, and he started to turn and look down the hall. She stopped him with: "They're saying you killed him. You should know."

Her words startled him, as he afterward knew she intended they should. He didn't turn around. "Killed who?" he asked tonelessly.

"Ed Merrill." Her look didn't leave his as shock rode through him in a wave that engulfed his vigilance of a moment ago. Then she was saying in a low, tense voice: "There's a gun on your back. I wouldn't move if I were you."

Getaway

Joe had hardly time to take in Jean Vanover's warning when he heard Roy Keech's voice close behind him saying: "Watch it, Bonnyman. You might get a busted spine."

Lifting his hands out and upward, slowly, to shoulder height, Joe felt the weight of his Colt leave his holster. Then there had been a reason for the sound of Keech's breathing letting off so abruptly as Joe climbed the stairs. Just as there had been a reason for this girl's strange behavior, her glances past him up the hall that he had failed to read. She had held him here by her evasive talk while Keech made good his surprise.

Joe forgot the indictment she had laid against him in the face of his sudden anger. A girl and a man who would ordinarily have been utterly incapable of this act had taken him as easily as they might have a gullible child.

He stood with hands lifted, not moving, the harsh edge of his glance striking the girl. "Thanks," he drawled. He nodded toward the bed, the foot of which was now outlined by the faint first light of dawn at the window. "You can tell Ruth how much of a help you were."

Her face flushed under the acid sting of his words. He had the satisfaction of seeing her angry and ashamed as he turned away.

"Is the county still feedin' its prisoners the food it used to, Roy?" he drawled.

"You'll eat well enough," answered Keech.

Joe noticed that his voice trembled. Remembering what he did of Roy Keech, the man's almost puppy-like manner of wishing to please, his ineffectualness, drove home completely his feeling of frustration as he headed down the stairs. He felt no anger toward Keech, only an edge of nervousness at the knowledge that the man held a gun on him. He had a healthy respect for a gun in the hand of a man who didn't know much about using it, and Keech didn't.

Scanning the carpeted stairs ahead, Joe saw the runner bulging loosely away from the two bottom steps, remembering how they had shifted under his weight on the way up. At the bottom of the stairs he paused and turned slowly to face the clerk.

"You might as well tell me what this's all about, Roy," he said casually. "Where was Merrill found?"

Keech had stopped five steps above, his head at ceiling level. He said in that same trembling voice: "You can't get away with anything with me, Joe!"

"No one's tryin' to." Joe lifted his hands outward. "You've got my iron. All I want is information . . . and a smoke while you give it to me." Again slowly, so that his gesture wouldn't be mistaken, he pulled his poncho aside and took a sack of tobacco from a pocket of his vest.

Keech stiffened until Joe had completed his move, then visibly relaxed. The clerk even lowered his gun as he bridled: "What information? You know how you gave it to Merrill as well as I do."

"Yeah. Shot him in the back, didn't I?"

"Like blazes you did! You clubbed him over the head with the butt of a gun!" Keech was watching his prisoner's hands as they sifted tobacco out onto a wheat-straw paper.

"Now that's interestin'," drawled Joe. "Where'd it happen?"

"In the alley behind the Land Office. You know as well as . . ." Keech broke off as Joe clumsily dropped the sack of tobacco close in to the bottom step of the stairs.

Joe grinned sheepishly. "Shakin' like a leaf," he declared, and stooped over to retrieve his tobacco.

"You ought to be shakin'," Keech began. "Anyone who'd . . ."

He got no further. For, instead of reaching for the tobacco sack, both of Joe's hands had closed on the loose end of the stair runner. He lunged erect, throwing all his weight against the long piece of carpeting. The tacks holding it pulled away easily. Before Keech could lift his gun, his footing was gone out from under him. He was falling frontward, hands outstretched to break his fall.

At the last moment he knew what was coming and cried out shrilly. The slam of Joe's fist striking the side of his jaw cut off his cry. He struck heavily, his chest across the edge of the bottom step, rolling onto his back. Joe had relieved him of both guns before he completed that roll.

Thrusting his own weapon into his holster, the other through the belt of his pants, Joe looked upward along the stairs, checking the impulse to go up there and confront Jean Vanover. Thus thinking of her, it surprised him a little when he saw her standing there, a lithe, erect shape only faintly visible against the darkness of the stair head.

A good-natured grin slashed his face as he drawled: "Better luck next time." When she made no answer, he said tauntingly: "Now whose face is red?"

"Poor Keech." Her low voice came down to him. "You needn't have hit him so hard."

"You should be screamin'," Joe told her.

He could barely make out that she shook her head. "No. It seems I made a mistake. You'd better go now. Someone's coming down the hall."

He pivoted around and headed toward the door as he heard the muffled tread of stockinged feet echoing down from that upper hallway. Going along between the buildings to Thrall's black, he wondered at the change in Jean Vanover. What had made her decide she'd made a mistake? Then he ceased wondering under the urgency of leaving this town as quickly as he could.

He was able to make out shadowy shapes through the swirling snow as he rode out of the head of the passageway, turning away from the hotel and up street. Knowing he was safe until someone in the hotel gave the alarm, he put down the impulse to kick the black into a run.

Through the grayness Joe saw a man trudging down the awninged walk, collar turned high about his ears, head down, hands in pockets. He held the horse in a slow trot, lifting a hand to the man as be passed. He smiled thinly as the man answered his wave. Farther along, he took the dogleg in the street and came abreast the big cottonwoods fronting the yards of the first houses; not all the leaves had left the trees yet, mute testimony to this storm's unseasonableness. He let the horse have its head and felt the animal's strong lunge into a run. Once again he found himself envying Thrall, the owner of the horse. The black had traveled some thirty miles tonight, and still had a lot left.

Joe rode hard and fast for an hour. When he judged he was half a mile or so short of Sommers's place, at the edge of the mesa, he left the trail angling directly north toward the shrouded hills. By that time the upcurling brim of his Stetston was filled flat by blown snow, and the wind howled with the same fierce intensity. But now it was warmer and lighter, and an occasional easing of the pall around him would give him a brief walled-in glimpse of a short reach of country. During one of those let-ups he got his exact bearing from a half mile distant spur of timber that he recognized. He swung off toward it, knowing that to follow its farther edge would shortly put him on the Troublesome.

He was faintly irritated by the knowledge that he was riding his own range, or land that had once been his, but was now Middle Arizona's. This brought alive again the sting of last night's welcome, of seeing Yace and of the fight with Ed Merrill. Merrill dead! For the first time Joe took in the full significance of the thing of which he stood accused. He could feel little regret over the man's fate. But his curiosity was alive now as to how they had come to fasten the murder on him. He had fought Merrill last night, yes, but what evidence had put Lyans and every able-bodied townsman out on the hunt for him? Only suspicion? No, he knew it couldn't be that. Bill Lyans wasn't a man to jump at conclusions; moreover, Joe remembered Bill as having been more tolerant toward him than the others five years ago. So it followed that the deputy must have some evidence that pointed directly to him, evidence that would have started inquiries. Clark had been in town and would have mentioned his leaving by the late freight. A wire to Junction would have brought the answer that he wasn't on the freight.

It fitted neatly, all the circumstantial evidence that last night had built against him—his fight with Merrill making him naturally suspect, the unknown evidence that had put Lyans on his trail, his leaving the freight. Now two more details would strengthen suspicion against him—his having gun-whipped Thrall and stolen the horse, and his encounter with Keech at the hotel. In another hour or two the word of his having been to Lodgepole would be out, and the hunt would he intensified.

He was lucky. The storm would hamper the posse while aiding him. He even stood a good chance of leaving the country if he chose, for rarely could he see more than 100 yards, and it would be a simple matter to avoid the trails that would surely be blocked by Lyans's posse men. But Joe put down that thought forcibly, and for a weightier reason than the one prompting him to leave the train last night. If he left now, with this murder on his head, he would spend the rest of his life as an outlaw. Merrill's family had influence. They would hound him for years.

So once again running was out. Instead, he'd head for the Broad Arrow cabin as he'd first planned, there to await Blaze, or maybe Clark. Between them, they should be able to work out a few leads that would eventually put them on the trail of whoever had killed Ed Merrill. And perhaps, just perhaps, that same trail would lead to a final security for Joe Bonnyman in this country.

* * * * *

By mid-morning Joe was well above the back edge of the mesa, high along Porcupine Cañon. Once he glimpsed two riders pushing a small bunch of cattle downcañon. He saw them barely in time to keep from being discovered. Turning off into the tall cedars, he waited while the riders passed. As he neared the head of Porcupine, close to the lower edge of broad Aspen Basin, he passed a cabin, with its sod-roofed barn and single corral, that was new to him. By the time he struck the basin the snow was falling heavily again, the wind had slacked off, and he decided to ride straight across the six-mile width of the bowl-like depression.

He made that distance without once being able to see farther than half a dozen rods, following the twisting line of the Troublesome, rather than chancing losing direction by the more direct way of riding point. He knew he was across when the trees closed in on either side. Shortly he came to the crumbling embankment of the old abandoned stage road that led over Baldy Pass and eventually to Junction. Lyans would have put a man or two up near the pass to watch the road, Joe knew, and his face took on amusement at thought of the miserable hours they and the rest would spend today looking for him.

He had impulsively decided on the Broad Arrow cabin as a temporary refuge back at Anchor, intending only to find some spot where he could meet Blaze without being discovered. Now that he considered it more deliberately, the cabin seemed perfect for a permanent hide-out. Bill Lyans would reason that a man being hunted for murder would take the quickest way out of the country. That ruled out a search along the upper Troublesome, for that tangled wooded country came to a dead-end against the precipitous foot of Baldy, the highest peak within sight of Lodgepole, and had but one outlet, that one downward as far as the stage road. So for the time being, the homestead cabin that had witnessed Hoelseker's last struggle against this upper country's bitter winters seemed the safest possible spot to Joe.

Ten stiff-climbing miles along the streambed took him into the aspen belt. The snow had stopped falling, but there was enough wind to sift over Joe's tracks. And now the steep-walled gorge that flanked the stream widened and there was an occasional small meadow, its lush emerald grass white-blanketed, edged by copper-leaved scrub oak thickets and the faded gold background of the aspens. Joe recognized a landmark, the mast-like finger of a lightning-killed pine centering one of those small glades. Directly beyond, he entered a thick stand of majestic blue juniper. Hoelseker's cabin should be at the far edge of the next meadow.

He sighted the cabin through the trees, and at once his curiosity came alive, and wariness was in him as he took in certain details. The roof was newly sodded, and the clear wall of the small barn, its top logs rotted and broken as he remembered it, showed fresh-peeled poles below the roof line. The corral, which had recently been rebuilt, had three horses in it. Someone had taken over Hoelseker's homestead.

A keen regret struck Joe as he reined the black around. At that moment a voice drawled, close to him: "Go right on in, stranger."

Joe's glance came around and took in a spare-framed man leaning idly against the trunk of a juniper twenty feet away. A Winchester was cradled carelessly under the man's arm, yet Joe had the feeling that the weapon could cover him before he had the chance to reach for his own. Then he saw how ridiculous it was to suspect the man of anything but friendliness. News that a posse was out looking for a killer couldn't possibly have traveled to this isolated spot.

So his lean face took on a smile and he drawled: "I was figurin' to spend the night. Didn't know anyone was livin' here."

The man considered this, his gaunted face remaining impassive. Finally he put a question: "Lose your way?"

Joe nodded. "Until about an hour ago. This seemed closer than town. Some storm, eh?"

"Yeah." His face impassive, the man motioned with the rifle's barrel toward the cabin. "Go on in."

Joe decided again that the rifle was intended as no threat. He turned the black and headed out of the trees, sitting sideways in the saddle and looking back at the man who followed. "Been livin' here long?" he queried.

"A month maybe."

Joe hadn't expected that answer. Spring would be the time for a family to move into a hill layout like this, with four months in which to raise a garden, gather hay, and get ready for the winter. His respect for the man had a quick let-down.

"Hoelseker didn't have much luck up here," he remarked.

"Who's Hoelseker?"

The question had a note of unfriendliness Joe didn't miss. He decided that the man was irritable at having to extend common range courtesy, the never turning away of a stranger who was in need of shelter. He wondered what he would find in the cabin. A woman, children? Would they take money for a meal and a night's shelter?

He came up on the cabin and started angling down toward the corral, when the man's voice sounded from behind, harshly now: "Never mind that! We'll go in first."

Coming out of the saddle, Joe gave the man a steady glance that was answered by one of suspicion, near hostility. He heard the cabin door open, and turned. Standing in the doorway was a man more broad than tall, a man who at first looked fat, but wasn't. His bulky frame was barrel-chested and gave hint of a hard-muscled compactness. His round face was set in an enigmatic half smile, and he wore a gun low along a thick thigh.

His eyes passed over Joe and went to the man beyond. "Well, Chuck?"

"Don't ask me, Mike," the man with the rifle replied. "Claims he's lost."

Mike's glance now came back to Joe and remained on him. Two other men came into view beyond the doorway. Abruptly Joe knew that this must be Mike Saygar, the rustler.

"Get his iron," Saygar said tersely.

Joe went rigid, then instantly ruled out any chance of drawing his gun. Chuck's rifle was now halfway lifted to shoulder, nicely covering him. Saygar's hand, as he spoke, had lifted to rest easily on the handle of his Colt.

As Chuck stepped in behind him and lifted his .45 from the holster, Joe asked quietly: "What is this?"

"You tell us," drawled Saygar. "Feel like talkin'?"

"About what?"

"Why you're here."

"Can't a man get lost without havin' to answer for it?"

Saygar's smile became genuine. "It's got to be better'n that, friend," he drawled. "This place is hard to find. Them outfits down on the mesa ain't. If you was lost, you'd have gone downcountry and made it a sure bet on runnin' into a warm bunkhouse and good grub."

Joe saw he had been tripped up by the other's logic. All at once a wide grin eased the severity of is face. "You win, Saygar. Didn't know you were up here. I wanted a place to disappear for a few days."

The outlaw's brows lifted as he heard himself called by name, and he considered what lay behind this stranger's claim. In the end he shrugged and turned in out of the doorway. "We can arrange that," he said. "Chuck, grain his jughead and get back down the trail. Step in, stranger."

Joe entered the cabin, feeling better. But one thing betrayed the pleasant way Saygar made him welcome. There was no offer to return his gun. He was a prisoner.

Outlaw Powwow

After a prolonged and open inspection of Joe, Saygar said easily: "You look played out, stranger. Help yourself to food and some shut-eye." He motioned to a low hogback stove in the cabin's far corner, to the Dutch oven, and the can of coffee sitting on it, and to the pair of double bunks along the back wall, before he turned his back on Joe to add: "Your deal, Whitey."

Saygar and his two men resumed their interrupted game of stud at the makeshift table near the door, seeming to forget their visitor. Joe's edgy vigilance eased off as he took a tin plate from the packing-box shelf behind the stove, and helped himself to coffee and a generous portion of the pork and beans he found in the Dutch oven. He was hungry and he was tired. Sitting down on one of the bunks, he wolfed the food, the coffee hitting his stomach in a warm, satisfying wave. When his plate was clean, he built a smoke and eased back in the bunk, resisting the urge to stretch out and sleep. He knew he would sleep in the end. But before that, he wanted time to think and to size up this situation.

Over the next quarter hour, he studied Saygar, and the other two, Whitey and Pecos. Saygar presented an enigma at first, for there was little about him to suggest his being the leader of these men. Yet the fact that Saygar's wild bunch had been a force for the Mesa Grande ranchers to contend with five years ago, and still remained one after this long lapse of time, was proof enough of the rustler's native shrewdness. And, watching Saygar, Joe could finally put his finger on certain qualities in the man that explained him. Not once did the run of cards cause Saygar to raise his voice or by the slightest change of expression betray an emotion. His luck didn't seem particularly good, yet he was gradually accumulating most of the matches that served as chips.

Once Saygar broke a heavy silence to say levelly: "Put it back, Whitey. Put it back."

Joe saw Whitey's face take on a quick flush. Whitey pushed his chair back and appeared about to lunge erect. He stared at Saygar with cold, furious eyes. Then, abruptly, his quick rebellion left him. Smiling crookedly, he tossed a card onto the table and drawled: "It was worth the try."

At that moment, Mike Saygar stirred from his impassivity to say cuttingly: "When you begin a thing, finish it, Whitey."

The blond young outlaw considered this plain invitation to back his play, which had been holding out an ace. But in the end he merely shrugged, saying querulously: "It's among friends, ain't it?"

Saygar laughed, and in his laugh was mockery that stung Whitey. But nothing happened, and in that small incident Joe saw what a hold Saygar had over his men. For Whitey was a type that Joe knew to be dangerous, vicious, arrogant, a typical gunman. His supple uncallused hands gave as strong a hint of his talents as the low-thonged holster at his flat thigh. The fact that he had allowed Saygar to accuse him of cheating at cards, and let the accusation go unanswered, was proof enough that Saygar himself must be uncommonly adept at handling a Colt.

This small incident reminded Joe strongly of the life he had just quitted in that bunkhouse high in the Tetons. Here he found the same breed of toughened indrawn men, the endless loafing around camp while awaiting an outbreak of the violence that sustained them. And here, as in Wyoming, he found a misfit. Pecos seemed nothing but an amiable, outspoken cowpuncher. He had little luck at the cards and complained good-naturedly about it in direct contrast to the other two, who played a silent, sober game. Joe decided that Pecos's worth to Saygar must lie in his knowledge of the country and cattle. Somewhere along Pecos's back trail must be an indiscretion or a petty crime that had forced him into this way of living. One day he might pull clear of it and go back to his old life. If he did, he'd be lucky; if he didn't, he wouldn't survive, for his slow wits and ordinary talents couldn't match those of the men he was traveling with. Joe felt a little sorry for Pecos, for he had himself been green and untoughened when circumstances threw him in with men like Saygar, Whitey, and Chuck outside on guard.

He was thinking of Pecos, vaguely wishing he could help him, when he eased back at full length in the bunk, pulled a blanket up over his legs, and let the pleasing languor of sleep ride over him.

* * * * *

Clark Dunne left the stage road and started up the Troublesome better than an hour after Joe, pushing his roan hard. He blamed Bill Lyans for this delay that was putting him at the Broad Arrow cabin behind Joe, instead of before him, for he knew that Saygar had last week moved down out of the higher hills and was making the cabin his temporary headquarters. Back at Anchor, Lyans had made his suspicions of Dunne quite obvious. As a friend of Joe's, Clark wasn't to be trusted alone today. So the deputy had paired Clark with Bill Murdock, and sent them on a wild-goose chase to cover the old stage road that led up over Baldy Pass.

Murdock hadn't caught on. High up toward the pass, within sight of Klingmeier's stage station, he had rebelled. "Shucks, what good's this doin' us?" he had grumbled. "I'm for takin' a swing down into the breaks. If Bonnyman come this way, he's ahead of us."

"Go ahead. I'll loaf around with Klingmeier," Clark had answered, and it had been agreed that they should meet at the stage station at dark.

Once Murdock had ridden out of sight in the smother of snow below the road, Clark had reined his roan around and put him at a lope back down the trail, trying to make up his lost time. The money Clark had taken from Acme's safe had been an uncomfortable prodding bulk in his hip pocket. Once he left Murdock, he changed it into the inside pocket of his coat, holding it in his hand a moment and looking down at it, his pulse quickening at the realization of what it was to mean to him. He hadn't counted it yet, but Vanover had said the safe held close to $9,000. This big fistful of banknotes was going to buy him his present security and a future, a future so limitless Clark was almost afraid to begin planning it. Saygar would get $4,000. The remaining $5,000, judiciously used, would more than quadruple Clark's present land holdings. It might even do better than that.

He was tired and on edge, had been since the moment Ed Merrill surprised him at the Land Office's alley door last night. He felt little remorse over having killed Merrill; he felt nothing but a deep resentment toward the man for having complicated an otherwise comparatively simple situation. But for Merrill's clumsiness, no one would have stood a prayer of ever finding out where Acme's money had gone. Clark, as the land company's new president, would have been least suspect, and Mike Saygar would have kept his mouth shut so long as he was paid off and his future dealings in stolen cattle assured.

Now there was some risk involved. Sooner or later the law would ask for a reckoning. It was, Clark decided, up to him to furnish Lyans with a victim. He had Neal Harper vaguely in mind as that victim. But first he had to see to Joe's leaving the country. Or did he? The thought made Clark jerk his roan to a stand. For a full minute he sat the saddle stockstill, considering the implications behind his thought. When he went on, he had the rudiments of an idea. As he traveled up the Troublesome in the thinning fall of snow, that idea took on clearer shape.

In the end, he saw Blaze as the only stumbling block to his plan. He hoped he hadn't betrayed himself to Blaze. He knew he hadn't been able to conceal outright surprise when the Anchor man informed him that Joe was headed for Hoelseker's abandoned cabin. But, he now reasoned, Blaze would have expected that reaction in him. And Blaze had been insistent on his heading up here first on the chance of seeing Joe. Blaze would himself be on his way to Joe as soon as he could leave Anchor without being followed. He'd probably be up sometime tonight.

The chance that Blaze might stumble in on things before he was quite ready for him set up a thin flow of irritation in Clark. He was feeling that irritation as he caught a far glimpse of the cabin and saw Chuck Reibel step from his place of concealment nearby in the trees and come into the trail.

"More company," Reibel said as Clark rode up. "Why don't they run a road up here, Dunne?"

Clark was invariably annoyed at the man's caustic manner, and had more than once cautioned Saygar to get rid of him for he had long ago judged Reibel the only one of Saygar's crew astute enough to be in this game for more than his share of the spoils. Once again he made mental note of this fact, intending to remind Saygar of it for the last time. However, he let none of his dislike show in his face or in his voice as he drawled: "So he got here?"

His answer surprised Chuck Reibel. "You knew he was comin'?"

Clark nodded, tilting his head in the direction of the cabin. "Send Mike out, will you? And don't let Bonnyman know what's up."

"Bonnyman?" The outlaw was visibly impressed. "Yace's son?"

"The same."

An indrawn expression clouded over Reibel's eyes. He was plainly trying to see what lay behind Joe Bonnyman's presence here. "I'll go get Mike," he said, and trudged off through the trees toward the narrow meadow, his boots leaving toed-in marks in the snow.

Clark's glance followed until the other was out of sight. Then he reached up to unbuckle his sheepskin coat, for the first time really aware of the rise in temperature. There was no breath of wind now, and overhead the sooty clouds were motionless and low-hanging. The stillness was like that momentary hush that precedes a thunderstorm. It would be raining soon, Clark judged. With rain on top of snow, the creeks would be over their banks before morning. The roundup crews would have the devil of a time with mud and rain and the streams impassable. Well, it didn't matter much what happened, Clark thought. The money in his pocket meant he wouldn't have to clean his range of stock. Tonight, when he got back to the layout, he'd send the cook up to tell the crew to ease up and gather only the moss horns and culls. After that he'd pay Neal Harper a visit.

Watching the cabin, Clark saw the door open and Mike Saygar come out. The outlaw paused by the door to stretch and yawn, then sauntered over to the corral where he leaned on the gate and built a smoke. Clark was only momentarily puzzled by the outlaw's move. When he saw that the fringe of trees grew to within thirty feet of where Saygar stood, he started circling toward the spot, keeping the cabin out of sight.

Clark left his roan well back in the cedars and, the thick trunk of one tree between him and the cabin, walked in on the corral.

Saygar heard him coming and said, not loudly: "Chuck claims that's Joe Bonnyman in there. What's this addin' up to?"

"You tell me." Clark was behind the tall cedar now. "He's got a posse on his tail. Me, for one. Last night Acme's safe was blown, and whoever did it cut down Ed Merrill makin' his get-away. Lyans says it was Bonnyman."

Saygar whistled softly. "Merrill dead? No wonder Lyans picked Bonnyman." He paused a moment, considering this news, coupling it with what he knew of last night's fight. Then: "Who did it?"

"No tellin'," Clark replied. "Have any trouble with Bonnyman?"

"Not any. He packed away some food and went to sleep."

"I've got to get him out of here, Mike," Clark said abruptly. "Out and on a fast horse headed over the pass."

"And have him spread it around where to find me?" Saygar's thin, unamused laugh echoed faintly from the sheer wall beyond the trees. "Uhn-uh."

"But I tell you he'll hightail once he's left here. Who would he spread it to?"

Saygar was silent a brief moment. Finally: "It's up to you, friend. It's your neck as much as mine."

"Then tip off the boys." Clark's voice bore a note of relief. "Chuck can bring me in as though he's caught me on the trail. You can get careless and give me a chance at an iron, and Bonnyman and I will make a getaway. No one knows me, get it?"

"Yeah, but you'll have to play it plenty smooth, brother."

"I will. By the way, Mike, I've got that four thousand."

Saygar's head came quickly around in the first betrayal of his indolent pose against the corral poles. His eyes narrowed as he looked toward the tree's thick stem.

"Another of your uncles cash in?" he drawled.

"Call it that." Clark's tone was brittle. "I'll lay it here on the ground."

The outlaw's glance still clung to the base of the tree. When Clark moved halfway into view, their eyes met. Clark's look was clearly belligerent. The outlaw, reading his own meaning into that glance, smiled meagerly. "You'd be smart to turn someone in for that job, Clark."

"Why me?"

Saygar shrugged. "Why not? It'd set you pretty tight with Acme and Lyans."

"It's an idea." Clark's face now echoed the outlaw's smile. "Noticed how the weather's turnin' off warmer?" he drawled.

Saygar nodded. "There'll be the devil to pay for a week or so. Think the cabin here will be safe enough?" He tilted his head in the direction of the meadow, out of which the stream's rushing waters sent across a subdued echo.

"You won't have to worry about that. You're movin' out."

"Movin'? Where to?" Saygar's frown expressed his puzzlement.

In the next few minutes Clark answered that question for him in minute detail.

Bushwhacked

Whitey was feeding the hogback stove one of the big quarter rounds of cedar as Saygar came back into the cabin after his talk with Clark. The *clang* of the stove's door brought Joe fully and instantly awake. Saygar heard him stir, and glanced toward the semidarkness of the bunk wall. He resumed his seat at the table where now a lamp had been lit, trying not to let his irritation show. Now that Joe was awake, Saygar wouldn't have the chance to tell Whitey and Pecos of Clark's plan.

"Let's lift the lid off this game," Whitey drawled as he picked up the cards for the deal.

"Help yourselves," Saygar replied. "Dollar limit?"

Whitey's tone had borne an edge of truculence, and Pecos looked worried. It was obvious to Joe, who now lay watching them resume their game, that Saygar was so far the winner. The daylight showing through the cabin's single window was dimmer now and rain pelted against the sash and set up a faint pleasing murmur of sound as it slanted onto the sod roof. The air in the cabin was stale and damp. Joe kicked the blanket to the foot of the bunk and closed his eyes again, feeling the need for more sleep.

Presently the muted sound of a gunshot stirred him out of a brief doze to open-eyed alertness. He saw Saygar rise quickly from the table and head for the door, palming his Colt smoothly from holster. Pecos turned in his chair, breathing—"Not another visitor."—and Whitey half rose before deciding to stay in his chair.

At the door, Saygar turned momentarily and nodded to the back of the room, telling Whitey: "Watch him." Only then did he inch open the door.

The outlaw's brief glance outside made him swing the door wide and slowly holster his .45. From the back of the room, Joe could see a narrow wedge of the meadow, its snowy surface now grayed by the rain. Two figures trudged into sight less than 100 yards away. The one behind, with the rifle slanted into the back of the man in front, was Chuck.

Joe could almost feel the hard pressure of the rifle nudging his own spine as he recognized the tall, sheepskin-clad shape of the man ahead of the outlaw. That man was Clark Dunne. Joe swung his legs off the bunk and sat up.

"Stay set, stranger," came Whitey's threatening drawl.

Pecos reached over and turned down the lamp.

So Blaze had, after all, told Clark about the mark over the shelf in Anchor's wagon shed. Clark had come here expecting to find Joe alone, and had walked straight into Saygar's guard. For the second time today, Saygar was being compelled to take an unwanted prisoner. Only Chuck had encountered a little more difficulty in bringing Clark in. The gunshot bore testimony to that.

In the next few seconds, Joe saw that he and Clark had been placed in a precarious situation. Saygar would naturally assume that two men having come up the trail, more might be on the way in. Where he'd been fairly good-natured about Joe's appearing in his camp, he would look on this second intrusion with suspicion. A man in Saygar's position couldn't afford to let word of his whereabouts get out. It naturally followed that he would have to take every precaution to keep his two visitors from leaving and carrying word down about him. Joe and Clark might be held prisoners for days, at least until Saygar had finished whatever errand had brought him to this cabin.

Joe felt Whitey's glance on him, but didn't look toward the table as Clark approached. Clark stopped several strides short of the door. Anger touched his eyes as he looked at Saygar and said: "A little outside your fences, aren't you, Saygar? How much of this country do you call yours?"

"As much as I need to move around in," drawled Saygar. "Any objection?" When Clark made no reply, the outlaw looked beyond him at Chuck Reibel and asked: "Why the fireworks?"

"He was a little slow about reachin' for his ears. Had to help him make up his mind."

Clark cut in with a curt: "You've got Joe Bonnyman in there?"

"Supposin' we have?" was Saygar's rejoinder.

Joe's attention left them as their talk went on, his glance coming around to Whitey and Pecos at the table. Pecos was on his feet now and standing out from his chair to look out the door. Whitey no longer peered so intently toward the back of the room, his attention having momentarily strayed the way of Pecos's.

The blanket was within Joe's reach. He snatched it up as he came to his feet. Gathering it into a loose ball, he threw it hard at Whitey. The blond youth sensed movement behind him and turned. Seeing the blanket coming, he dodged, at the same time reaching for his gun. But the blanket spread out and caught him in the face. Joe lunged sideways as Whitey's .45 arced up and exploded. The next instant Joe was across the room, numbing Whitey's wrist with a quick downward slash of his hand and wrenching the gun from the outlaw's hand as Saygar spun around.

Joe rocked the gun into line with the outlaw. "Go ahead, try for it," he drawled, for Saygar's right hand had lifted part way to holster and frozen there.

Out in the yard, Clark said—"Nice, Joe."—even though Chuck had moved in and was prodding him in the back with the Winchester. Whitey finished clawing the blanket from around his head and stood straight, holding his hurt wrist.

For a moment it looked as though he were going to throw himself at Joe until Saygar said sharply: "Whitey!" Pecos had already seen the look on Joe's face and lifted his hands.

"Tell your understrapper out there how to behave, Saygar," Joe drawled.

The outlaw briefly considered the rock-steady gun aimed at his belt, then called: "You heard what he said, Chuck!"

A moment later Clark had the rifle. Joe made a motion toward the door with the .45. "The air's better outside, gents."

When they stood grouped a few steps out from the doorway, Joe, in possession of the two remaining six-guns and a rifle he had found over by the bunks, moved over to where Clark stood.

"Hold 'em while I get a horse," he said, and started out for the corral, his bare head tilted against the slant of the rain.

As soon as he was out of hearing, Clark smiled at Saygar. "Better than the way we planned it, eh?"

Whitey, in ignorance of what was being referred to, bridled. "Just what in blazes is this?" he demanded.

"Later, Whitey, later," Saygar said. Then to Clark: "What'll you do with him?"

"See him up the pass road a ways."

"That all?"

"That's all," Clark said.

"How about our irons? And that bronc'?" Saygar nodded toward the corral, where Joe was throwing his saddle onto a stocky chestnut horse.

"You'll get 'em back."

The answer brought a thin smile to Saygar's face. Although he said nothing, he was sure now of something he hadn't been at all sure of when he and Clark talked near the corral an hour before.

When Joe came back from the corral, he went into the cabin, and reappeared with his Stetson and poncho. He made the outlaws cross to the lower edge of the meadow, where Clark's roan was standing. Then, with Clark in the saddle beside him, he looked down at Saygar.

It's a fair trade on the horse," he said. "I'll hang your guns from a tree a ways down the trail. Much obliged for the meal, Saygar."

"Sure," the outlaw said, his face bearing its customary meaningless half smile. "Stop in any time you feel like it."

Joe and Clark headed down through the trees. Just below the meadow Joe left the three Colts hanging by their trigger guards on the stub branch of a dead cedar close to the trail. He took more pains with the rifles, hiding them in the high crotch of a big pine farther on. Clark, who hadn't spoken since leaving the meadow, now said: "It looked to me like we'd be coolin' our heels there a few days. How'd you do it?"

"Luck," Joe told him.

Clark shook his head. "You call it that. But it took something else, too." He spoke in honest admiration. "Here's some luck you maybe weren't countin' on. The road over the pass is clear. Lyans put me and Murdock up here to cover it. Murdock's made a swing down into the breaks and is to meet me at dark up at Klingmeier's. So you can get through."

"Why should I?"

Clark looked quickly around at Joe. "Why shouldn't you?"

"Clark, I hopped off that freight out by Baker's last night because I was tired of runnin'. I still am."

"Hang it, man, they're tryin' to saddle you with killin' Ed Merrill! Or didn't you know?"

"I know," Joe answered, and told Clark about his visit to town that morning. He finished with a question: "How were they so sure it was me?"

"Your horsehair hatband," Clark answered. "You must've lost it in the fight. Someone found it and framed you by leavin' it on Merrill."

Joe nodded. "And you still say I should hightail?" He laughed soberly. "Not this time, Clark. I ran once and it didn't work. Then it didn't matter what people thought of me. Now it does."

"It shouldn't."

"That's where you're wrong. But we'll skip that. What I can't skip, though, is this bird that takes the trouble to hang a robbery and a murder on me. I reckon I'll stick around and find out who he is."

Their arguing grew more heated, Joe clinging stubbornly to his decision, Clark naming every reason he could think of to counter it. Unconsciously they rode a little faster, flanked most of the way by the swollen stream that was already crowding its banks and giving promise of what was to come tomorrow when the rain and the melting snow had their effect. The rain was a thin spitting at their backs and the light was failing.

When they came to the stage road above the basin, Clark drew rein and turned in the saddle to face his friend. "Still stickin' to it?" he queried. "Where you headed to?"

Joe nodded downward: "Home. They won't be lookin' for me there. Blaze and I can think out something."

"Why not my place? I'll go up and meet Murdock and be down around midnight."

"No. Anchor's better. Thanks anyway."

Clark shrugged and grinned. "See you, then. I'll keep in touch with Blaze." He reined out into the road and started up it.

Joe sat watching his friend for a long moment, thinking how lucky he was to be having Clark and Blaze to side him during this bad time. The brief interval just ended had brought back a little of the feel of the old days. He and Clark had been wild and carefree then, with nothing much depending on the outcome of their tomfoolery. This was different. Whatever they did now counted. It was a good bracer for a man to find that his friends were still with him.

* * * * *

Half a mile above the place he'd left Joe, Clark took a backward look along the trail and swung sharply away from it, striking downcountry through the jack pine. He went faster now, cutting across occasional draws whose beds already ran water. He climbed a ridge and paused there long enough to scan the timbered reach of country in the direction Joe was traveling. The rain had turned misty and a thin fog obscured Clark's sight of the basin and the timber this side of it. But he knew this country well and slanted off the ridge a little eastward.

Twenty minutes' travel brought him abruptly to the upper edge of Aspen Basin. Reining in before clearing the trees, he came out of the saddle and tied his roan. He took his Winchester from its scabbard and deliberately levered a shell into the chamber. Moving several paces to the left so that a broad rounded boulder lay between him and the open ground ahead, he looked out and downward to the twisting black line that marked the Troublesome's far bank.

He had a long wait, longer than he had counted on. As the minutes dragged by, he fidgeted restlessly, first sitting on the boulder, then standing behind it. He changed the rifle from one hand to another, and finally leaned it against the boulder's back face, choosing a patch where the snow had melted to rest the heel of the stock. Twice his hand went automatically in under his sheepskin coat to the pocket of his shirt that held his tobacco; each time the hand came away empty. And during this seemingly endless interval his glance clung to the narrow indentation in the timber that marked the line of the Troublesome. His eyes were squinted, for he was facing into the misty slant of the rain.

The light wasn't so strong now and Clark imagined that the fog was thickening. Down by the creek it seemed to be rising from the foaming water in a billowy cloud as if purposely obscuring what lay off there. All at once a shadow moved through the murky fall of mist edging the creek. It moved down and out of the trees and along the stream's far bank. Clark stiffened and went to one knee, reaching for the rifle and laying it across the boulder. For a moment he saw the slow-walking chestnut horse plainly, saw Joe riding with his head down as though deeply in thought. Clark laid his sights on Joe's chest, but at the instant his finger tightened on trigger the mist closed in again, and all he could make out was a vague shape moving on away from him.

His sights picked up the target again. Only now Joe's back was toward him, and that fact heightened a strong nervousness that was in him. Only by a concentrated effort could he keep from trembling as he took a deep breath, exhaled slowly, and squeezed the trigger.

At the last moment the gray mist made Joe indistinct once more. The rifle's sharp *crack* seemed deadened by the blanket of thin fog. He saw Joe's outline move violently as the chestnut shied. Then Joe was falling sideways from the saddle, and the horse was running back toward the trees.

Clark stood up and slowly levered the empty from the .30-30. He put the empty in his pocket. His face was drawn, bloodless, gray. Momentarily the fog thinned and he could see Joe lying there, 200 yards away, close to the creek. A sure instinct told him his bullet had gone where he wanted it. The shot had felt right.

He turned and without another backward look went across to the roan. Swinging up into the saddle, he rode back the way he had come.

A Hide-Out

The faint far-off *snap* of the rifle shot sounded above the hoof *thud* of Blaze Coyle's pony and the murmur of the rain. The Anchor foreman pulled his gelding to a stand and sat stiffly, listening. A quarter minute failed to bring him any further sound that might explain the first. At length he muttered—"We're spooky, fella."—and put the gelding on up along the line of the Troublesome's left bank. He was a little better than halfway across the basin.

As the gray dusk thickened about him, Blaze knew he should be hurrying, making the most of what light there was left. But he didn't hurry. He was reluctant to meet Joe without quite knowing why he felt that way. All day he had puzzled over the details of Merrill's death and the fact of Joe's sudden change of mind about leaving. His thinking had netted him little beyond a vague, indefinable uncertainty over Joe; this uncertainty he stolidly refused to recognize, for it was something he didn't have the right to think upon until Joe had had his chance to explain. It was because he was afraid Joe couldn't explain that Blaze was taking his time, delaying his arrival at the cabin up along the Troublesome.

Blaze had had a full day. This morning he had ridden up Porcupine in the height of the storm to check on the crew. Back at Anchor shortly after noon, he had found Yace saddling a horse. The rancher wanted to go across and see John Merrill.

"He'd likely shoot you," had been Blaze's caustic comment when he found where Yace was going.

"Joe didn't kill Ed. John knows that," Yace had said briefly.

He and Blaze had ridden west from Anchor on the Brush trail. They hadn't talked with Merrill. Coming in on the layout, they'd spotted the doctor's buggy under the lean-to shed alongside the barn and another by the main hitch rail at the house. As they rode up to the house, Fred and Jean Vanover had come out the door with Ruth Merrill.

Her father, Ruth had told them quietly, had had a stroke on learning of Ed's death. The doctor wouldn't say how bad it was, but Ruth was afraid it was quite serious. Blaze and Yace had expressed their sympathy and offered their help. The girl thanked them. She wanted to know what the posse had accomplished in the hunt for Joe and seemed glad when Yace said stoutly: "Nothin', ma'am. And they won't."

Vanover and his daughter had driven out the lane with the two Anchor men. At the forks in the trail below Brush's big pasture, Vanover had pulled in to say: "Bonnyman, what about this talk I hear?"

"What talk?" Yace's tone had been curt.

"That I had my own men break open that safe."

"Whoever claims that is a fool." Yace had been emphatic. "What's more to the point is that Harper might have been riled about losin' his job, riled enough to collect what he figures you owe him."

Vanover had showed a steady check on his temper. He had said merely: "I'm looking into that matter, Bonnyman. Good day."

The rain had seemed to push Yace down into a deeper mood of depression. He had retired behind a wall of testy silence ever since Lyans's departure this morning. Consequently Blaze had been glad to give the excuse that he was going back up Porcupine to spend the night with the crew. Yace had accepted his explanation without comment.

It was now plain to Blaze that more lay behind the Acme robbery than any of them had supposed this morning. It had erased the last remnant of good feeling bred by last night's meeting. The old suspicions had come to life once more. Even Fred Vanover couldn't be sure that his own men hadn't betrayed him. Vanover had made a mistake in disclosing his uncertainty. He was the wrong man for his job, always had been. The cattle company needed a man with Vanover's brains and Harper's cold mercilessness. Vanover was too soft, too reasonable. Blaze felt sorry for the man as he saw what might be coming. He liked Vanover.

He now shrugged away these unwelcome thoughts and touched the gelding lightly with spurs, sending the animal on at a faster trot. Ahead, the broad sweep of the basin was a dusk-bordered sodden gray reach of melting snow. Close to his left the creek roared an ominously strengthening note. Until now, Blaze hadn't given much thought to what tomorrow would bring. At this moment, he did; there would be maybe a week's delay in driving down to the railroad and in shipping. To an outfit as big as Anchor, which hired ten extra men for roundup, that week's delay represented a sizable expense. And, as always, Blaze accepted this unlooked-for trouble as a personal one, so conscientiously did he take his job. The storm was bad enough. This matter of Joe's trouble made it . . .

The gelding's sudden sideward shying cut in rudely on Blaze's thoughts. He said—"Whoa, you jughead!"—glancing toward the creek to see what had frightened the animal.

An instant later he was vaulting from the saddle, dropping reins and running over to the sprawled figure he had already recognized. Transfixed by horror he knelt beside Joe, peering down at the crimson stain on the snow around his friend's head. Then, gently, he lifted Joe's upper body. The head sagged back loosely at what Blaze first thought was an inhuman angle.

"Joe! Joe, boy! Answer me!" he cried hoarsely.

His hand went to Joe's chest, and his panic subsided as he felt the even beat of the heart. His eyes moistened as relief and thankfulness hit him.

Calmly, methodically Blaze made the next few minutes count for all they were worth. He took off his poncho and put it under Joe. He unlaced his blanket from the saddle and wrapped it around the unconscious man. For the moment, he could do nothing about the wound, which was an ugly deep bullet crease high along the side of Joe's head.

As Blaze worked, he looked up from time to time, his glance sweeping the slowly narrowing circle of plainly visible ground nearby. Finally he left Joe and, mounting again, rode toward the timber. The position in which he had found Joe gave him no hint of where the bushwhacker had hidden. But before the light was completely gone, he intended to try and find the killer's sign, knowing that the rain would have obliterated it long before morning.

And now, as Blaze began what appeared to be his almost hopeless search, his earlier doubt was gone. The fact that Joe had been shot and left here, apparently dead, to be discovered by the first stray rider who happened along was proof that someone had a reason for not bringing Joe in himself. What that reason was, Blaze had no way of knowing. But there was a reason, and it might tie in with Ed Merrill's murder. That small possibility did more to bolster Blaze's belief in Joe's innocence than anything that had happened today.

Riding into the timber, Blaze began circling, knowing that the trees offered the best protection to a man wanting to shoot from cover. He crossed the creek and noted that the water had risen from its normal fetlock depth to his gelding's knees. Beyond the stream he angled back along an open stretch, skirting it. Farther on, he climbed along a low rising spur of ground. Beyond that, in a shallow draw, he came across horse sign.

The light was now so feeble that Blaze had to lean down in the saddle to get the details of that sign. The horse had worn light shoes and, from all appearances, had been a fairly big animal. Blaze turned toward the basin, following the sign. He found the spot where the horse had been tied and its rider gone on afoot. But out here, where the force of the rain wasn't broken by the trees, the sign was already badly washed. There was nothing but the badly melted outline of boot prints to go by. They might have been made by a man wearing a size seven boot or by one wearing a twelve.

The boot tracks led to a boulder. It was behind the boulder, under its back vertical face, that Blaze found the still clear print of a rifle's butt plate. He knelt and examined it closely, even striking a match and cupping it in his hand against the rain, to see clearly every detail. The mark was coarsely etched in cross lines, a Winchester. That was discouraging, for probably 100 men in Lodgepole alone owned Winchesters.

Then, almost when he was ready to drop his match, Blaze saw a raised line angling over the cross-hatching. It ran obliquely across the plate, from a point midway on it almost to the heel. It was obviously a scar put on the butt plate made by rough handling; perhaps a deep branch scratch, or the mark left by the rifle's owner dropping the gun's stock carelessly onto a sharp edge of rock.

When he straightened and climbed onto his gelding again, Blaze knew that he would be able to recognize the killer by his rifle, if he could ever get a look at the gun. And from now on he'd inspect every Winchester he came across.

Back with Joe again, he faced a knotty problem. Where could he take the wounded man? Anchor was out, for Yace wasn't to be trusted; besides, the posse was making the ranch house its headquarters for tonight at least. Joe would need care, more care than Blaze himself could give him. A doctor's care would be best. Doc Nesbit was at Brush. But, reasoned Blaze, Nesbit would be as anxious as the next man to turn Joe in as a suspected murderer. So he couldn't go to Nesbit.

Ruth Merrill! The instant Blaze thought of her, he was sure he had found the right person to help him. The next, he wasn't.

Hadn't Ruth kept stalling Joe five years ago when Joe openly admitted she was the girl of his choice? Why, Blaze asked himself, would Ruth now go out of her way to protect a man she didn't love? He had never liked Ruth much; her ways were too high and mighty to suit him, and her treatment of Joe had done little to increase his respect for her. In fact, Blaze still looked on Ruth Merrill as one of the primary causes of Joe's having sold out to Middle Arizona before he left home.

He thought of Jean Vanover and at once discarded her as a possibility. She, like the others, wouldn't hesitate to give away Joe's whereabouts to the law at her first opportunity. Also, to bring Jean up here would mean telling Vanover about Joe. And that would seal Joe's fate as surely as though the bushwhacker's bullet hadn't missed its mark.

As total darkness settled over the basin, Blaze knew that he would have to do this on his own. He tried to think of a place to take Joe, and abruptly knew where it would be. Two miles from here, up a narrow box cañon, was a cave where he and Joe and Clark had once smoked out a mountain lion their dogs had cornered.

Blaze had a hard time lifting Joe and getting the gelding to stand while he roped his friend across the animal's withers. But in the end he managed, and left the creek, striking eastward. The rain came harder now, no longer a misty vapor, but a pelting downpour. Blaze began to worry about Joe's catching cold, even though he had bundled his friend tightly in the poncho. He wondered how long Joe would remain unconscious. He wondered what he could do about feeding him. He wondered, all at once, if Joe would die.

From then on Blaze hurried, as though his friend's life depended on how soon he could find the cave and get a fire going. He found the brush-choked mouth of the box cañon and rode its narrow bed for better than half a mile before he was sure he had passed the cave. He turned back, his impatience blending with his worry to set up a strong and futile anger in him. He went almost as far as the mouth of the cañon without seeing the cave, and knew he had again missed it. Then, stubbornly, he got down and led the gelding, stumbling through the scrub oak along the east wall. He was ready to give up. He started thinking he had come up the wrong cañon.

Then he saw the tall, jagged finger of a high rock outcrop, and suddenly knew where he was. Fifty yards up the cañon he found the cave entrance. It was hidden by a tangle of a hackberry thicket he hadn't remembered. Leaving the gelding, Blaze crawled into the low opening on hands and knees, lighting a match to inspect what lay beyond. The long low tunnel was some fifteen feet deep, broadening out and shoulder-high at its rear wall. It was dry and warm in here.

He scraped the floor clear of twigs and branches left by some small animal that had once made the cave its home, then went down for Joe. He fell once on his way back to the cave and had a moment's bad fright when Joe's limp body rolled off his shoulder and into the mud. Hardly had his panic subsided than he was in the cave and hearing Joe's breathing now as a throttled, choked gasping. That awful sound lasted even after he had stretched Joe out at full length on the blanket.

Helplessness and near desperation were strong in Blaze now. He sat alongside Joe with the conviction that his friend was dying, that the strangled breathing sounding so ominously out of the darkness was a prelude to the end. The pitch blackness made it seem as though this cave was a tomb. As though he had found a way of helping Joe, Blaze went out into the night again and stumbled around until he had gathered a big arm load of wood, mostly dead branches broken from windfalls and the bottoms of the stunted cedars higher up along the near wall. He found some pitch pine, too, with which to kindle the damp wood.

The fire helped. Now that he could see, Blaze made his first close inspection of Joe. It was with a start that he saw the bandanna around the unconscious man's neck knotted hard and drawn so tightly that the neck muscles bulged. He loosened the knot and pulled the bandanna free. And at once Joe's breathing became easier, quite normal. Somehow, in that fall Blaze had taken when he was lugging Joe up here, the bandanna had been drawn so tightly that it had constricted the unconscious man's breathing.

Blaze sat back on his heels, keen relief striking through him. He might have killed Joe back there. Tragedy had nearly struck Joe a second time, proof to Blaze now that he wasn't capable, alone, of looking after his friend. No matter how often he told himself that Joe's color was good, that his friend would presently regain consciousness, he couldn't put down the urgency of the belief that he should go for help. Supposing Joe should die because he didn't get that help? Supposing his death should be caused by some simple thing like that tightly drawn bandanna that another person could readily see and correct?

Blaze knew finally that he was going to get help. Once again he tried to think of a person he could trust. There wasn't one but Clark Dunne. And Clark would be little more help than he himself in a situation like this. In the end, Blaze settled on Jean Vanover as the likeliest possibility. He went out and gathered more firewood. As he wrapped his poncho around Joe, took a last look, and finally stepped out into the rainy night, he thought he knew a way to get Jean Vanover up here without anyone knowing where he had brought her.

Night Ride

At Diamond Ranch, headquarters for Middle Arizona, Fred Vanover and his daughter were sitting before the fire that blazed on the hearth of the big stone fireplace. Vanover had been restless and distracted since supper, and now he said abruptly: "I can't wait any longer, Jean. I have to know."

"What, Dad?" His daughter's head tilted up from the book she was reading. She was sitting on the couch, her legs curled under her.

"About Harper. Yace Bonnyman was right. It could have been Harper that looted the safe and killed Merrill."

"But, Dad, he isn't . . ."

"He's entirely capable of it," Vanover anticipated what she was going to say. "Harper's been an enigma ever since they sent him down here to me. Last night, when I told him he and his men were through, it was as though I had remarked on the weather. He's the coolest proposition I've ever come across."

"But to rob the man he's been working for, to kill that way? I can't believe it."

"What has he had out of this beyond wages?" her father asked, reasoning aloud more than putting a question to be answered. "His kind are never in a thing for wages alone. It's an admitted policy of the company to reward their hired gunfighters with something besides pay. Take their Phillipsburg operation ten years ago. Dooley came out of it with a ranch of his own. He was nothing but a hired gun boss for the company when he went down there." Vanover rose from the chair and went out of the room, to reappear a few minutes later, pulling on a poncho. He had his Stetson. "Don't wait up for me," he said. "I'm going up to the camp."

"Be careful, Dad," Jean said, and walked with him to the door, kissing him before he went out. She knew that nothing she could do or say would keep her father from riding up to the chuck wagon tonight to see Harper and have it out with him. This was part of her father's job. The only reassurances she had against the gun boss resorting to violence was that her father never carried a gun, and that several of the roundup crew had little use for Harper and would side with her father if it came to a showdown.

She stayed at the door until he rode from the yard, then went back to the couch and picked up her book again. But now she stared sightlessly at the page, her thoughts too insistent to be turned aside. The rain drummed gently on the roof, reminding her as it had this afternoon that the fifty men on the hunt for Joe Bonnyman must be having a miserable time of it.

As had happened several times since early morning, Jean's thoughts turned to the tall, pleasant man who had come to Ruth Merrill's hotel room in that dawn hour. She wondered again why she hadn't called out for someone to stop him after he had struck down Roy Keech. But now an answer came to her. She didn't really believe that Joe Bonnyman was guilty. She hadn't believed it this morning as she stood at the head of the hotel stairs and listened to his mocking words. It didn't do any good to reason that she had found him attractive and was giving in to a little wishful thinking. It went deeper than that, to an instinct she couldn't deny, one that seldom was wrong. That instinct told her that Joe Bonnyman wasn't capable of having committed the crime for which he was being hunted. The brutality of striking down an unarmed man with the butt of a gun wasn't in his make-up, or she was no judge of a man.

She had told Ruth of Joe's visit, and Ruth had bitterly resented the fact that she hadn't been wakened. She hadn't even bothered to thank Jean for staying with her through the night. She'd had two opportunities, once before Jean left the hotel, another when Jean and her father had gone over to Brush to offer their help this afternoon on learning of John Merrill's collapse. Both times Ruth had assumed that proud cloak of cool aloofness so irritating to most people who didn't know her well. But instead of taking offense, Jean had felt sympathy for the girl. She wished now that she had wakened Ruth and let her talk with Joe for she saw even more clearly than she had last night, when Ruth so blandly admitted it, that the girl's feeling for Joe Bonnyman was sincere. So, in her generous way, Jean Vanover blamed herself rather than Ruth for the coolness of feeling that lay between them. She would have given anything to be able to relive those few minutes with Joe in the hotel's upper hallway, so as to make good what she now saw as a grave error.

She was thinking this when she heard a rider coming in across the yard toward the house. Her first thought was that it was her father returning, then she knew it couldn't be, for he hadn't been gone long. She had a disquieting moment of realizing she was practically alone, until she remembered that Harley, the cook, was close enough to be wakened if she called. His room was beyond the kitchen, which adjoined this main living room. So when the solid clump of boots crossed the porch and the knock sounded at the door, she answered it unhesitatingly.

It was the Anchor foreman who stood in the light of the lamp shining through the door when she opened it, a sodden, drawn-faced, poncholess Blaze Coyle, who wrung from her a quick: "Blaze! You're soaking! Get over by the fire!"

"Thank you, ma'am," he drawled, and took off his hat as he came in, revealing his sorrel hair matted wetly to his head. He crossed the room and stood with his back to the fireplace, puddles forming quickly around his boots as he said: "Sorry to butt in on you this time o' night." His glance roved the room and came back to the girl. "Your father around?"

"No. He had to ride up to see the crew."

Blaze's eyes went narrow-lidded a moment. "Then how'll he know where you've gone?" he asked.

"Am I going somewhere, Blaze?"

"It's up to you, ma'am. John Merrill's worse, a lot worse. Ruth ain't much help, and the doc sent a message over to our place that I was to send a man across to get you. I come myself to make sure."

"I'll leave Dad a note," Jean said, and at once turned toward the hallway that led to her bedroom.

In the following moments, Blaze's face assumed an unaccustomed gravity even though the fire's warmth was relieving the bone-deep chill of his two-hour ride. He liked Jean Vanover, and it hurt him to have to lie to her. But he forgot that in the face of the urgency that drove him. Thinking of Joe now, remembering his fright over that labored breathing, and the deep wound channeled in his friend's head, he doubted that he would ever again see him alive. A stark fear took hold of him, sent him across the room to call down the hallway into which Jean had gone: "I'll go out and saddle you a horse! We'll have to make some fast tracks!"

Blaze not only saddled a horse for Jean at the big corral, but roped a fresh mount for himself, choosing a big-headed animal that had the look of a stayer. He turned his Anchor-branded pony loose, knowing the animal would find its way home. Back at the house, Blaze entered the living room as Jean came out of the hallway. He saw that she wore waist overalls and a sweater and warm jacket under her ankle-length slicker.

She carried a spare poncho over her arm and gave it to him. "You'll need this. What happened to yours?"

"I'm a bum judge of the weather, I reckon." Blaze grinned ruefully. "Hate to wear the darn' things. I thought it was through rainin' when I left our layout." He thought of something to take her attention from his lame explanation and added hastily: "I missed supper. Mind if I see what I can find in the kitchen?"

"I should have thought of that," Jean said contritely. "I'll wake Harley and have him get you something."

"No. Don't. A cup o' coffee'll do."

His relief was keen as Jean led him into the kitchen without approaching the door at the far side, which he knew to be that of the cook. There was coffee on the stove and a pan of tamale pie in the warming oven. Blaze sat down to a big plateful of ground beef and browned cornmeal mush, for the first time aware that he was ravenously hungry. But he grudged this waste of time; he had wanted to get into the kitchen alone, to get his hands on food he could take to the cave, but Jean's endeavor to be helpful had spoiled his chances of that.

As the girl got him bread and butter and a second cup of coffee, she questioned him about John Merrill. Blaze pretended ignorance of everything but the errand he had been sent upon. Jean wanted to know about the posse, if there was any word yet of their having taken Joe. No, the redhead said, no word yet. He was slightly puzzled by the girl's obvious relief at his answer.

As his hope of taking any food up to the cave left him, she said abruptly: "The note. I'd almost forgotten. Help yourself to anything more you want, Blaze. I'll be back in a minute." And she went out into the living room.

Blaze was up out of his chair the instant she was gone. He found half a sack of flour in the bin under the bread board, emptied it quickly, and started looking for things to put in the sack. In the storage cupboard he found canned tomatoes; he took three cans. Next came a coffee can full of flour, the big salt cellar on the stove, an unopened can of baking powder, one half full of coffee, a big slab of bacon from the ice box. He had run his belt through the handle of a small frying pan and was buckling the poncho over it when he heard Jean's steps crossing the room beyond. He fastened the last buckle barely in time to keep her from seeing what was underneath the poncho as she entered the room.

Blaze said—"All set."—and opened the outside door. Jean paused close to him before she went out, taking a last look at the kitchen. Then the darkness swallowed her and he was groping his way over toward the horses, pulling his Stetson low against the slanting rain, breathing a long sigh of relief at not having wakened the cook.

By the time they came to the yard gate, Blaze had tied the flour sack to the horn of his saddle, knowing it was too dark for Jean to see it.

"'You'd better follow me close!" he called, and spurred his horse into the lead. The animal seemed eager to go, and Blaze was relieved to think he'd made a wise choice.

The one danger, Blaze knew, lay in their getting lost, for the pitch blackness of the night was unrelieved. It was also necessary that, for a mile or two, he keep up the pretense of heading for Brush.

When he did swing off the trail, the girl called from close behind: "You're too far to the right, Blaze!"

His answer was inspired, coming to him quickly. "Short cut," was all he said.

For close to half an hour his explanation seemed to satisfy Jean, for she stayed close, even though he rode hard. But at the end of that interval, when he finally swung up into the timber that backed the mesa, she called out again: "Blaze! Let's stop. I think we're lost."

He reined in and let her come alongside, a ready answer again occurring to him. "I was supposed to sleep with the crew tonight. Thought I'd swing up Porcupine and tell 'em I couldn't be in until mornin'. It isn't much out of the way."

The girl was close enough so that he could distinguish faintly the outline of her face. He imagined that she was smiling. When she spoke, he knew it wasn't his imagination.

"Blaze," she said softly, "where are you really taking me?"

He was at first astonished, then angry as he realized that his ruse had failed. The girl was suspicious. He groped a moment for an explanation, and in the end knew there was none. Just as surely he knew that he couldn't carry out the idea that had sent him down to the Diamond. He couldn't lay a hand on this girl, force her to come with him; no matter how badly he needed her the innate sense of decency in him rebelled at that.

"There's a man bad hurt up in the hills," he told her simply. "I wanted someone to help me look after him. I reckon you can go back now."

"It's Joe Bonnyman, isn't it?" Jean said.

Blaze nodded wearily, not surprised that she should have guessed to whom he referred.

"You didn't think I'd have come if I'd known he was the one, did you?" Without waiting for his reply, the girl went on, her voice edged with gravity. "Is he badly hurt, Blaze? How did it happen?"

"Someone shot him and left him lyin' by the creek at the upper edge of the basin. Thought he was dead, I reckon. The slug hit him alongside the head, knocked him out. I've got him in a cave up there. His breathin' didn't sound any too good."

"Why didn't you tell me?" She was angry now. "We could have brought iodine and bandages. Now we'll have to get along with what we have. What's in that sack, Blaze?"

"Grub," he said sheepishly. So she had known all along of the sack tied to the horn of his saddle.

"We can at least be thankful for that." Jean paused a moment, then: "Well, we're wasting time. Show me the way."

"You mean you'll help?"

"Of course. I couldn't let a man die, could I?"

"And you won't give it away where he is?"

"Blaze, I'm terribly poor at telling directions. For all I know, we're on our way to Lodgepole."

As he touched his pony with spurs and went on, Blaze let his breath out in a long sigh of keen relief. You could never tell about women. Jean Vanover was no more lost than he was.

Homesteaders with Guns

Mike Saygar drew rein at the edge of the timber, within 100 yards of the spot where Joe Bonnyman's horse had thrown his rider at dusk yesterday evening. He let the others come up with him before he said, his voice lifted against the roar of the swollen Troublesome: "You got it straight what you're to do?"

Whitey and Pecos nodded, but Chuck Reibel's look was sullen as he said: "The devil with this sleepin' on the ground. It stiffens me up too much, Mike."

"You can travel any time you don't like the way you're treated, mister," came Saygar's smooth drawl. Ignoring Reibel, then, he lifted a hand, indicating the snow-patched reach of the basin baking under the hot early sun. "Run your lines each side of the creek. If you have trouble gettin' wire, forget your fences. Whitey, watch your temper in town. We don't want the law on us. Remember, you've come in here peaceable and all you want is to be let alone. Now go ahead and make it look right."

So saying, Saygar turned back into the trees. The others sat watching him go, until Pecos drawled: "Well, let's get goin'."

On the ride down out of the hills, they talked chiefly about the weather, and the way the sun had risen into a cloudless sky at dawn, two hours ago, to start the rapid melt that would see every creek on this side of the peaks over its banks by noon.

"There'll be hell to pay for what we're doin' tonight," Pecos commented once.

"What you worryin' about?" was Reibel's acid retort. "It ain't you they'll skin for it."

They rode into Lodgepole shortly after ten, going straight to the Land Office. The clerk there was only mildly interested when they asked to look over the plat maps in his big file case. Busy with his work, he left them alone.

But in half an hour, when Reibel politely asked for three sets of homestead papers, the clerk's curiosity came alive. He got the papers from his desk, handed them to Reibel, and queried: "Settlin' down here, are you?"

Reibel gave him little satisfaction beyond a nod before he returned to the office's side counter, where Whitey and Pecos were closely inspecting one of the maps. For the next twenty minutes, while the three strangers filled in their papers, the clerk had to control his curiosity. But at the end of that interval all three came over to his desk and laid their papers on it. The clerk picked up the first, Reibel's, and glanced at it.

He suddenly straightened in his chair at something he saw on the printed form. Hastily picking up the other two, he examined them. His jaw sagged open a moment. Then he laughed.

"You're out of luck, boys," he said. "That's closed country."

Reibel's brows lifted. "Closed? How come? There's a notice over in the post office at Junction that that land is open to lease or homestead. We looked it over and like it. We're movin' in."

"But you can't." was the clerk's smug rejoinder. "You'd have half a dozen of the biggest outfits in the country ganged up on you inside of a day."

"It's legal, ain't it?" Whitey drawled.

"Legal? Sure. But that basin's summer range for the Mesa Grande outfits, Anchor, Brush, Yoke, and a few others."

"Never heard of them brands," Pecos offered.

The clerk's eyes widened. "You haven't? Well, brother, you'll hear plenty if you stay around here. Where you from?"

"Colorado."

The clerk shook his head. "Sorry to disappoint you, gents. But it's no go.

"You mean we can't file on that creek up there?" queried Reibel.

"You can. But it won't do you any good. You'll be run out."

"That's our worry, ain't it?" Reibel drawled. He nodded down to the papers. "Go ahead and register those. We're movin' in."

The clerk argued, reasoned, and finally lost his temper. But in the end he wrote the names of Henry Jordan, Cyrus Smith, and Edward Tolley in his recorder's book, their titles to their quarter-sections being subject to their proving up on their basin homesteads in the next three years.

When Reibel, Pecos, and Whitey left the office, the clerk ducked out the back way and told the first man he met about the three strangers who were homesteading Aspen Basin. If Saygar's men hadn't stopped in at the Mile High for a drink before they went to the hardware store, they might have had better luck with Whitlow, the store owner. As it was, Whitlow knew who they were when they came back to his office and wanted to buy a wagonload of barbed wire.

The storekeeper's expression was sympathetic as he shook his head. "Sold my last spool yesterday, gents," he told them. "And that fool son-in-law of mine forgot to order any last week. So you'll have to wait."

"How long'll it be?" asked Reibel.

Whitlow shrugged. "Two weeks, maybe three. I'm sure sorry about this. Where you plannin' on puttin' up your fence?"

"Aspen Basin," Reibel answered.

Whitlow lifted his brows and said merely: "That's nice country up there. Closes in a little early in the winter, though. Thought about that?"

"We've thought about it," Reibel assured him. "Then we'll see you when the wire gets here." He led the others out of the store.

Bill Lyans was waiting for them on the walk out front. The deputy had had only four hours' sleep the night before, and his voice showed it as he stepped in front of them, asking brusquely: "You the three gents that're homesteadin' the basin?"

"That's us," Reibel said.

The deputy's stony glance appraised each one for a longer than polite moment. "You know what you're lettin' yourselves in for?" he asked sharply, finished with his inspection.

"Just what the devil is this?" Whitey drawled, and his voice wasn't pleasant. "We see a notice posted that good land's open to homestead. We look it over. We decide to file on it. Now every jasper we talk to warns us off. This is a free country, ain't it?"

"All of it's free but the basin," Lyans said.

"And why isn't it free?"

"Because for twenty years the basin's been summer range for the mesa outfits."

"Meanin' there ain't room for us?" Reibel queried.

"Meanin' Yace Bonnyman and Workman and a few others will swarm over you like a pack o' dogs on three crippled rabbits. You're playin' against a pat hand, gents. My advice is to forget the basin."

Reibel's glance narrowed. "These range hogs hire you, do they?"

"The county pays me." Lyans's face darkened under the insult.

"Then it's up to you to enforce the law," Reibel said easily. "Which means you arrest anyone that takes a notion to run us out. Correct?"

Lyons was on the spot and knew it. He didn't like the looks of two of these three; the third appeared to be a harmless enough cowpuncher. He was trying to find the patience to explain exactly how he stood in the matter when someone hailed him from out on the street.

Looking that way, Lyans saw Fred Vanover reining a sweat-lathered horse in toward him. Because he couldn't think of anything to say to the three strangers, he purposely ignored them and stepped out under the tie rail as Vanover came up.

The look on the Middle Arizona man's face warned the deputy that something more serious than the trouble he had just postponed was in store for him. Vanover looked tired and worn as he stared bleakly down at the deputy and said: "Lyans, something's happened to Jean. She's been kidnapped."

Before the deputy could say anything due to his surprise, Vanover was going on: "She left a note last night, saying she was going across to Merrill's, that the old man was worse, and the doctor had sent for her. I got home late and didn't think much about it. This morning I went across to Brush and found she hadn't been there, and hadn't been sent for. The rain last night washed out all the sign there was in the yard. I don't have a thing to go on."

"Come up to the office, Fred," Lyans said wearily. "Either the devil's got a hand in this or I've been on a straight diet o' locoweed."

* * * * *

Clark Dunne knew something was wrong several minutes after he got to town and stopped at the jail, where he saw Bill Lyans. That something was that there was no word of Joe's body having been discovered.

Two hours ago Clark had followed the Troublesome into the upper end of the basin and seen that Joe no longer lay where he had last night. About an hour before that a Brush rider had brought him and Bill Murdock the news of Jean Vanover's disappearance, along with orders from Lyans that one man was to stay on duty above Klingmeier's station in the pass, while the other came down to Lodgepole to join the hunt for the girl. On the ride down here, Clark had swung over to Diamond, Middle Arizona's layout, and had had the luck to talk briefly with Neal Harper.

Now, a little after five in the afternoon, as Clark relaxed in a barber chair and let Sid Ordway begin work on his three-day beard, he had time to think things out—or thought he did. The net result of his thinking was only a heightening of his uneasiness.

Joe's body had been moved—that much Clark had seen with his own eyes. Yet no word of this had reached Lyans. Someone, for some obscure reason, was hiding the fact that Joe was already dead.

The more he thought about it, the more puzzled Clark became. Added to this puzzlement was irritation at Sid Ordway's insistent talk. Ordinarily the barber was a quiet man. But too much had happened today for Ordway to maintain his usual reserve, and he told about being on the street when Fred Vanover rode in to talk to Lyans. He became eloquent. "There was Bill, madder'n a pup with a new-docked tail, talkin' to these three strangers that say they're movin' into the basin. Then along comes Vanover with fresh trouble. You should've seen Bill. Fit to be . . ."

"What about the strangers?" Clark interrupted.

"Ain't you heard?" asked the barber. "There's three of 'em. Goin' to homestead along the Troublesome in the basin."

"You don't say!" Clark suppressed a smile with an effort.

He had momentarily forgotten his plan for Mike Saygar and his men, forgotten the arrangements he had made with the outlaw while talking with him at Hoelseker's cabin yesterday, before Chuck Reibel brought him into the cabin with a rifle at his back. He should have known. Saygar and his men had come down to the basin early this morning. Of course. They were the ones who had found Joe's body. Because of what was to happen tonight, Saygar would naturally want to keep the posse at work, keep as many men as possible away from the thinned roundup crews working the country in back of the mesa.

As Ordway finished shaving him, Clark became quite genial. If the barber noticed the difference in his manner, he gave no sign of it. It was with an effort that Clark kept from laughing outright when Ordway told him of the sensation created in Lodgepole by the appearance of Reibel, Whitey, and Pecos.

"There'll be hell to pay if they fence in that water," the barber predicted.

* * * * *

123

Out on the street a few minutes later, Clark wondered how to take advantage of this newest development of Saygar's hiding the fact that Joe was already dead. It would be hard for him to get up to the basin and see either Saygar or his men, for Lyans was gathering everyone available in the search for Vanover's daughter. This afternoon close to fifty men had set out for the high country in what Lyans himself admitted was a pretty feeble effort.

"Trouble is," Lyans had said, "we don't have anything to go on except that note she left her father. Who do you reckon the man could have been that came after her, Clark?"

Clark hadn't been able to make even a guess. Engrossed as he was with his one problem, he hadn't given the circumstance of Jean Vanover's disappearance much consideration. Now he did, seeing in it that same mysterious quality he had first associated with the disappearance of Joe's body.

He was sauntering up the walk toward the hotel, having decided to use this extra hour before he was due at the jail over a leisurely supper. His stride broke and he halted abruptly. For a full minute he stood at the edge of the walk, deep in thought. From a hard concentration, his face eased into a smile. Presently, when he went on to the hotel, he was whistling softly.

Before he went in to the four-table dining room to eat, he climbed the stairs to his room. There he tore the back from an envelope and, sitting at the washstand, spent several minutes laboriously printing out a message on the segment of raggedly torn paper. Finished with that, he blew out the lamp and went to the window; he touched a match to the remainder of the torn envelope. When the match burned down to his fingers, he dropped it out into the alley.

He spent some forty minutes over a steak supper, topping it off with a piece of pie and three cups of black coffee. During this interval, several men came up and spoke to him. Most of them were men joining the posse tonight. One, Sam Thrall, wore a bandage on his head.

As Thrall approached the table, his face was set in a heavy scowl. Clark, seeing that scowl and knowing the reason for it—the Brush crewman this afternoon had told him about Joe's theft of Thrall's horse—schooled his expression to one of concern.

"Tough luck about your horse, Sam," he told the Emporium owner.

"To the devil with the horse," Thrall said. His hand went to his bandaged head. "This's what Bonnyman's goin' to answer for."

"Hurt, does it?"

"Plenty. I've already spoken for a seat in the jury box when they try that jasper."

"Think they'll bring him in?" asked Clark.

"They will," Thrall said flatly. "Even with you and Blaze tryin' to hide him."

Clark looked at the store owner levelly a moment. "What makes you think Blaze and I are hiding him?"

"You're his friends, ain't you? And wasn't Blaze in here this afternoon lookin' for you?"

"Was he?"

"He was." Thrall shook a finger at Clark. "Watch your step, Dunne." He glared at Clark and, turning, went out of the dining room.

Clark lingered over his last cup of coffee, considering the inference to Thrall's remarks. He decided finally that nothing in what the man had said could influence the thing he had set out to do. He was sorry he hadn't been able to see Blaze this afternoon. The redhead might have had something important to tell him. What that could be, beyond the fact that Blaze had possibly been up to Hoelseker's cabin this morning and found it deserted, Clark didn't know.

Paying for his meal, Clark left the hotel, crossing the street to the Emporium. He went to the back end of the store, stopping at the counter alongside the wire cage with the window placarded *Post Office*. Behind the counter a clerk in thick-lensed spectacles sat on a stool.

"'Evenin', Brad," Clark said. "Any mail for me?"

"Ought to be. You ain't been in for a couple days." The clerk stared near-sightedly at Clark, left his stool, and stepped behind the wicket, turning his back as he reached into the rack of pigeon-holed compartments making up the far side of the cage. A similar rack occupied the side of the cage nearest Clark.

Glancing quickly behind him and up toward the store's front, Clark made sure that no one was watching him. While the clerk's back was still turned, he took the torn piece of envelope from his pocket, reached around the end of the cage, and thrust it in the pigeonhole numbered **4**. That compartment, he knew, was for Acme's mail.

By the time the near-sighted clerk faced around, Clark was leaning idly on the counter, well out of reach of the cage.

"You made a good haul tonight," Brad said, handing a thick packet of letters across.

Clark thanked him and left the store.

* * * * *

A good half hour later, Sam Thrall burst in through the door of Lyans's jail office. He was out of breath and red in the face. Half a dozen men, Clark among them, were there with the deputy. Thrall tried to speak, couldn't get his breath, and instead tossed a scrap of paper onto the desk before Lyans.

"What's ailin' you, Sam?" the lawman asked, picking up the paper.

"Read it!" Thrall managed to gasp.

Lyans looked at the paper and straightened suddenly in his chair, his face losing color. He glanced quickly up at the store owner, asking tonelessly: "Where'd you find this?"

"Acme's mailbox."

"Who found it?"

"Brad." Thrall wiped his perspiring face. "Vanover got his mail right after the train come in at noon. So the box should've been empty. Brad always takes a pretty careful look at things before he closes up the cage. He found this just now as he was lockin' up for the night."

"What is it, Bill?" one of the others asked.

Lyans handed the scrap of paper to the speaker, not saying anything.

They all gathered about the man. Clark, looking over his shoulder, read his own crudely penciled message:

Vanover:
Have Lyans call off his dogs, or you don't get the girl back.
Bonnyman

For the interval it would have taken a man to draw in a slow breath and as slowly exhale, no one spoke. Then Clark gave a toneless laugh.

"What's so funny?" Lyans growled.

"Nothing. Only Joe Bonnyman didn't write that."

"Yeah? How come you're so sure?"

Clark hesitated, as though lost for an explanation. At length he said lamely: "It just isn't like Joe. He'd never lay a finger on a woman. He . . ."

"He clubbed Merrill to death!" Sam Thrall cut in. "He meant to do the same to me! Why the hell wouldn't he do this?"

The man to whom Lyans had given the note looked at Clark, and there was open hostility in his eyes. "Sam's right, Dunne. Joe and me used to get on pretty well, and up to now I ain't been sure about him. Right now I am. If it ever comes to hangin', I'll take the job of springin' the trap out from under him!"

An angry murmur of agreement came from the others. Then, seeing Clark properly silenced, their attention came back to Lyans.

The deputy knew it was being left to him to make a decision. From the deadly serious expression on his face, it was obvious that he was weighing all the possibilities. Finally he stood up, reaching around to take his shell belt and holstered gun from the back of the chair. As he cinched the weapon to his waist, he said: "We'll go see Vanover. But we'll do it on the quiet, just in case Bonnyman's here in town watchin' us. Split up when you go out and let on like you're goin' home. Half an hour from now meet a mile out the trail." His glance rested briefly on Clark. "You needn't come along, Clark."

Rustlers Work at Night

That late afternoon saw Charley Staples's main Singletree shipping herd, along with 150 head of Anchor steers, bunched far and near the mesa's edge in the triangle formed by the confluence of the Troublesome and the Porcupine. Sherman, the Anchor straw boss, took a look at the swollen waters of the two creeks, at the white water, racing into the mouth of Rainbow Gorge close ahead, and opined: "I'll let the seat o' my pants take root right here before I try a-crossin' through that water, Charley."

An hour ago Staples had come up with the herd to see what luck his crew was having. He had already made his decision, which coincided with the Anchor man's. But, because he was an owner, he pretended to give the matter more careful deliberation, especially in view of the fact that tomorrow a thirty-car freight was due on the siding ten miles west of Lodgepole to take his first beef shipment.

He glanced off south to the head of the gorge. Rainbow was little better than a mile long, but even with the Troublesome at its lowest, the waters foamed along the steeply dropping and rocky bed of the gorge with a swiftness neither man nor animal could stand against. From a certain angle at the foot of the rim, where the deep notch emptied out onto the flats 400 feet below, a man could most always see a rainbow thrown up by the water spray along about sunset.

Noticing where Staples was looking, Sherman said: "Wonder what that'd do to a critter that got swept into it?"

"Ground beef and bone meal," was Staples's sparse but eloquent answer. He turned in the saddle and looked out across the mesa, along the line of the Troublesome.

Again the Anchor man read his mind. "There ain't even footin' for a horse, Charley. I know. I tried it and didn't think I'd get out alive. Horse is still bloated with all the water he swallowed."

Staples nodded, reining around and speaking to his men as he went away: "You boys are due for some sleep. There's plenty of grass and water here, and these critters won't drift overnight. If I was you, I'd get back to the layout."

Which advice his men and Sherman acted upon at once. By nightfall, Singletree's cook was back in his shack at headquarters and serving up a meal for nine men.

* * * * *

From a high point in the timber above the mesa, Mike Saygar observed all this across a distance of some three miles. He saw the dark smear of the herd drift into the wedge of land between the two creeks, saw it pause there, and then, along about dusk, spread out and away from the creeks. Before the light completely failed him, he spotted a chuck wagon going in along the trail leading to Staples's spread, two miles to the east. and nestling close in to the hills, out of sight.

An hour later, Saygar drifted in on the fire before the lean-to close to a pine-topped knoll along the Troublesome at almost the exact center of Aspen Basin. He could see no one around the fire, so, as he approached, he called: "All right, you rannies! It's me."

Whitey and Pecos, and, finally, Chuck Reibel drifted in out of the shadows. Pecos hunkered down by the fire and pulled a Dutch oven out of the coals with a forked stick, putting a half-gallon coffee pot in its place.

"Come and get it," he drawled, tilting the lid from the oven.

Mike Saygar liked to eat. Tonight, as usual, he relished the meal Pecos had prepared, an onion-and-tomato-flavored beef stew. Along with this there was pan bread and coffee. As he wolfed down his heaping plateful of the stew, the rustler chief listened idly to the talk of his men that was concerned chiefly with the minor sensation they had created in town this morning in taking out their homestead papers.

Saygar rarely spoke when he ate. But once, when Whitey turned to him and queried—"What's all this addin' up to, boss?"—he took pains to answer carefully: "A nice stake for us, if we work it right. What we're doin' tonight ought to split the ranchers and the cattle company again. Each outfit'll think we're workin' for the other. If they don't start usin' their guns after this, we'll give 'em even a better reason for it."

Whitey's look was still skeptical. Presently he drawled: "The thing that's itchin' me is Dunne. What's he gettin' out of it?"

"Don't be nosy, feller," Saygar said quietly.

Whitey's look turned sullen, but he was through with his questions. After that they ate in silence.

When Pecos returned from the creek after sand-washing their tin cups and plates, Saygar said without preliminary: "Let's go."

Ten minutes later they headed away from the camp, going downbasin, Saygar leading them well into the edge of the creek. The horses made work of it, with the insecure footing of the flooded stream's rocky bank. But Saygar kept to the stream all the way to the lower edge of the basin, a good half hour's going, where they came upon a ridge that marked the beginning of a rocky and treeless tangle of hills falling gradually toward the mesa.

Saygar rode with even more care now, making long detours to avoid crossing the occasional areas of topsoil. They left the roar of the Troublesome far behind, until it became but a faint murmur almost inaudible over the *clatter* of their ponies' hoofs on bare rock.

The night's chill was settling down and this slow going made Reibel, who had foolishly worn only shirt and vest, hunch his shoulders for added warmth. Overhead, the dusting of myriad stars in a cloudless sky gave them enough light to see plainly where they were going. The faint breeze carried with it the clean-washed smell of pine and juniper that flanked this narrow strip of barrens. Once their horses spooked as a startled steer crashed away through a nearby tangle of scrub oak in the bed of a wash. Saygar stopped as they neared the lower margin of the rocky breaks, better than two hours out of camp.

"Can we hit that Diamond trail without leavin' this rock, Pecos?" he asked.

Pecos thought a moment. "Try it off to the left," he said then.

Saygar turned east and presently, without leaving the rock, they came to the line of a trail and took it, not caring that now they were leaving sign, for this trail was used fairly heavily.

Twenty minutes more of steady going brought them to within sight of Diamond's bunkhouse lights. Those lights of Middle Arizona's headquarters were less than half a mile away as the four men rounded a spur of the hills backing the mesa. At that point Saygar swung sharply off the trail and southwest across the lush grass flat of the mesa. He rode neither fast nor slow, but at an alternate walk and trot. Close to an hour of this riding brought the sound of the Troublesome close again.

Finally Pecos pulled up abreast of Mike. "This ought to be about right, boss," he drawled.

They halted. Saygar squinted, trying to pick out details of what lay ahead. At length he said: "Whitey and Reibel will work off to the right. You stay left, Pecos. When you come on 'em, push easy until they begin jammin' up. I'll give you half an hour. When I shoot, you do the same. The rest ought to take care of itself."

"You want 'em all pushed in, Mike?" Reibel asked.

"No. There's too many. Dunne said not to bother if even half of 'em broke away. One thing more. We're goin' back the way we came, across that rock. You're to hit that Diamond trail and ride it a ways before you head for the basin. Go ahead now. And make it good."

They separated, drifting away to be swallowed by the night. Saygar sat his horse, motionless for many minutes. Then, lifting his reins, he put the animal straight south at a slow walk. Shortly he came upon a bunch of grazing steers, and reined over toward the bunch. They lifted their heads, wheeled, and lumbered away at his approach. He saw more cattle. Patiently he reined from side to side, pushing them on after the others. Soon those gathering bunches made a broken black line close to the outward limit of his vision. Saygar rode in on them obliquely, pushing first against one segment, then another, until he had them moving slowly in the direction of the distant angry mutter that was the pounding of tons of water down the mouth of Rainbow Gorge.

When they started breaking out of line, loping back the way he had come, Saygar drew his .45, lifted it above his head, and sent one shot, then another, racketing into the confusion of sound. As the explosions cut loose, the nearest steers plunged away from it, into the massed animals ahead. From off to Saygar's left came other muted gunshots. Then Reibel and Whitey opened up far away to his right. The bawling of the cattle was drowned by a growing hoof thunder. Fear-crazed animals reared and plunged, pawing the backs of those blocking their way. A few turned and ran back away from the main body of the herd. Saygar let them go. Time and again he shot into the air. When his gun was empty, he reloaded, taking his time, sensing the relentless forward surging of the herd now.

Up along the creekbank, the inky, fast-swirling waters formed a barrier the closest animals shunned with greater fear than that which had made them run from the sudden press of animals closing in on them. But the press of those gun-shy steers farthest behind pushed them relentlessly on, to the edge of the water, into it, then on until they lost a foothold.

Rank after rank of animals plunged into the creek, lost footing, and tried to swim to the far bank close at hand. A few made it. But the powerful rush of the current caught the rest, swept them relentlessly on toward the roaring rapids that marked the Troublesome's precipitous plunge into the depths of the gorge. The bawling of the lost animals was drowned in that roar as they were swallowed by the curving high crests of the mounded waves racing across the jagged humps of huge boulders.

Saygar felt the forward motion of the herd slow. In another moment it stopped and he emptied his gun over the heads of the nearest steers. The sounds seemed to drive them completely mad, for they suddenly turned on him. He wheeled his pony around barely in time, driving home his spurs. His horse ran for his life, urged on in stark fear at the thunder of hoofs on all sides. A plunging steer came close to knocking the horse from his feet. Saygar lost a stirrup and thought he was going to be thrown. Then, miraculously, the horse pounded into the open and away and he was safe.

Behind, the bawling of the herd faded gradually until finally the night's serenity remained unbroken by anything but the steady slur of the pony's hoofs sliding through the knee-deep grass.

Saygar struck the Diamond trail a quarter mile beyond the point he and his men had left it. He turned in toward the Middle Arizona Ranch and rode the trail in that direction until he saw the lights once more. Then, heading back up the trail, he started for the basin.

Danger Signals

The glowing coals of the cedar fire tinted the cave's walls with a ghostly pinkish light that lacked the strength to cast a shadow. Jean Vanover sat in the feeble outer radius of that light, near the blanket-draped figure that gave out but a faint whisper of shallow breathing. It had been this way last night and all day today, and now, at the beginning of this second night, there was no change that Jean could see in the unconscious man.

Last night there had been something to do. Before Blaze had left, they had bathed the deep gash in Joe's head and bandaged it with a cleanly washed strip of the flour sack. Then, with Blaze gone in the hour past midnight, Jean had heated some condensed milk in a pan on the fire and tried to make Joe drink it. He hadn't seemed able to swallow. The girl tried every way she could to make him, as he lay flat on the blankets, finally lifting his upper body onto her knees. It was while she held him that way, his head lying in the crook of her arm, and looked down into his face, that she felt the first unaccountable stir of feeling toward him.

Before that moment, Joe Bonnyman had been simply a man hurt badly and in need of help, a man who perhaps piqued her curiosity in a strange, indefinable way. But, as she held him close, feeling his solidness and strength, and yet knowing that he was as utterly helpless as a small child, that new and stirring emotion took her. He was hers to watch and protect, to bring back to life, and since that very moment she had wanted Joe Bonnyman to live, wanted it more than she'd ever wanted anything. She couldn't define her reasons for that fervent hope. It was there and it was all that seemed to matter.

The day had dragged. Jean cooked and ate a meal, not relishing it. Many times her imagining had taken her quickly across the cave to kneel beside Joe in a breathless expectancy, thinking she had heard a change in his breathing, or that he had moved. Each of those times had brought a deep disappointment. He was always the same, lying the way he had when she last looked down at him; she would feel his pulse and it would be strong, betraying her fear that his shallow breathing was a prelude to death. Through the long hours she had been half sick with fear of his dying. At times she imagined she could feel another presence in the cave, a sinister presence, and in those moments she would go to Joe and lift his head into her lap and hold it close, as though shielding this man who should be a stranger, but wasn't, from the beyond.

Now, with the total darkness of this second night, Jean was fighting a battle of her own. Sleep was relentlessly crowding in on her. She fought giving in to it with all her will, drinking the coffee she had brewed at midday, bathing her eyes with cold water, even rubbing them to make them stay open.

She invented a problem to keep awake, going across to sit beside Joe and thinking back on what little Blaze had told her or the circumstances surrounding the shooting. Trying to remember what little she had learned from the doctor about dealing with emergencies like this. Had she forgotten anything? Was there anything at all she could do to help this man keep his slender hold on life? Trying to think of something helped her fight her drowsiness.

When she had exhausted every possibility, Jean's thoughts turned to something else. Ruth Merrill loved Joe Bonnyman, and Ruth was the one who should be here now. Jean knew that Ruth had been Joe's choice years ago. More than likely, Ruth was one of the reasons Joe had come back home. Jean thought of the two, what the future might hold for them, in an angry, defensive way that had no logic or reasoning behind it. It became as though she, not Ruth, had some rightful hold over this man and was unwilling to relinquish it. She finally realized the absurdity of her attitude and tried to be amused by it. But that feeling of possessiveness stayed with her, regardless of the effort she made not to let it.

In late afternoon she had dozed for a few minutes, stirring out of a deep, dreamless sleep with an acute feeling of guilt. As dusk settled prematurely in the narrow cañon, she had gone out and gathered more firewood, knowing that Blaze might not have the chance to get back here tonight. He had said he wouldn't come if there was the slightest possibility of being followed, and with another night's lonely vigil in prospect, the girl was counting on the friendly glow of the fire to drive out her despairing mood.

When she could no longer make out the light at the cave mouth, when the darkness in the cañon was complete, that feeling of despair became so strong that she wanted to cry out. She was sure now that Joe Bonnyman would never again be alive and well. The injustice of the thing galled her. For, from what Blaze had said last night, she saw now that Joe was more the victim of circumstances than the unprincipled betrayer of family and friends. She was a little ashamed of her father's share in giving Joe the name he bore on this range.

So engrossed did Jean become in trying to see how Joe was to come out of this, provided he lived, that she let the fire die. When the sound of a pony's hoofs striking rock beyond the cave mouth echoed in to her, the cave had become a sinister place. She was badly frightened.

She reached for the Colt Blaze had left with her the night before, and, pushing back into the shadows at the rear wall, she waited, hardly daring to breath.

Then Blaze's cheerful—"Anybody home?"—sounded hollowly down the short tunnel, and the quickness of easing nerve strain hit her and left her almost too weak to speak.

"Just the two of us, Blaze," she said, trying to make her tone casual.

When Coyle crawled into the light, his freckled good-natured face showed a wide grin. "Then he . . . he's hangin' on?"

"He's just the same."

They knelt alongside Joe, Blaze reaching down to feel of his friend's wrist. When he straightened, he gave the girl a look, and his expression sobered. "You're tuckered out. Better get some sleep while I sit with him."

"I'm not sleepy," she insisted. "How is Dad taking this?"

"Sort of hard," he admitted. "They've got men out. I wanted to tell him, but . . ."

When he didn't go on, she said: "I know. It wouldn't be fair to Joe. Dad will understand when it's all over."

Her face flushed after she had spoken, and Blaze knew that she instantly regretted her choice of words. Pretending not to notice, he said quickly: "They've put a reward out for Joe. A thousand dollars. Want to turn him in and we'll split it?"

"Blaze!"

He laughed softly, glad to have prodded her from her dark mood. He went on then, telling her of the three strangers who proposed to homestead the basin, and how the mesa ranchers would be too busy until the hunt was over to do much about them, how if they thought much about these homesteaders, they'd probably decide they were hired to come in by Middle Arizona. But he saw that Jean wasn't listening. Her eyes seemed to be staring through him at something beyond, and whatever she was seeing patterned her face with sadness, an expression that changed her prettiness to outright beauty.

Blaze paused a moment, then asked quietly: "What is it, Jean?"

It was the first time he had ever called her by name. It seemed to bring them closer. Abruptly she choked back a sob and whispered: "Blaze, I'm afraid, terribly afraid."

"What of, girl? Joe? He's tough, I tell you, hard to kill. He'll be all right."

What he said didn't change her wide-eyed and alarmed look. "We can't stop hoping, can we? He'll wake up tonight, won't he?" She lifted a hand and ran it over her eyes. "Don't pay any attention to me, Blaze." She tried to smile. "Build up the fire. Let's see if he'll eat something."

Blaze reached across Joe to get a stick of wood. Hand outstretched, he all at once froze in that attitude. Then he was saying hoarsely, gladly: "Joe, boy! It's me . . . Blaze."

And Jean was hearing Joe's evenly drawled: "You always were a sucker for a wake, you red-headed bum."

Blaze hunkered back on his heels and let out a whoop that made the cavern ring. Tears glistened in Jean's eyes. She brushed them away as Joe's glance came around on her. His smile broadened and he seemed about to say something when a grimace of pain crossed his face and he closed his eyes.

He lay that way a long moment in which Jean's breath wouldn't come for fear of the thing she had been dreading. Then, gradually, his expression eased and he was looking at her once more.

"Does it hurt much?" she asked.

"It did there for a minute. You . . . you've been here all the time?"

"Since midnight last night," Blaze told him. "I couldn't think of anyone else to bring."

"They know where you are?" Joe still looked at the girl.

"No one knows," she assured him. "You're safe. We'll keep you here until you're well again."

"What will they think?" he said.

"It doesn't matter what they think." She spoke defensively. "What does is that you're alive. We . . . we weren't sure you'd ever be this way again."

"Who was it shot from behind that rock, feller?" Blaze queried.

"What rock?" Joe asked absently. "There are lots of rocks, big ones and little ones, all falling up the hill. Up, not down Blaze! It sure was a . . ." His voice trailed off and he closed his eyes..

Blaze gave Jean a queer look. "You were lyin' along the creek up at the edge of the basin when I . . ." He broke off to reach over and shake Joe by the shoulder. "Joe!" he said urgently. "You hear me?"

But Joe's eyes remained closed. His breathing was deep, even. After a moment Blaze said: "He's passed out again." He didn't look at the girl.

Jean sat back. " Does it mean he won't . . . ?" she began lifelessly.

"He'll be all right," Blaze quickly assured her. "But you've got to get some rest. Here, take this blanket. He can have my coat." He pulled the blanket off Joe and spread it out for her.

This time she made no protest, but lay on the blanket and closed her eyes. Blaze, putting wood on the fire, thought she dropped off to sleep immediately. But just as he decided this and faced the sobering possibility that Joe might this time not regain consciousness, she spoke: "I'm going to stay here until he can be moved. And, Blaze . . ."

"Yes?" he answered when she paused.

"I'm not afraid any longer."

"Neither am I. Never was," Blaze lied. "Now get some shut-eye."

A moment later her even breathing told him she was really asleep this time.

In the next two hours Joe wakened three times, each time seeming a little stronger and more rational. At last he asked to sit up. At first Blaze wouldn't let him, but then he gave in, moving Joe so that he could sit with his back to the wall. For a minute or two Joe's face paled. Then his color seemed better.

"I could eat a side o' beef," he said finally. "Anything around?"

Blaze filled a tin cup with steaming coffee he'd put on the fire after Jean had gone to sleep. "Try this."

Joe downed the coffee. "Anything else on the menu?"

Blaze heated a cupful of the condensed milk. Although Joe made a wry face when it was offered, he drank it.

"Better?" Blaze asked.

"Some. If that wall across there would only stop spinnin'. Sit still, can't you?"

"All right," Blaze said, realizing that the aftereffects of the concussion must be severe. "Here's something to steady you down. Three homesteaders filed on quarter-sections in the basin this mornin'. They're movin' right in."

"No," Joe breathed, and it seemed to Blaze that his eyes were more alert. "Who are they?"

Halfway through Blaze's description of the three strangers, Joe cut in with: "Saygar's crew."

"What about his bunch?"

"That's them, those three. The young one was blond, sort of tall? Did you notice the way he wore his iron?"

When Blaze described Whitey in detail, Joe was sure. He told of his ride up the Troublesome, of running into Saygar at Hoelseker's cabin, of his escape with Clark.

"Then it must've been one of that bunch that bushwhacked you and left you layin' there for someone else to find," Blaze said. "No one in this country has ever laid eyes on those sidewinders, only a few on Saygar himself. He probably put a man after you to make sure you wouldn't give away this play he's making for the basin." A look of worry came to his face. "Do you reckon he could have sent another man out after Clark? Clark wasn't in town today."

"You'll have to find out," Joe said, his lean face going grave. "I should have done like Clark said, headed out. Then I'd have been with him as far as the pass. Blaze, there's a gent that don't happen often. He invited a slug in his guts just to save me when we made that break."

Blaze eased the somber run of his friend's thoughts by saying: "If anything had happened to him, I'd've heard of it. Murdock would have reported down to Lyans."

"That's so," Joe agreed, and seemed relieved. "How do you figure this play of Saygar's? He's a rustler, not a rancher."

"I can't figure it."

"He's workin' for someone."

Blaze frowned. "Middle Arizona?"

"Maybe." Joe looked down at Jean and gave a slow shake of the head. "But not for Vanover. What's his foreman like, this Neal Harper? Would he be smart enough to hide behind Vanover and set out to take over the country for the outfit the way they tried to in the beginnin'?"

"Search me. That jasper's a hard one to figure. I've had him pegged as a brain-shy gun boss. But maybe I'm wrong. Vanover agreed at the meetin' the other night to let him go. Accordin' to the girl, he's agreed to pull out tomorrow."

"Without any fuss?"

"So she says. Vanover never liked him much, because him and that crew he brought in made it seem like Diamond was cocked for trouble. The way she makes it look, Vanover's been just as bogged down over this mess as the rest of us."

"Maybe she's tellin' the truth, Blaze."

Blaze shrugged. "I'd take her word before most anyone else I know. But if it ain't been Middle Arizona, who has been stirrin' up all this trouble?"

"The same party that's behind Saygar."

Blaze sat a little straighter, eying Joe sharply. "That don't hold water," he said patiently. "There's just two sides to this, and only two. There ain't no in-between."

"There could be one we don't know about."

"But who, damn it?"

Joe shrugged. "We could find out by makin' Saygar talk."

"Providin' we could find Saygar. And providin' he talks in his sleep. Or maybe we should go to him and say . . . 'Please, Mister Saygar, tell us who you're workin' for?'"

"We'll have a try anyway." A grin broke across Joe's pallid, lean face.

"When?"

"Why not tonight?"

Blaze laughed. "You ain't strong enough to hold a cup steady, let alone stick a saddle. A lot o' help you'd be. Besides, I've got to be back at the layout tonight to keep Yace quiet. If he suspected anything, it'd be tough on both of us."

"He's ready to turn me in?" Joe asked tonelessly.

"I can't make him out, and that's a fact," the redhead said. "First I think he's thinkin' one way and then he'll do somethin' to make me wonder if he isn't thinkin' the other. But we can't take any chances on him."

"Then you can come back tomorrow night with a spare horse. We'll see Saygar then."

"I'll try to make it," Blaze agreed.

"How about the girl?" Joe asked softly, looking across at Jean.

"She's on our side, friend," Blaze said quickly. "She'll do whatever we ask."

"Even to keepin' quiet about me?"

"If she thinks it'll help, she'll tell her old man anything we say. No one was at Diamond when I went after her but the cook, and he was asleep. I tolled her away with a story about John Merrill bein' sick. She left a note for her father. It was just plain fool luck that she didn't mention me in it. So there's nothin' to connect us with where she's been."

Something Blaze had said had taken Joe's attention. He appeared reluctant to mention it, but asked finally: "How's Ruth?"

"Haven't seen her." Blaze's tone was curt. "Old John's had another stroke. I reckon she's pretty busy takin' care of him." He studied Joe closely. "Don't stick your neck out by tryin' to see her," he advised. "The farther you stay from the mesa, the better off you'll be."

"Did I say I wanted to see her?" Joe bridled.

"No. But you were a sucker for that honey-colored hair o' hers once, and you're actin' like you'd like another try." Blaze came slowly erect. He glanced toward the pile of firewood, down at Jean, finally to the corner where the provisions he'd brought from Diamond lay. He was obviously embarrassed at having said too much. "I'll have to be goin'. Can you get along?"

"Easy enough," Joe drawled.

"About Jean. See if you can't figure out a story for her to give Vanover."

"I'll think of something."

"Then I'll see you tomorrow night. Could I get you some grub before I pull out?"

Joe shook his head, still stung by Blaze's outspoken condemnation of Ruth. "Couldn't eat it right now."

Blaze hesitated, knowing that his uncalled-for indictment of Ruth had put a barrier between them. His impulse was to get out of here, now, before he really had to. He should be staying a little longer to make sure that Joe was able to take care of himself. But that reminder that Joe still cared for a girl who had once made a fool of him, and that Ruth herself might encourage him if she were given the chance, had filled Blaze with a savage anger. He had tried to hold it in check, but couldn't. So now he said abruptly—"Be seein' you."— and went out along the short tunnel, stooped over, and not looking back.

It wasn't until he was out of the cañon and halfway down across the basin, with his rancor toward Ruth Merrill gradually lessening, that the let-down hit him. He started trembling. At first, he thought it was the biting chill of this late hour, then he realized he was quite warm, and that it was something else. His rein hand shook so that he had to rest it on the horn to steady it. A weakness hit his knee, and it was easier to sit the saddle than to stand in stirrup as was his habit.

144

He knew he was tired. But this was something else. Without a clear awareness of the surge of feeling that was in him, yet knowing it was this feeling and not his fatigue that was making him feel this way, Blaze was for the first time struck by the full significance of Joe's being alive and not dying. Things seemed all right now, damned fine in fact! Two hours ago nothing had been right. Looking back on those hours tonight and last night while he and Jean sat waiting for something to happen, yet dreading that it should happen, Blaze felt momentarily ashamed of the way he'd unburdened himself to the girl. No, he wasn't ashamed, he decided. Jean Vanover was a fine woman. So fine, in fact, that tonight he had forgotten who she was and talked to her the way he'd have talked to a man, a close friend. And now Joe was going to live. Together they'd lick this thing, whatever it was, whoever it was. He and Joe Bonnyman, the lanky kid he'd seen grow into manhood, would take this thing by the horns and throw it. Throw it hard and clean. They'd be a hard combination to beat.

Suddenly Blaze felt good, so good he rammed his spurs to his horse's flanks and raced across the last, flat open stretch of the lower basin. The chill wind knifing against his face braced him; the excitement of having come through as bad a two days as he'd ever lived drove out his weariness. He didn't want to wait for another night to get started at this thing. Right now he could walk up to Mike Saygar and beat the truth out of him, the truth about whom he was working for, what lay behind his men homesteading the basin. But, more importantly than this, and something that must come first, was a heart-to-heart talk with Yace. The hard-headed old fool needed to be told a few things, such as that his son was worth two of him, and that he couldn't any longer hide behind that high and mighty way of his and expect to get away with it. From now on Yace was either going to have to throw in with them to lick this thing, or lose his foreman. Blaze decided that definitely, where never before had his threats to quit Anchor been anything but a soon regretted impulse. Now it was the real thing. Yace would back his son all the way or to hell with him.

Blaze was thinking this as he rode clear of the trees flanking the rim of Porcupine Cañon and saw, far to the west, the lights of Anchor ablaze. He came a little straighter in the saddle, a quick glance at the wheeling stars showing him it was past two, lacking a couple hours of dawn. The crew was always up and about early, but not this early. Something was wrong at Anchor.

As he rode down toward those lights signaling danger, Blaze was gripped by a grim sense of foreboding. Things were moving fast toward a showdown on this dynamite-packed range, and without anything definite to back up his feeling the red-headed Anchor foreman had a premonition amounting to conviction that tonight would see that showdown.

Murder at Brush

Clark Dunne rode in on the lights of John Merrill's Brush Ranch a little before midnight. The two hours it had taken him to make the slow fifteen miles out from town had brought some sobering thoughts and much worry. First off, he'd tried to puzzle out the answer to the disappearance of Joe Bonnyman's body and his death not being reported to Bill Lyans. Secondly, he wondered if his talk with Mike Saygar at the cabin yesterday had been convincing. Would Saygar come in on this thing for the money he was to get out of it? Clark had no illusions where the outlaw was concerned. Saygar could be trusted only so long as he stood to profit from a thing; beyond that point, he would sell out to the highest bidder. Just now the outlaw looked to Clark for those profits. Soon—maybe sooner than Clark knew—Saygar might transfer his loyalties. It was up to Clark to keep that from happening.

It took a man like Mike Saygar to see the possibilities in taking a long shot like the one he was taking tonight, or, rather, Clark hoped he was following orders. It might take several months for Saygar to cash in on the partnership he had joined. Until then, Clark decided, the outlaw was to be trusted. What happened after that was another thing. If worse came to worst, a man could always use a gun. Saygar bore no charmed life; a bullet would stop him as quickly as the next man.

Clark eyed the night-shadowed layout as he rode in toward the house lights, near now. He couldn't see plainly in the darkness but his mind's eye built the picture of the spread from the few scant details that showed through the obscurity. The lights were coming from the house, the big tile-roofed stone house with the two long wings that was crammed with tasteful furnishings shipped out from the East.

John Merrill was unlike these other mesa ranchers; he came from a moneyed, aristocratic family, and Brush had always seemed an outpost of culture and refinement, untouched by the cruder life of this cattle frontier. The Merrill family's tradition was in part responsible for Ruth's aloof ways. In a poorer land, John Merrill's extravagance would soon have impoverished him. But here on Mesa Grande wealth grew up out of the ground faster than a man could spend it. So Brush remained a fairly prosperous outfit even for the expensive taste of its owner who had been bred to the purple. If John Merrill had had the drive of a Yace Bonnyman, Brush would have been a more powerful outfit than Anchor.

That Brush would one day be the power on this range had long been a dream of Clark's. Until lately, it had been a far-fetched dream, one that included himself and Ed Merrill as partners in a vast, hazily developing enterprise. Now Ed was dead and there remained only old John Merrill to share what Brush represented. Thinking of it in this new light, Clark was all at once struck by the wish that old Merrill would die quickly. But once that wish materialized, he put it down quickly. Even though he had killed twice in two days, his sense of decency was not yet dulled to the point where he could tolerate such a thought.

He was challenged as he crossed the yard toward the tie rail near the house, and he recognized the voice of the man who called out. "You're up late, Mel," Clark said. "How's the old man?"

The Brush man sauntered up and waited until Clark had swung aground before replying: "Bad, I reckon. They ain't told us much. Doc Nesbit and the girl are stayin' up with him. Go on in. She'll be glad to see you."

Ruth answered his knock on the door. As Clark stepped into the lighted, low-ceilinged main room, he saw that her face was lined with care and weariness.

"I came as soon as I could, Ruth," he said. "Lyans has had me up coverin' the pass road. How's your father?"

"No better and no worse, Clark. What . . .?" She hesitated and her eyes were afraid. Then her words came in a rush. "What about Joe? Did they find him? Is he . . . ?"

"Not a sign of him yet." Clark tried to overlook the quick relief that brought tears to Ruth's eyes. "My hunch is he's left the country."

The gladness that had been in her faded. "That would be safest for him, wouldn't it?" she said lifelessly. "But I . . . I hoped he hadn't."

Again he had to overlook her betrayal of a more than casual interest in Joe. He said: "You're tired. Why don't you turn in for a while?"

As he spoke, he heard the door at the far end of the room open. Before the girl could answer, Doc Nesbit was saying: "I've been tryin' since dark to tell her that, Clark. She hasn't had a wink in twice 'round the clock."

The doctor appeared to be in little better shape than Ruth. His old face looked haggard; there were dark circles under his eyes, his coat was off, and his collar and tie loosened where ordinarily he was fastidious about his appearance.

"You could stand some sleep yourself, Doc," Clark declared. "Why don't both of you turn in for a few hours and let me take over? Is there any reason why I couldn't?"

Nesbit scratched his head and ran a hand over his beard-stubbled face. "It would be nice to shave and lie down a bit. How about it, Ruth?"

"Is he still asleep?" the girl asked.

The medico nodded. "Will be, until time for his medicine. Clark could give it to him." He paused only a moment before he decided. Then, coming across, he took Ruth by the elbow, gently urging her toward the hallway that led to the bedrooms. "So we needn't worry. Come along, Clark. I'll show you what has to be done."

Ruth turned to Clark as she came abreast the open door to her room. Lifting her face to him, she said softly as the doctor went into the room opposite: "Put your arms around me, Clark. Kiss me. I'm . . . I'm so lost."

He took her in his arms, gently, and kissed her on the lips. She smiled as she drew away. "Thanks," she said wistfully. "I needed that. So much has happened that I can't take it all in. You're sure Joe's safe? Hasn't anyone seen him?"

Her concern at this moment for another man dulled the quickened interest that had been in Clark as he held her yielding body in his arms. "Don't worry about Joe," he said levelly. "He can take care of himself."

Ruth's door closed softly, and Clark entered John Merrill's room, going quietly across to the sick man's bed as the doctor motioned him to silence. Nesbit indicated a bottle and a teaspoon on a small table beside the bed.

"He's to have a spoonful of that every hour, on the hour," he whispered. "You may have to wake him to give it to him. It's what keeps his heart goin', so be sure you don't miss. Another thing. He seems to want to talk, thinks he's going to die and that he has to get things squared away before he does. Don't let him talk. Tell him he'll be better in a couple of days."

"And will he?" Clark asked.

Nesbit shrugged. "Maybe, maybe not. If the medicine takes effect, he has a good chance." He took his watch from his pocket, wound it, and laid it on the table. "Twenty minutes until he gets the next dose. Well, I'll turn in. If anything goes wrong, if his breathing or color changes, wake me. I'll be in the next room."

Alone with the sleeping man as the sounds in the next room, the doctor's, finally quieted, Clark sat in the rocker by the bed and tried to keep his eyes from straying to the bottle of medicine close to his elbow. He tried to think of other things, of Jean Vanover's strange disappearance, of what Saygar and his men were doing tonight, but always his eyes would go back to the bottle and his thoughts would turn to what it represented—life or death for John Merrill.

He hadn't until now seriously considered Merrill's dying. It came to him quite suddenly, and for the first time, that, should the old man's stroke prove fatal, Ruth would inherit Brush. All that went with it, social eminence, prestige, and power, would be hers, to be shared by the man of her choice.

Clark remembered the kiss Ruth had given him. What had followed had made her gesture of turning to him less symbolic than he would have liked it. But wasn't Joe dead? And after Joe, wasn't he the man of Ruth's choice? Wouldn't she be alone after this was over? Wouldn't marriage ease her grief?

Staring at the bed, at the man who illness seemed already to have wasted away, Clark saw the blankets move and John Merrill's gray-haired head turn. Merrill's eyes were open, looking at him.

With an effort, Clark put the vicious thoughts that were dogging him from his mind and forced a smile. "Hello, John," he said quietly. "Feeling better?"

"Clark." The old man's whisper was barely audible. The faint trace of an answering smile came to his sunken-cheeked, pale face.

Clark leaned closer. "Ruth and Nesbit have turned in for a little rest. I'm going to sit up with you. Try and sleep again."

Merrill's mouth came open. He seemed to he trying to swallow, unable to do it. His breathing became audible, very labored. He gasped a whispered word: "The medicine!"

Clark looked at the watch. It was already fifteen minutes past the hour. A wicked and concise impulse struck him and he said easily: "Not time yet, John. Ten minutes to go. Try and rest."

John Merrill's eyes widened with alarm. He tried to speak again but couldn't summon the strength. A beady perspiration stood out on his forehead. He lifted a hand and reached out, fastening Clark's wrist in a surprisingly strong grip. Clark drew his hand away, wrenched loose from the old man's hold.

"You'll tire yourself, John," he said soothingly, unable to keep from smiling.

He felt a cool draft on his neck and only then realized that the door to the room was open. He turned quickly in his chair, panicked by the thought he might have been overheard. Rising quickly, he went to the door and peered out into the hall. Ruth's door, directly opposite, was closed. Clark tiptoed along the hall to the next room's entrance. It was open. Standing there, breathing shallowly, he listened.

The doctor was asleep. Clark could hear his breathing, deep, even, the breathing of an exhausted man. Soundlessly he returned to John Merrill's room and closed the door, every muscle in his body taut as the hinges grated.

When he looked down into John Merrill's face again, the old man's eyes were closed. The mouth was still open. The paleness was gone and now the parchment-like skin bore a bluish tint. And Clark couldn't hear the sick man breathing any longer. He leaned down and listened and then could hear it, faintly.

Clark sat in the chair once more, and now the silence was oppressive. Gradually a panic rose up in him. It became so strong that he reached for the bottle and spoon. He uncorked the bottle, thinking: *There's still time to save him, to let him live.* Then, because the vision of the power that could be his for the asking came to him at that moment, he placed the cork back into the bottle and set it back on the table.

He wasn't going to look at the bed now. He got up and paced the length of the carpet, his glance picking out details of the room's furnishings he hadn't noticed before. On the dresser was a daguerreotype of a handsome woman, no doubt Ruth's mother.

Clark had never known her. She had that same exotic beauty as her daughter. The picture's frame was of intricately wrought gold, somehow symbolic of John Merrill's quiet, tasteful affluence. A set of military brushes with engraved silver backs lay near the picture. Another sign of wealth. It quickened Clark's pulse to think that countless other objects in this luxuriously furnished house were of great value. Just thinking of it, of all this wealth that was to be his one day, made him want to shout.

In this moment, Clark Dunne was half crazed with the lust for power. He had nearly forgotten John Merrill. Returning to the bed, he leaned down over the man, seeing that the bluish tone to the skin had deepened. He listened for Merrill's breathing. There was no sign of it. Hurrying across to the dresser again, he took one of the brushes and held its silvered back close to the old man's nostrils. No telltale fogging of breathing showed on the cool, polished metal. Clark felt of Merrill's pulse. Feebly— or could he feel it?—came the beat of the old man's fighting heart.

Clark returned the brush to the dresser and started for the door. Halfway there, he paused and came back to the table. He uncorked the bottle, poured some of the syrupy liquid into the spoon, then poured it back from the spoon to the bottle again. Then, sure that he had thought of everything, he laid the spoon on the table again and went out the door.

Nesbit was awake at the first touch of his hand on shoulder. "Better get in there, Doc," Clark said, low-voiced. "I think something's happened."

His tone brought the medico quickly out of bed. Clark followed Nesbit's nightgown-draped figure along the hallway and back into John Merrill's room. Reaching for the old man's wrist, Nesbit felt of it. He stooped quickly and took his black kit bag from beneath the table. Out of it he brought a cedar-necked stethoscope and a small vial of a char-colored liquid. "Pry his mouth open, Clark," he said curtly,

Together, they managed to pour some of the liquid into Merrill's mouth. But Nesbit slowly shook his head. "Too late," he said. "How did this happen? Why didn't you call me sooner?"

"I wouldn't have had it happen for anything," Clark said in a voice heavy with regret. "I gave him his medicine at one. He wanted to talk. I told him not to, but there were some things he thought he had to say. Then, when he was through, he dropped off to sleep. I reckon I was sittin' here daydreamin', not watchin' him very close. Then just now I saw his color had changed. I listened to his breathin', couldn't hear it, and called you."

Nesbit gave a weary shrug of his shoulders. "I don't suppose anything could have saved him. Don't take it too hard, Clark. It would have happened, even if I'd been . . ."

"Clark, what is it?"

Ruth's low cry sounded from the door. They turned to her as she slowly advanced into the room. She had thrown a robe about her shoulders. Coming to the bed, she stood staring dully down at the face of the dead man. All at once she turned to Clark, put her head on his shoulder, and sobbed: "I knew it! I knew he wouldn't live till morning! Clark, I'm so alone!"

He took her by the shoulders and pushed her a little away from him, looking down into her tear-brimming eyes.

"He wanted me to wake you, wanted you to hear what he had to say," he said quietly. "Now I wish I had."

"He . . . he said something? What, Clark?"

"He made me promise we'd be married. Tomorrow, he said. He was sure he wasn't going to live. He wanted to be sure there would be someone to look after you. He . . . he said you love me, Ruth."

The girl's choking sobs came as Clark drew her to him once more. Nesbit turned from them and busied himself at repacking his bag. As an afterthought, he reached over and pulled the sheet up over John Merrill's face. Then he left the room.

When they were alone, Ruth lifted her head. "He said it was to be tomorrow?" she asked.

Clark nodded to the watch on the table. "Today," he corrected her. Tilting her chin up so that he could look into her eyes, he asked gently: "Are you as sure of it as he was, Ruth? That I'm the man you want?"

"Yes, Clark," she answered after a moment, and in that slight pause he knew she was thinking once again of Joe. "Yes, he was right. I do need you."

Six-Gun Parley

Two and a half hours ago Luke Sherman and two other Anchor crewmen had ridden the Troublesome toward the herds' bed ground, curious over the sound of distant gunfire heard by a wakeful cowpuncher. They had come across half the answer to what had happened, a thin scattering of cattle where the main herd should have been. The darkness had hidden the rest.

Now, as dawn's light strengthened in the east, Blaze and Yace and nine other Anchor men—all but the cook—sat their horses at the edge of the rim and looked downward the 400 feet to the edge of the flats to see the final answer. The gorge lay off to the right, obscured by the lack of light. Below, at its mouth, lay evidence of destruction beyond any man's imagining. Some fifty of the carcasses dammed the creek and diverted it in a quarter-mile-wide pool beyond which the swollen muddy waters swirled back into the main channel. As far back as they could see, clear to the gorge mouth, other bloated carcasses lined the banks of the stream or turned lazily in the side pockets out of the current. Occasionally they would glimpse the scarred Anchor brand on a distended belly, but more often it was a Singletree-branded animal. No one bothered to ride to the gorge rim and look down into the roaring chasm deeply gashed by the stream; it would be the same there, they knew, maybe even worse.

Only five minutes ago Blaze had taken a careful look at the small bunches of grazing steers and told Yace: "I make it a slim half hundred, boss." Last night nearly 500 cattle had been left near the junction of the Troublesome and the Porcupine to graze.

"This is the damnedest thing I ever set eyes on," Sherman drawled as he turned and put his horse far enough back from the rim so that he wouldn't have to look any longer.

"In a few days it'll be the damnedest stink your nose ever got hold of." For once, Yace's tone lacked bluster and was one of outright incredulity. He took his last long look at what would undoubtedly mean ruin to Singletree, although Anchor would not be so hard hit, and turned to Blaze. "This is nice, comin' right after I find I've got a son that takes a fancy to carryin' off women."

"Blast it!" Blaze said savagely. "If you weren't an old man, I'd lick the livin' daylights out of you for that! Joe no more carried off that Vanover girl than I did."

As soon as he'd spoken, amusement tempered Blaze's anger. There was a moment in which he wondered what Yace's reaction would be if he knew that Blaze had in fact been the man who had taken Jean Vanover from Diamond night before last. Then both his amusement and anger were gone before the look he caught on Yace's face. The old man was baffled, the fight gone out of him. The news of Joe's note found in the post office last night had been hard for him to take. Now this other was piled on top of it. Yace Bonnyman was hard hit, too troubled with his own loss and what he considered a second betrayal by his son to take Blaze's words seriously.

"Well, what now?" he asked quietly.

The near docility of his question did more than anything to prove to Blaze how deeply the old man's pride had been wounded. Blaze had never seen Yace this way, so strangely humbled and looking to someone else for an idea. So it was a long moment before the redhead could find a reply. When he spoke, it was to say as quietly as Yace had: "We might get something out of that sign . . . unless you want to wait here for Staples."

"He can take care of his own end of this." Yace motioned his foreman to take the lead and for the next twenty minutes Blaze heard no word spoken in the file of riders strung out behind. At the end of that silent interval, Blaze reached the spot where he'd seen sign on the way out. As he came stiffly out of the saddle, he drawled: "May not mean nothin' at all, Yace."

But it did. Here, along the slope of a barren and sage-studded knoll, one of the few grassless spots on the entire mesa, the tracks of three shod ponies struck a straight line across the knoll toward last night's position of the herd. Stranger yet was the fact that, looking the opposite direction along the line of those tracks, Diamond's clutter of buildings lay shadowed in the strengthening light some four miles distant.

Blaze started to say something after the others had gathered around him but thought better of it. Sherman, too, appeared to have an idea, but he had nothing to say. Instead, he glanced at Yace as the others did.

Yace's color didn't seem any too good this morning. His face looked tired. And now, as they waited for him to say something, he appeared hesitant. But in the end he nodded toward Diamond. "They came from over there," he said. "Didn't bother to ride around this bare ground because no one would think of comin' way over here to take a look."

What he said was true. This spot was well isolated from any trail. Cattle rarely grazed this far back on the mesa, for the grass was thicker and taller farther out. Blaze saw the conviction that was gradually building in all of them. It scared him a little.

"Let's make sure before we go any further," he suggested. He went into the saddle again and followed the line of the sign over the crest of the knoll and down the far side, where it came out of the thin stand of grass. He didn't stop there but went on, the others coining up on him. And once again they rode without speaking.

The sign was hard to follow. When Blaze lost it, he didn't stop to study it out. He went on. Luck was with him, for occasionally he glimpsed faint patches of flattened grass and once or twice the clear print of a horse's shoe along a bare patch of soft ground. When he came to the trail that led from Diamond on up to the basin, he had to make a cast of less than ten rods to pick up the sign again. It came from downtrail, in the direction of Diamond, now less than a mile distant.

Once again the men closed in around Yace, waiting for what he had to say. He seemed to sense that he had a grave decision to make. Deliberating over it, his glance went down the trail, and for the first time that morning Blaze saw his face set doggedly in the old familiar look of gathering anger.

"It was Harper," Yace said finally, with a suddenness that startled them all. "It's the sort of a play he'd make, blamin' us for costin' him his job. It's a good thing we thought to bring along our irons. Sherman, you take five men and . . ."

"Hold on!" Blaze cut in. "We've got a law in this country. Lyans is the man we ought to see first."

"The devil with the law!" Yace flared. "Besides, Lyans is out lookin' for the Vanover girl." He turned, one hand on the cantle of his saddle, the other resting on the horn, and looked at his men. "Any of you want to head for home? No one'll hold it against you if you do."

No one spoke or made a move to leave. Yace's glance went to Sherman. "Me and Blaze and a couple others will go on. You take the rest, Sherman, and circle up into the timber and come down back of the barn where you'll be handy. If we buy into trouble, you're to bail us out. Got it straight?"

Sherman nodded, saying only: "Better give me a couple of rifles."

The three riders with rifles in saddle scabbards reined over alongside him. As Sherman left, leading his men over into the timber, Yace called: "If it comes to burnin' powder, make it count!"

Yace, Blaze, and two others sat watching while Sherman disappeared into the trees immediately beyond the trail.

"Better give 'em time to get set," Blaze advised.

As he spoke, the *clang* of Diamond's meal iron sounded clearly across the distance, summoning the crew to breakfast. The man beside Blaze, Shorty Adams, drawled: "I could do with a feed about now." No one so much as smiled at the remark and Shorty's gaunt face flushed at the silent reprimand.

"Let's go," Yace said finally, and he and Blaze took the lead down the trail, going slowly at first until Blaze drawled: "Now would be a good time to arrive, while they're eatin'." After that Yace set the pace to a fast trot.

The six of them came into Diamond's barn lot from behind a flanking row of outbuildings. Across the way was the rear of the low adobe bunkhouse, beyond it the grove of locust trees that hid the house.

"I take one side, you the other, Blaze," Yace said curtly as he swung to the right to round the bunkhouse. Blaze struck left, one man following him.

Blaze hurried a little, not wanting to let Yace get there first. Along the side wall of the building he came abreast a window and glanced in but could see nothing. He was keenly aware of the weight of the gun at his thigh and let his hand fall to it, lifting the heavy .45 a little out of the holster. Having made sure that it rode free, he let it drop back into leather again.

He reined in around the front corner of the building and in close to one side of the door, seeing Yace do likewise opposite. A man came out the door, stopped abruptly at sight of the pairs of riders flanking him, and took an involuntary backward step before he caught himself. His look was wary as it went to Yace.

"What'll it be, gents?" he asked flatly.

"Harper," Yace snapped. "Send him out."

The man's look was impassive as he said: "He ain't here."

"Where is he?"

"Over there." The man nodded out across the space separating the bunkhouse from the trees.

Blaze's glance went to the trees. Neal Harper stood within an arm's length of the thick trunk of the nearest locust. His boots were apart in a firm stance. He held a gun in each hip-high hand, carelessly almost, but those guns covered Anchor's two pairs of riders.

Harper waited a moment, seeing Yace's massive frame go rigid, Blaze's relax in a seeming slacking off of tension. Then he drawled: "You wanted me, Bonnyman?"

It was obvious that the Anchor men had been spotted on the way in and that Harper was taking no chances. Yace saw this and it heightened his anger to think that he had been taken in by such a simple ruse. Sherman, in the timber directly backing the big barn, couldn't possibly see Harper and know what was taking place and he was too far away to hear voices.

Yace was stumped on how to begin. His ideas on how easily he was to deal with Harper underwent quick revision. Still, he didn't know what to say.

As had happened many times before in a tight spot, it was Blaze who came to his rescue.

"We wanted you and Vanover," Blaze told Harper. "A little something to talk over."

"Vanover's somewhere up in the hills lookin' for his daughter," Harper said.

Blaze's brows lifted in polite interest. "So?" he drawled. "Then we'd better go find him. Because we've located the girl."

Harper's guns dropped an inch or two. His look narrowed. He eyed Yace, then Blaze, and what he saw in the Anchor foreman's expression made him drop his guns into his holsters.

"Why didn't you say so?" he said, smiling meagerly. "You looked like you were huntin' bear when you rode in here." He nodded to the man who had come out the bunkhouse doorway. "Tell 'em it's all right, Bill."

"But it ain't all right," Blaze drawled, and rocked a gun up into line, resting his forearm on the horn of the saddle.

A moment ago, seeing Yace cocked for making the most of his first chance, Blaze had settled on the only possibility of turning Harper's advantage into one for himself, and had given that inspired reply. For a brief instant Harper's glance had gone to the man at the door. As Harper had holstered his guns, Blaze's right hand, away from the Diamond foreman, had lifted his .45 clear. Now his forehead was cool with beads of perspiration, so close had the margin been between Harper's seeing and not seeing his move.

As Blaze's drawled words struck across to Harper, the man froze in a posture with his elbows out, cocked for the draw. Quickly he calculated his chances and saw there weren't any. Blaze was well out of line with both the door and the single front window. His gun wasn't quite in line but would be before Harper could get a weapon clear. And the tree Harper had intended as a shelter in the last extremity was a long stride away, too far to be reached before Anchor's foreman could get in a shot.

Harper had little respect for Yace Bonnyman but a healthly one for Blaze Coyle. Most redheads, Harper knew, had hair-trigger tempers and were unpredictable in a spot like this. He didn't know Blaze well, but something about the man warned him that here he faced a cool brain and a judgment keener than his own perhaps. A cold fury took him when he saw how nicely Coyle had used his mention of Vanover's daughter to trick him and dull his wariness.

He lifted his hands out and away from his guns, saying nothing, waiting, as Yace and the pair of Anchor crewmen drew their weapons.

"Call the others out, Harper," Blaze said. "They're invited to this party."

"You call 'em," Harper drawled.

Blaze shrugged briefly and said to the man at the door, without looking at him: "Harper's a little shy, Bill. Get your side-kicks out here unless you want a new boss."

Bill looked at Harper and, getting no signal from him, called: "You heard what he said in there! Pile out!"

Five men filed out the doorway. All wore guns and all surrendered them to Billings, the Anchor man who had rounded the north end of the bunkhouse with Blaze. Harper came last, after Billings had taken a quick look in the bunkhouse, then crossed the yard to the Diamond foreman, keeping well out of line with him and Blaze.

"There, Yace," Blaze said, as Billings stepped away from Harper, the gunman's twin belts slung over his shoulder. "What'll you do with 'em?"

"There's a jail in town," Yace said. "Shorty, go give Sherman a call and get him down here."

As Shorty Adams rounded the bunkhouse, headed for the barn lot to call to Sherman, Neal Harper drawled: "Is this a guessin' game? Or do you tell us why you're takin' us in?"

"You got a little careless last night," Yace said. "We picked up your sign on that sage knob four miles out."

Blaze saw Harper's face break from its impassiveness into puzzlement. "Not our sign, Bonnyman."

"You can tell it to Lyans when . . ."

"Hold on, Yace," Blaze cut in, intrigued by the genuineness of Harper's surprise. He eyed the Diamond foreman sharply. "You claim you were here last night, Harper? All night?"

"All night," Harper said. "We were gatherin' together our possibles, gettin' ready to pull out. Maybe you hadn't heard, but you rannies cost us our jobs."

"Any way of provin' where you were?" Blaze asked.

Yace snorted. "You're wastin' time, Blaze. Get 'em . . ."

"Let him have his say!" Blaze cut in. "Well, Harper?"

The Diamond foreman shrugged. "If it's proof you want, we don't have any you'd take. It's our word against yours. What are we supposed to have done?"

"Stampeded my herd and Staples's into the head of the gorge," Yace told him.

The look on Harper's face underwent a quick change. His lips became tightly drawn. Blaze thought he could see his face lose color. Then Harper was saying: "So you're not only runnin' me out but framin' me, too! You're a pack of low . . ."

The flat explosion of a gunshot, sounding from behind the bunkhouse, cut off his words. Hard on the heels of the first came a second, prolonged by a third. As a pony's hoofs pounded around the far side of the adobe building, the glances of the Anchor men went that way. Harper wheeled unnoticed behind the nearest tree as Shorty Adams, who had gone to call Sherman, rounded the corner of the bunkhouse.

Shorty's pony shied away from Yace's horse. The abrupt move unseated the Anchor rider. His spare high frame fell loosely from the saddle and he rolled over twice from the momentum of his fall, then lay still. The riderless Anchor pony ran up the slope toward the timber close above. From out behind the bunkhouse a man called hoarsely: "Harper! Sing out, Harper!"

Blaze, as startled as the others, only now thought of Neal Harper. He looked over toward the trees, saw that Harper was gone, and touched his pony's flanks with spurs, sending him across there. Behind, Yace shouted something Blaze couldn't make out. Blaze reined his horse in through the trees, bringing the house and Harper, making for the door, into sight.

Blaze took a snap shot at the Diamond man, at the last moment pulling his gun out of line, in the hope that the mere sound of the shot would stop him. But Harper made the door and disappeared into the house. Back beyond the trees two guns spoke, one the heavy pound of a .45, the other the sharper report of a .38. Blaze heard Yace yell—"Head him off! Over there by the barn!"—and knew that one of Diamond's crew must have been busy at some chore in one of the outbuildings when Anchor rode in. That man had undoubtedly awaited developments on the hunch that the mesa crew was looking for trouble. That he had made the best of his chance was now evidenced by the fact that one Anchor man lay dead, or badly wounded, and that Harper had made the house where he could get hands on a gun.

Blaze heard the glass go out of a house window with a shattering *crash*. He wheeled his pony sharply around and in behind a tree barely in time, for Harper's first bullet struck the tree trunk and ricocheted away in a high whine. Blaze struck on back through the trees, going fast.

When he came into sight of the bunkhouse, it was to see Shorty lying exactly as he had been before.

Billings was back in the saddle, his gun trained on three Diamond men. There should have been five. The remaining two had disappeared, along with Yace.

As Blaze rode up, Billings spoke without taking his glance from the trio before him: "Yace is out back somewhere. A couple of these jaspers grabbed irons while I wasn't lookin'. What'll I do, boss?"

"Make tracks," Blaze told him. He lifted his voice, shouting: "Yace! Get back here!"

His answer came in the form of a single gunshot from out behind. Fear was suddenly in Blaze. He put his horse around the near side of the bunkhouse and brought the barn lot into sight in time to see Yace ride, bent low over the saddle, from the shelter of a shed to that of a larger crib.

As Yace crossed the open space, he lifted his gun and emptied it in the direction of the barn. Two guns answered from the loft door, and Blaze saw them stab flame from the shadows in the big opening under the roof's peak. One of those bullets found its target. Suddenly, with ten feet to go to get out of line, Yace's pony fell in a frontward roll. Yace, thrown clear, landed hard. But Blaze saw him lunge to his feet and run to cover.

Blaze put two shots into the barn loft and reined back behind the bunkhouse wall. Billings came up behind him. "What about Shorty?" Blaze asked his crewman.

"They got him," Billings said. "I'm goin' to take him back with me or I don't go."

"Hurry up," Blaze warned. "Harper made the house. He's got a gun."

From up in the timber a rifle shot broke the momentary stillness. Another of Sherman's Winchesters joined the first. Twice his fire was answered by the deeper-throated explosions of six-guns from the barn loft. Blaze saw Yace run back and up toward the timber from the big crib he had hidden behind, keeping it between him and the barn. But presently it no longer sheltered him and the guns in the barn spoke again. When Blaze saw the bullets sending geyser-like puffs of sandy dust close to Yace's feet, he reined out into the open once more and lined three swift shots through the loft door. The rifles on the hill joined him, not breaking off until Sherman had ridden down out of the trees and helped Yace up to the saddle behind him.

Once he saw Yace and Sherman safe, Blaze turned and rounded the bunkhouse again. Billings was lifting the body of the dead man across his horse's withers, ahead of the saddle. No Diamond men showed in the bunkhouse doorway now. Blaze looked off toward the trees that blocked a view of the house. He said urgently: "Get going, Billings!"

Shortly Billings was in the saddle and they were making a wide circle around the bunkhouse toward the trail they had taken in. Blaze's glance was constantly directed toward the rear until they were out of rifle shot from the trees screening the house, where he expected Harper to appear at any moment.

"This makes it a sure thing, don't it, Blaze?" Billings said at last.

"A sure thing?"

"This business we been steppin' around the last year or so. A showdown with Diamond."

"The part that makes it bad is that Harper and his men didn't push that herd down the gorge," Blaze said. He kept his glance away from the limp form ahead on Billings's saddle.

Billings gave him a queer look. "No?" he drawled mildly. "Then who did?"

"I don't know."

"I'll say you don't. As for me, them hardcases will do till someone better comes along. Hell, they gut-shot Shorty, didn't they? You goin' to let that pass?"

Blaze didn't answer. Some minutes later, riding up on Yace and Sherman and the others, he knew he wouldn't stand a chance of even beginning to explain his doubts.

Yace waited until they had come up and reined in. His bleak glance went briefly to the body slung across Billings's saddle.

"We split up here," he said then. "Blaze, you'll head up to Clark's and pass the word to him. Andy goes to Workman's. Sherman, yours is Merrill's. Don't bother the girl any more than you have to. She's got enough on her hands as it is. Abe, give me your horse. I'll go across to Staples. We'll bring back every man that can be spared. Meet at Yoke. It's closest."

"What about Vanover?" Blaze asked.

"What about him? He's responsible for his men. Whatever they do is his look-out."

"Killin' included?" Blaze drawled.

"Great jumpin' Jehoshaphat!" Yace's deep voice boomed. "You want us to take this sittin'? Look at Shorty there!"

"We could go in and get Lyans. He'd put Harper under arrest."

"If we could find Lyans . . . and if we happened to catch Harper gone blind or deaf!" Yace gave a mirthless laugh, eying his foreman coldly. "You turnin' yellow on us, Blaze?"

Blaze's only answer was to rein out from the others and start out along the trail.

"Where you goin'?" Yace demanded querulously.

"Clark's!" Blaze called back. "That's where you said I was to go."

Blaze's hot anger didn't cool until he was well up into the trees, out of sight of the others. He would follow this trail, he decided, leaving it short of the basin to cut across the hills and reach Clark's layout, which sat far back in a peninsula of grass high along the Troublesome at the northernmost point of the mesa. He'd talk things over with Clark. Maybe, between them, they could get an idea that would stop Yace and the others before there was more killing.

Hearing a sound close to the left in the trees, Blaze looked that way in time to see Shorty's loose pony, reins caught on the horn, trot deeper into the timber. The riderless Anchor horse had already worked the saddle down under his belly. Before long, if he stayed in the timber, he might catch the reins on a tree or bush or ruin the saddle. He was a good horse, a big-chested bay. Blaze, knowing the outfit might lose a good horse and saddle, reined off there. After a brief chase he caught up the loose animal, a little irritated at the thought of having to lead it all the way to Clark's where he could turn it loose in the open. Abruptly he had another thought. Joe needed a horse. It would cost him an extra hour at least to go up to the cave. But it would give him the chance to talk to Joe, and he was badly in need of talk with someone who could consider this new development rationally. Leading the dead Anchor man's pony, he turned up on the trail.

Plans

"So he's framed me with this, too," Joe said. He gave Blaze a long, level look. "In three days he's built up four counts against me. Murder, robbery, horse stealin', and now kidnappin' a woman. Can they hang a man more than once?"

"Not that I ever heard of. But it was me that brought the girl here. They can't saddle you with something I did," Blaze argued.

"You didn't leave that note in Acme's box."

"No," Blaze admitted, "he did. Who's *he*?"

Joe shrugged and hunkered down in the shade of a nearby piñon. They were below the cave mouth, close to the spot where Blaze had two nights ago staked out Jean's horse on a patch of grass. Shorty's bay now grazed near the Diamond branded animal at the end of a picket rope twenty feet away.

Joe studied the animal, its sturdy clean legs, its big chest and high withers. "Shorty cut himself out a nice chunk of horseflesh this mornin'," he remarked.

"He's a little hard-mouthed. Shorty liked to ride the bit." Blaze picked up a pebble and flicked it into the narrow stream made from melted snow that foamed close by along the bed of the ordinarily dry cañon. They'd had their brief words about Shorty, who had been too good a friend to both to occasion any more talk. "You're still seein' Saygar tonight?"

Joe nodded. "After I take care of something else."

"What?"

"How fast is this bay?" Joe asked in seeming irrelevance.

"Plenty o' legs," Blaze answered. "But what's that got to do with this other thing you're takin' care of, Joe?"

"We want to stop a shoot-out between Vanover's bunch and the old man's, don't we?"

"Sure. But how?"

"With Shorty's horse."

"All right," Blaze drawled bitingly, "let me in on it when you get good and set."

"Don't think I will," Joe told him. "What you don't know can't hurt you. Since you're goin' back down there, you might give it away. Can you be up here tonight right after dark to side me across to Saygar's camp?"

"I'll be here," Blaze said. "But what's this other about Shorty's jughead?"

Joe smiled meagerly and gave a slow shake of the head. The motion set up the throbbing ache again and he held his head in his hands until it had passed. Then: "I'm going to send the girl on down."

"With what kind of a story?"

"That'll depend on what she has to say when I talk to her. Hadn't you better head for Clark's?"

"I should've a half hour ago." Blaze stood up. "Ain't you goin' to let me in on it, whatever it is?"

"No."

"You didn't make out so well the last time you were on your own. There's too many against you, Joe."

"That's one thing I'm countin' on."

"On too many bein' against you? I don't get it."

"I don't want you to get it. You'd better hightail."

Blaze showed his disappointment and a little anger as he picked up his reins and climbed into the saddle. But when he looked down at Joe, his expression softened. "Whatever it is, be careful, son," he finally drawled.

"I'll be careful."

Joe watched the redhead until he rode out of sight around a near bend in the cañon. Back there a minute ago he had caught himself when on the verge of telling Blaze what he was about to do, deciding on impulse that his friend already had too much to worry about and that he might not approve anyway. Now he was filled with a nervous anxiety to put his idea into motion. But a look skyward at the sun at its zenith told him it was too early to start.

Last night Joe had slept fitfully after Blaze left. Waking at dawn, he had felt more like himself. He had tested his legs and found them weak. The throbbing in his head had eased off except when he moved too abruptly. He had spent a long time looking down at the sleeping girl, realizing what she had done for him. Then he had gathered some of the food stacked in the corner and crawled out of the cave as quietly as he could so as not to wake her. He'd built a breakfast fire of smokeless dry cedar on the shelf directly in front of the cave mouth. While waiting for his coffee to boil, he had walked upcañon and stripped and washed in the stream. The icy chill of the water had put new strength in him. He had relished his meal.

Twice before Blaze had ridden in, Joe had crawled back into the cave to see if Jean was awake. Each time he had found her sleeping soundly. She had moved only once during the night, a plain indication to him that she was exhausted and needed as much rest as she could get.

The clash between Anchor and Diamond seemed to be a part of a slowly emerging pattern Joe was beginning to recognize. The destruction of Singletree's and Anchor's herd and the note, pointing directly to him as being responsible for the girl's disappearance, were both pieces of that pattern. Mike Saygar was part of this puzzle, one of its key pieces, perhaps. But the outlaw was in no position to feel accurately the pulse of what was going on in town and on the mesa. No, someone was behind Saygar, a man shrewd enough to make the most of every chance, wise enough to stir up trouble between the cattle company and the mesa outfits to gain his own ends. What those ends were, Joe had no way of knowing. His hunch was that he would find out when he saw Saygar. But before Saygar came this other thing, the stopping of more of the killing that had already cost one loyal Anchor man his life.

Joe heard a sound above and looked up there to see Jean step into sight at the edge of the broad shelf fronting the cave mouth. Looking at her in that unguarded interval before she saw him, seeing her tall figure outlined against the sky, he was struck by something that had passed unnoticed that early morning in the upstairs hall of the hotel and last night in the cave. The bright sunlight edged the girl's chestnut head with coppery highlights; her face held a startling quality of freshness and fragile beauty of which he was only now aware. And in this moment, for the first time since Blaze's outburst last night, Joe's thoughts turned briefly to Ruth Merrill. Then Ruth left his mind, obscured by the newly found loveliness of this girl.

Jean's glance came down to him and her look was momentarily startled before her face showed outright relief. As she hurried down the gravelly slope to him, he was keenly aware of her grace and poise and her swinging boyish stride.

She stood before him a little breathless, high color on her cheeks, giving him a glad smile. "You are better," she said. "I thought you'd gone." She seemed to realize only then how openly she was betraying her gladness at finding him. "Is the head better?"

His hand went up to the bandage and he felt of it gingerly, a wide smile on his lean face. "Lots," he said. "I had a good doctor." His smile was gone then as he added: "You got yourself in for something when you let Blaze drag you up here."

"I'm glad he did, Joe. Besides, I knew where he was taking me."

"You did?" Outright admiration came to his face. "One day I'll try and make this up to you."

"There's nothing to make up. You didn't deserve to just . . . just die."

Joe's grin was wry. "There's some that wouldn't agree with that."

"I know. And maybe I'm a little selfish in wanting to see you get well. You see, some of the things that have happened lately have . . . well, they've been things neither Dad nor I could understand. Blaze has told me enough to let me know you couldn't give the answers to all those things. I think you're the only one who can help us."

"And you're the girl who helped Keech get that gun on me," he drawled.

"I'm sorry for that, terribly sorry. You must believe me." There was no mistaking her sincerity. "If I had known what I know now, I would have warned you, hidden you there in the room. You could have seen Ruth. That's something else." She paused, studying him intently. "I'll go tell Ruth anything you want me to. Perhaps that will help make it up to you."

He tried to find something to say but couldn't.

She went on to cover his embarrassment: "Ruth didn't like it at all. I don't suppose we're friends now."

"Let's forget her," he drawled. "What's more important . . . what will you tell your father?"

"The truth." Her head tilted up in a determined way. "When I tell him, he'll believe as I do, that you're innocent. Naturally I wouldn't let anyone know where to find you."

"There's been trouble this morning, trouble that may change that," Joe told her gravely. "Blaze was in on it. Last night someone pushed a herd into the gorge below Anchor. Staples lost heavily, Anchor, too. This morning Yace took a crew over to Diamond. They tangled with Harper and lost a man. They're gathering more men now to go back."

"Where was Dad?" Jean asked quickly. Her face had gone pale.

"Out somewhere with Bill Lyans, lookin' for you. If he'd been there, it wouldn't have happened."

"Why would this change what I think of you, Joe?" she asked.

"You'll have to take sides. They've got it that I'm the one that carried you off the other night. Someone left a note in Acme's mailbox and signed my name to it."

"But you didn't! I'll tell them it's a lie!" Her look became alarmed. "Who's behind this, Joe? Someone's doing everything they can to make trouble."

"I know. We can have a try at findin' out. You could help by tellin' your father to hold off until I see him."

"How will you find out? You're sick, weak."

"Not as bad as you think," he told her. "Let's get you some breakfast and then start down. I'll ride a ways with you."

"You can't, Joe. What if they see you?"

He drawled: "That's what they're supposed to do . . . see me." He told her why.

Vengeance Riders

By 2:00 that afternoon thirty-one saddled ponies stood at Yoke's yard tie rails and along the near side of the holding corral by the barn. Down-headed and hip-shot, they drowsed in the sun, tails switching at the flies. Inside the house, the talk was muted and sparse. John Merrill's death had done as much to sober these men as had the fight and the loss of Shorty Adams at Diamond this morning. Added to that was Staples's predicament. Singletree had been all but wiped out.

Clark had brought four men from Brush and sent out for six more who were gathering Merrill's shipping herd. Staple's crew was there in its entirety, angry and chastened over what they considered a betrayal of their owner—their having left the herd the night before in favor of their bunkhouse. The rest of the count was made up by Anchor and Yoke, with more Yoke men expected down out of the hills shortly.

They were waiting for the return of a man they had sent in to try and locate Bill Lyans. Yace Bonnyman had had no scruples about immediately returning to Diamond and settling matters any way that seemed best. But Slim Workman had said flatly: "Damned if I want any hangovers when this winds up. We're law-abidin' citizens, always have been. I don't budge from here until we get the law to witness what we do."

So Yace and the rest had agreed to wait until Lyans was summoned. As Clark Dunne put it: "We can do all the better after dark anyway."

When Blaze rode in, Clark was talking to Charley Staples off in one corner of the plainly furnished main room of the house. Blaze came up to them, said—"Like to see you when you're finished, Clark."—and drifted over with some others. Clark was puzzled by Blaze's look and tone, which was urgent, but he had reached the crucial point in his talk with Staples and didn't want to leave it unfinished.

He went on now with the point he'd been making when Blaze interrupted: "I'll leave it up to you, Charley. It'll take some time for Ruth and me to get John's affairs settled. We may get away for a short honeymoon. A rest, I mean. This isn't any time to be talkin' a honeymoon, considerin' what's happened. But when we get back, I reckon Ruth and I can see our way clear to helpin'. Either by buyin' your spread outright or through a loan."

Staples's look was that of a man worried and harassed beyond endurance. "I'm through with this country," he said vehemently. "Clark, I saw six thousand dollars of mine layin' at the foot of that creek this mornin'! Six thousand! All I'll get out of it is a few hides."

"I know. But that's no reason to quit. What'll you do if you sell out?"

"Take what's left over and move to town. Olson's been after me for quite a spell to come in with him on that feed mill. It ain't much of a livin'. But it's better'n seein' half your life swept away in a flood."

Clark's look of sympathy revealed none of his inner excitement. The destruction wrought by Mike Saygar and his men last night was bringing more dividends than Clark's wildest imagining had hoped for. He had made some shrewd guesses, first about the thaw making the Troublesome impassable, second about Staples's shortness of money and what the loss of his shipping herd would mean. He had assumed that Staples would have to borrow to keep his head above water. But never had Clark dreamed that the man would be crowded into selling the Singletree, or that he would be in a position to buy it. He'd had some vague notion of handling a loan for Staples through his capacity as Acme's new president and maybe, years from now, taking over the loan himself. But old John Merrill's death last night had changed all that. The news of the Anchor-Diamond fight had caught him about to start for Lodgepole with Ruth; they had planned a simple wedding at the preacher's house. Now that she believed Joe was gone, Ruth seemed more than willing to follow what she understood to be her father's dying wish.

Clark found himself in a position hard to grasp. He was, in fact, already owner of Brush. Here was Staples ready to sell the Singletree, which adjoined Brush on the west. Across a triangular piece of Yoke range was his own layout; maybe Workman would one day sell him that piece, thus throwing together a vast stretch of land that would make Brush bigger by far than Anchor. And there was the basin that would eventually be his, with Saygar's men already homesteading it.

He was a little drunk with a feeling of power, with disdain for these men whom he now looked upon as pawns to be used or pushed aside as he willed. Tonight it would be a finish fight. When it was over, Clark hoped Harper and his men would he dead, unable to betray him. Saygar was safe until he collected his share in this; there was time to deal with him. Vanover would be recalled by Middle Arizona.

Jean Vanover. There was something Clark didn't understand, something he had puzzled over in the hours after John Merrill's death this morning. At first he hadn't worried about the girl. But finally he saw her mysterious disappearance, along with that of Joe's body, as the only two factors bearing on the accomplishment of his plan that he didn't understand. He'd have to get up and see Saygar tonight and make sure the outlaw was the one who had found Joe. Perhaps Saygar also knew something of the girl.

Now Clark looked down at short-framed Charley Staples and put a friendly hand on the man's shoulder. "Just don't worry about it, Charley. It's done and can't be helped. Name a fair price on Singletree and I'll . . . we, Ruth and I . . . will pay it. I want to see you get another start."

Staples sighed wearily but with some relief. "Clark, you're sure white to do this. If it wasn't . . ."

A shout from the yard cut in on his words. They both turned toward the porch door and joined the men crowding out of it. By the time they joined the others, Fuzz Tonkin, one of the riders Workman had summoned from his roundup crew, was saying: ". . . on that white-stockinged bay of Shorty's. We thought it was Shorty at first and tried to come up on him. Then's when he spooked. He cut up into the timber east of Dunne's place. Jim was close enough to recognize him. So Jim and the others went after him."

"Who?" Staples asked.

"Joe Bonnyman!"

Color left Clark's face. His hand, thumb hooked in his sagging shell belt, began to tremble. His throat felt dry and he swallowed, trying to clear it. He heard himself saying: "But that couldn't be! He's . . ."

Blaze's look came around to him quickly. "He's what, Clark?" the Anchor foreman asked sharply.

"Left the country," Clark said haltingly. His glance, on Blaze, became angry. "I saw him two days ago, had a talk with him. I . . ."

"You saw him?" It was Yace Bonnyman whose explosive words cut him short. The men between Yace and Clark moved aside. "Why didn't you tell us?"

Clark had himself under control now. He smiled wryly. "And let you string him up when he wasn't guilty?" he drawled. "Hell, Yace, I don't treat my friends that way. I tried to help him leave, clear the country. He didn't want to. But I supposed he had. No one's come across him since we parted company."

Yace was undecided now where a moment ago his righteous indignation had made him almost threaten Clark. As he hesitated,

Slim Workman's nasal tones drawled: "I reckon we know how you feel, Dunne. Well, what're we waitin' on? If they've sighted him, we got from now till dark to run him down. Plenty of time for this other."

They poured down off the porch, running for their horses. Someone shouted—"Better throw a saddle on a fresh horse, Tonkin!"—and the riders milled in the yard until the Yoke man who had brought the news had cut out a fresh horse from the half dozen in the corral.

Meantime, Staples reined over to the porch where Clark still stood. "Not comin', Clark?" he asked.

"No."

"Me, either." It was Blaze, approaching, who spoke.

"I'm sure sorry to have to do this," Staples said, and wheeled his pony out into the yard to join the others.

"You knew Joe hadn't left?" asked Clark as soon as Staples was out of hearing.

"He couldn't," Blaze answered. "Someone tried a bushwhack on him. He was out colder'n a side o' beef for near two days."

"Why didn't you tell me?"

"Haven't seen you so I could. What difference does it make?"

Clark was nearly caught off guard but saw the danger in time. "I could've helped, couldn't I?"

"He had all the help he needed. It was me that got the Vanover girl. She's been up there with him in that cave east of the basin where we smoked out the mountain cat that time. Remember?"

"Was he hurt bad?"

"Bad enough. The slug dug a nice groove in the side of his head."

Just then Yace called stridently from out in the yard: "You and Clark get across here, Blaze!"

"Count us out, Yace," Clark answered.

"We're not askin' you to side us!" Yace called back. "It's somethin' else."

So Blaze and Clark went out to where the men, ready to go, waited. The horses milled restlessly and a thin fog of dust lifted over the yard. Workman cursed deliberately but in a gentle voice as he tried to quiet his black gelding to a stand so that he could tighten his cinch. The attention of the riders was divided between his difficulty and what Yace had to say to Clark and Blaze.

"We figured someone ought to keep an eye on Diamond while we're gone," Yace began. "You willin' to go over there for the rest of the day and lay on your bellies in some nice cool shade and see what goes on?"

Clark looked at Blaze, and, in a moment, the Anchor foreman drawled: "Suits us."

"We want to know how many men Harper can count on besides his own crew of hired fighters," Yace said. "And keep an eye out for Vanover. He's been with Lyans. When he hears about this, he'll probably head for home. It wouldn't hurt if you stopped him on his way in and brought him here. We'll get back as soon as we get our man . . . or as soon after dark as we can make it. Meet us back here."

Clark frowned. "I oughtn't to let Ruth stay alone so long," he objected. "Blaze can tell you whatever's necessary. I'll get back to Brush when we leave Diamond and meet those extra men and wait till I hear from you. It won't take you long to get the word across if we're needed."

Yace nodded. "What matters is that we know what we're headed into tonight. Find out if you can." He glanced around at the others. "Let's ride!"

A long broken line of grim-faced men, they boiled out of the yard, Yace Bonnyman in the lead, heading north toward the foothills, to scour the country for one who stood condemned by all of them as a thief, a murderer, and a kidnapper of women.

Bullet Bait

Joe Bonnyman spotted the Yoke riders from a distance of better than a mile and cut down out of the timber so that they could see him. Presently they angled over in his direction and he held the bay to a slow trot, close to the edge of the timber, pretending he hadn't noticed them. When they were less than 200 yards away, he suddenly spurred the bay into a lope and reined over toward the trees. Workman's cowpunchers had been close enough so that Joe recognized two of them, Jim Lansing, the foreman, and Ed Bundy. Joe heard Lansing shout and then a gun exploded flatly, its echo slapping back down off the timbered slope ahead. He climbed the sparsely grown incline and put some trees behind him before he looked back. He was in time to see five of the riders come on, Lansing in the lead, while the sixth man headed out across the mesa at a fast run.

During the next hour and a half Joe played a game to which Shorty's bay horse seemed a perfect partner. The horse was a stayer and fresher than Joe had hoped. When he thought it necessary, it wasn't hard to draw away from his pursuers. Occasionally, as he gradually climbed higher along the tangled hills toward Aspen Basin's eastern boundary, he would slow his pace to breathe the bay and let the men behind get a glimpse of him. Once, while he walked his horse along the crest of a hogback, clearly skylining himself, a bullet kicked up an exploding puff of sand barely a foot ahead of the bay, and, as he quickly dropped down the far side of the small ridge, the sharp *crack* of a rifle sounded from below. After that he kept more distance between himself and the Yoke men.

Joe purposely changed direction time and again so as not to get too far from the mesa. Only when he caught a far downward glimpse of many riders crossing an opening in the timber did he ride point for the basin. He was better than two miles across it when rider after rider raced from the margin of the trees behind and lined out after him. From this distance he couldn't accurately tell how many newcomers had joined the chase. But his guess put the count at upward of twenty and he was satisfied, for he judged that these were the men who would otherwise be riding now for a shoot-out with Diamond. By the time he had put the bay across the belly-deep Troublesome, he was riding in earnest.

By late afternoon Joe had swung abruptly north, toward the higher hills. With the sun's last light a reddish blaze on the new snow of the peaks directly above, he was pounding up the stage road at a hard run, pausing only briefly to breathe the bay. Now, he told himself, was the time that counted. He wanted to be seen passing Klingmeier's stage station.

Close below the station's clutter of log buildings, as dusk was settling, Joe pulled the bay down to a steady trot. He came abreast the corrals and windmill, then the squat log building of the station itself. Lights showed at the windows. A man sitting tilted back in a chair on the roofless stoop by the main door eyed him speculatively. Joe lifted a hand and got an answering wave. To all appearances, he was a rider trying to cross the pass before making camp.

But, to give the lie to that judgment of him, he spurred the bay to a fast run once he was out of gunshot of Klingmeier's, knowing the man back there would see something odd in his hurried flight. He held the bay to the lope until he judged he was out of hearing. Then he pulled in, reined steeply downward off the road into the trees, and rode point for the basin. Crossing it two hours ago, he had spotted in the distance the makeshift lean-to Mike Saygar's men had thrown up to the west of a clump of timber cresting a knoll that flanked the Troublesome.

This morning Joe had told Blaze to meet him at the cave at dark, that he would have company when he made his call on Saygar. But time was too pressing now to make the long ride across to the cave, then back to the outlaw camp. Blaze would have to wait. Joe was going alone to meet Saygar.

* * * * *

"So you're to meet Joe up there at dark." Clark gave Blaze a sideward glance. "What good does he think it'll do to see Saygar?"

"He figures he can make Saygar talk. You'd better come along."

Clark deliberated the suggestion. He would have liked to be present when Joe Bonnyman saw Saygar; not that he didn't trust the outlaw, but because he wasn't too sure of Whitey or Pecos. Thinking on it, though, he decided Saygar was capable of looking out for both himself and his men. Besides, his wasting half the night riding the basin would mean he would be out of touch with things below, and what was to happen down here tonight was the more important.

So he told Blaze: "You go with Joe like you planned. I'll get back to Ruth. Yace won't make a move before he sends a man down to find out from me what happened across here this afternoon."

Blaze's look became worried. "It'd be a heap better for everything to wait on what Joe and I run onto. Don't you see? If Joe's hunch is right, and if he can get Saygar to talk, we'll be huntin' only one man instead of goin' off half-cocked after Harper's crew. Harper's nothin' but an understrapper. He can come later."

Clark shrugged and lay back, hands locked behind his head. "We'll have to take things as they come. Maybe you can get down before things open up tonight."

"I don't like it, Clark. For a fact, I don't."

Seeing that Blaze wasn't looking his way, Clark permitted himself a meager smile. He had found the last few minutes' conversation quite profitable. Blaze knew just enough to bear watching, not enough yet to represent a serious threat. And Clark sincerely hoped the redhead wouldn't become one; he was really fond of Blaze and hated the prospect of having anything interfere where another friend was concerned. Time and again today, before learning Joe was alive, Clark had lived through those last few moments of that rainy afternoon in the upper basin as he laid his sights on Joe's back and squeezed the trigger of the Winchester. Now, since finding that his shot had been high, that Joe was still alive, he put off thinking of having to do the job again.

He and Blaze had picked this spot high on the hill that backed Diamond for the reason that from here, a good 200 yards above the nearest outbuilding, they could get an unobstructed downward view of both the bunkhouse and the house yard beyond the trees. The house itself was hidden by the locust grove. Only one thing marred the perfection of their look-out; they couldn't see the line of the trail striking out across the mesa and thus spot Vanover coming in, provided he wasn't already down there.

The two men didn't speak for several minutes, Clark lying back on the soft cushion of pine needles, Blaze sitting with hands locked about his knees and doing the watching. Finally Blaze looked around, a wide grin on his face.

"Shucks, I ain't even given you my sympathies on gettin' hooked," he said. "Goin' to let me stand up as best man?"

"Like the devil! This'll be a respectable weddin'."

Blaze's look sobered. "All jokin' aside, friend, I'm wishin' you well."

"Glad you approve," Clark drawled.

Blaze went on, speaking more to himself than to Clark: "It's a funny thing, but I always reckoned Joe and Ruth would get hitched. He was sure gone on her there for a while. But she never felt quite the same as he did."

A faint uneasiness laid its hold on Clark. Supposing Ruth heard that Joe was still alive and had been seen? Suppose she still cared for him, as she had seemed to last night, cared for him enough to postpone the wedding? She was capable of it, Clark knew. Then he remembered how much Joe knew, how close he was to discovering the answer to all this trouble, and felt easier. This time he'd have to make sure of Joe for the simple reason that with Joe alive he'd always be in danger.

Clark wondered, idly, how much Whitey would take to do the job for him. Whitey or Harper. Either man could be bought at a price, although he doubted that either had ever stooped to bushwhack for other than purely personal reasons. Later tonight, at Saygar's camp, when this other was over, he'd feel out Whitey. Saygar himself needn't know anything about it. Mike already had too much on him; no sense in letting him in on more.

"Y'know, I'm sort o' glad it happened this way," Blaze said, startling Clark from his preoccupation. "Not that it's anything ag'in' you, understand."

"What?"

"You and Ruth. Joe and her never hit it off right. Now take that Vanover girl. If Joe ever settles down here again, there's my idea of a good match. She's the salt o' the earth, Clark. Pretty as a pure-bred filly, too."

"Aren't you the matchmaker." There was irritation in Clark's tone. He was as well aware of Jean Vanover's attractiveness as he was of Ruth's shortcomings.

"Funny thing is, she seems sort of soft on Joe. Up there in the cave, while Joe was layin' there, I'd catch her lookin' at him in a funny sort of way, like . . ." Blaze straightened a little, glancing fixedly at something below. "There's Vanover. We're already too late to stop him. What'll we do?"

Sitting up, Clark peered down through the trees to see Fred Vanover crossing the clean-swept graveled yard toward the house. In a moment, Middle Arizona's manager was out of sight.

Clark shrugged. "Nothin' we can do." He looked off through the trees into the west where the sun already edged the low spur of hills that marked the mesa's far limit. Then he thought of something that made him look sharply at Blaze. "How about takin' a last look-see and then headin' for the cave? You work off to the left and down as close behind the house as you can. I'll take the bunkhouse and try to get that count Yace wanted. Meet you back here in half an hour."

"What good'll it do us?" Blaze plainly didn't like the idea of going so far afoot.

Clark shrugged. "We can't miss any chances."

Blaze agreed grudgingly and they started down the slope, the redhead soon out of sight among the trees off to the left. As soon as he was sure he couldn't be seen, Clark broke into a run. He moved carelessly, so that when he neared the lower margin of the trees a Diamond crewman who had been standing at the front of the blacksmith shop had stepped around the building and was looking toward the hill, attracted by the sound of his coming.

Clark advanced boldly a few steps into the open and beckoned to the man. He was impatient over the other's slow approach and showed it when he snapped: "Get Harper up here. Right away, Tillson."

"He's over at the house with Vanover." The man's face bore an ugly scar over the right eye. He wore a holstered gun, butt foremost, high at the left side of his waist.

"Get him anyway."

Crossing the back lot toward the trees that screened the house, Tillson's stride was no longer indifferent, proof of how much weight Clark's curt order had carried.

Tillson was gone nearly five minutes. When he reappeared, he went across toward the bunkhouse and out of sight. Clark was about to call to him when Harper walked out of the trees.

"Anyone see you come out here?" was Clark's first question.

"No. Vanover and the girl are still talkin'."

"She's back?" Clark asked, for Blaze hadn't known when Jean was to return to Diamond.

"Rode in around noon. When I asked her where she'd been, she looked kind o' funny and told me I needed a shave." Harper ran a hand over his freshly shaven and hawkish face. "Didn't want to talk. You know anything about it?"

"You'll get that later," Clark said. "Bonnyman's goin' to raid the layout tonight. It'll probably be late. I'll try and swing it so he'll split his men. Maybe I'll get the chance to send word over on exactly what to expect. In case I don't, take half your men and . . ."

"There won't be no powder burned," Harper drawled. "Vanover's gettin' ready to go see Bonnyman and make his peace with him. If I'm guessin' right, he'll try and have me jailed. Or at least Tillson. He's the one who cut down that Anchor man this mornin'."

"Don't let Vanover see Bonnyman," said Clark. "Keep him and the girl here. This fight has to come off, Neal. And you won't lose a man if we work it right. After it's over, later on tonight, you and your bunch can ride the pass across to Junction and hop that early morning express."

"How do I keep from losin' my men?"

"Easy enough. How many can you count on?"

"Only six. The regular crew is actin' a little shy." Harper smiled wryly.

"Then put four men about half a mile out the basin trail, the other two in the timber east of the house. They can pick off Bonnyman's crew as they come in. Stick to that arrangement unless I get word in to change it."

Harper's smile broadened. "So it's that easy, eh? Any particular scalps you'd like to collect?"

"Bonnyman's." Clark was going to let it go at that when he added, on impulse: And Charley Staples's." He could make doubly sure of getting the Singletree by having only Staples's widow to deal with.

The gunman nodded. "This ought to call for sweetenin' the kitty, hadn't it?"

Clark unbuttoned his shirt and reached under it to unfasten a money belt. He let Harper see the bulging pouches of the belt but opened only one. He unwadded the bills he removed from it. "Here's four hundred. You get four hundred more from Saygar on your way out. I'll get it up to him later tonight."

Harper frowned. "I don't trust that jasper, boss," he said, but took the proffered banknotes.

"You'll get your *dinero*. Mike's too deep in this to try a double-cross. Here's another thing. You're to head up to Saygar's camp now. Get there as quick as you can and tell him Coyle and Joe Bonnyman are droppin' in on him in a couple hours. Tell him Bonnyman's primed to make him talk. He'll know what to do."

"Bonnyman! I thought you said you . . ."

"I know," Clark cut in. "But he's still alive. We'll make sure of him tonight. Got everything straight?"

"Do I get back down here before the ball starts rollin'?"

"You'll have plenty of time. And remember to keep Vanover here. You can do it without bein' rough with the girl, too. Don't let a man like Tillson handle it."

"Gentry gets that job," Harper said. "That's all?"

"That's all."

Clark waited until Harper had walked back as far as the trees, out of six-gun range, before he turned his back and started up the slope. He had caught the narrow-eyed way in which the gunman eyed his money belt.

Saygar Wins a Hand

It was from across the Troublesome, the west bank, that Joe made his careful inspection of the outlaw camp. He was out of the saddle, holding the bay's bridle close on the chance that the animal might try to signal the horses he knew must be across there somewhere.

It was obvious that Saygar's men were making no attempt to hide their presence here, for a big blaze lit the shoulder of the timber-crested knoll, throwing into dark relief the nearest jack pines and glinting dully from the oily, mounded swells of the creek. Pecos worked by the fire, spending some minutes over a batch of biscuit dough that he finally dropped into a Dutch oven lifted above the coals by a forked stick. Several times Reibel and Whitey crossed boldly before the fire. Joe, well acquainted with the habits of men on the hoof, realized that they must be enjoying this brief relaxation from their wary ways that had put them here for the outwardly legitimate purpose of homesteading.

Knowing that they had relaxed their vigilance, and also that the roar of the stream would hide the approach of a rider, Joe rode downstream a short distance until he came to a point where the creek split up into two channels around a narrow neck of high ground. Here he put the bay across to the east bank, the water rising above the stirrups. Less than five minutes later he looked down from the timber above the camp to see Mike Saygar's arrival.

Joe felt a keen disappointment at sight of Saygar, having hoped that he could talk with the others in the absence of their

189

leader, whose shrewdness he respected highly. So he waited a long moment before he started down toward the camp, rearranging his ideas on what he was to do.

Chuck Reibel, who had led Saygar's horse over to the rope corral, saw him first as he rode into the light and called to the others: "Heads up! We got company."

Joe came on, reining in close to the other three at the fire. He caught Whitey's angry scowl and the lift of the gunman's hand that put it within finger spread of holster. Saygar's look was the same impassive half smile of the other afternoon at Hoelseker's cabin. Pecos merely turned and looked up at the newcomer, not bothering to stand, his expression politely curious.

"You again," Saygar drawled.

"Yeah." Joe got aground deliberately, moving slowly, keeping his hands in plain sight. "Where can I turn this horse in and feed him?" he asked as Reibel sauntered over into the light.

His question obviously surprised them. "Did we ask you to stay?" Saygar asked.

Joe tried to school his face to an expression of puzzlement. "Didn't he tell you?" he asked.

"Didn't who tell us what?" Saygar's tone was cool, suspicious.

"That I was to meet you here and wait until he showed. It's set for tonight."

Saygar's glance narrowed. "This's the first I've heard of it."

Joe shrugged. On impulse, he turned and handed his reins to Reibel, saying: "Grain him. He's had a real workout this afternoon."

Reibel hesitated only a moment, then took the reins. As he started off toward the corral, Saygar said flatly: "Stay set, Chuck!" Then to Joe: "What kind of a sandy you runnin', Bonnyman?"

"Sandy?" Joe asked blandly. He laughed. "I see. He didn't get the word to you. Well, it doesn't matter. I can give you the set-up. Diamond and Anchor swapped some lead this mornin'. Harper came out on top. So Bonnyman's goin' back with more men tonight. That is, if his crew's in shape to." He nodded in the general direction of the pass road. "He's up there somewhere lookin' for me. That was part of the job, to toll him up there after me until we could get ready for him. We're supposed to go down to Diamond tonight, soon as we get the word. Harper doesn't have enough men to handle this."

It was Whitey who drawled into the following silence: "This must be what Clark was after when he had us push that herd into . . ."

As the youth spoke, Saygar wheeled, quick as a cat, and struck him across the mouth with an open hand. "You loose-mouthed pup," he breathed. Ignoring Whitey, he faced Joe again. "Who let you in on this?" he asked tonelessly.

Joe was only vaguely aware that the outlaw had spoken, so intent was he on Whitey's mention of Clark's name. "What about Clark?" he demanded. "What's he got to do with this?"

"Something Dunne told Chuck the other day when Chuck held the gun on him," Saygar explained hastily.

But his answer lacked conviction. Joe stepped around him to face Whitey, whose pale-blue eyes were cloudy with mute rage as he stared venomously at Saygar.

"What about Clark?" Joe asked again.

Before Whitey could answer, Saygar reached out, laid a hand on Joe's arm, and jerked him roughly around. In that moment Joe knew only that Whitey had made an attempt to couple Clark's name with last night's raid on the herd at the head of Rainbow Gorge. His one and only thought was that these men had planned this mention of Clark's name for just such a circumstance, to confuse anyone who might connect them with the mounting trouble and be curious over their part in it. Here they were, four men who knew the answer he sought, trying to pin the guilt for their work on one of his best friends.

As Saygar's hold jerked him off balance, Joe was thinking this, and suddenly he knew he would get nothing from these men unless he beat it out of them. He used the side fall of his frame to add surprise to his staggering lurch against Saygar. His Stetson fell aground. He rammed the outlaw hard with his shoulder, the shock setting up a burst of pain in his head. But he ignored that, his hand blurring to holster as Saygar stumbled and sprawled awkwardly backward to the ground. Whitey reached for his gun, saw he was too late, and jerked his hand away from his side. Beyond the blond killer, Pecos, still hunkered by the fire, remained motionless.

Joe's glance whipped around to Reibel, to the gun arcing up into line with him. The expression of viciousness on Reibel's face was eloquent of his danger. He dodged, bringing his own gun into line. Reibel's .38 exploded deafeningly close. Joe felt the bullet's tug at the sleeve of his shirt and he squeezed the trigger of the Colt. He didn't hear his gun's explosion, only saw the front of Reibel's vest stir and the man driven backward in a wheeling fall. He didn't look at Reibel again. He didn't have to.

Saygar's spurs scuffed long marks across the grassy sod as the outlaw got his feet under him and slowly came erect. Whitey stood awkwardly stooped at the waist, having frozen in that posture at the beginning of his draw. Pecos, some of the color gone from his face, now moved out of line with Joe and Whitey.

"I ain't in on this, Bonnyman," he said hoarsely.

Joe's look settled on Saygar. He was breathing heavily, waiting for the last aching throb of his head to subside. "Now what was it about Clark?" he said flatly, taking a stride that brought him within arm's reach of the outlaw. "Talk, Saygar," he drawled. "This crease you had put in my skull is just a scratch to the one I'll carve in yours if you don't open up. Who paid you to push that herd down the gorge?"

"You've got one thing wrong, Bonnyman." Saygar's glance went to the bandage on Joe's head. "No one of us did that. Unless . . ." He looked around at Whitey before asking: "When did it happen?"

"You sent a man after me that afternoon Clark and I got away from the cabin."

Saygar's anger seemed to vanish before the importance of denying this accusation. "You're wrong, Bonnyman. I didn't . . ."

Joe's knuckles slashing him across the mouth cut off his words. His head rocked around and blood welled from his mouth. "Talk while you're able, Saygar," Joe said. Again he struck, this time harder. His fist caught the outlaw along the jaw, tilting the man's head back.

Saygar's long, heavy arms came up. He made an ungainly attempt at knocking Joe's arm down, one that went wide of its mark. Joe hit him again, this time with his gun; it was a numbing short blow squarely on the thick muscle below Saygar's neck. The outlaw groaned and, a hand clamped to his shoulder, sank to his knees.

Whitey had watched all this closely. Now he thought he saw his chance and the hand he had held rigid, clear of his side, once more started toward his Colt. Joe let that hand reach the handle of the .45 before he rocked his gun around and shot. Whitey spun halfway around, right arm dropping limply. He cursed savagely as he clamped his good hand to the spreading stain of crimson on his right shoulder.

Joe stood, straddle-legged, above Saygar. "Who had you do it?" he said tonelessly. "Who had you push that herd down the gorge?"

Saygar seemed to sense then that the gun in Joe's hand was dangerous only as a club would have been, that Joe wouldn't shoot him before he talked. As he pushed erect, all the cunning and viciousness of the outlaw's nature came into play. A submissive look was on his face. He held up a hand.

"I've had enough," he whined. "Let me get my wind and . . ." He threw himself headlong at Joe, his long arms locking about Joe's waist, all the terrific power of his heavy shoulders tightening that bear-like hold. Joe's back arched. He tried to club Saygar alongside the head with the gun, but the man's skull was thrusting at his chest, too close to get in a telling blow. Joe forgot the gun and let it fall as he brought his knee up hard into Saygar's groin. The outlaw groaned in pain but his hold didn't slacken. Pain as sharp as a burn coursed down Joe's spine as his back muscles were wrenched. Again he brought his knee up; when that failed to break Saygar's back-breaking hold, he tramped hard on the outlaw's boots, twisting his heels.

Saygar's howl of pain echoed back from the trees. Suddenly his arms came loose and he sank to the ground, writhing in pain. Joe snatched up his gun, seeing that Pecos had moved over to where Whitey sat and was reaching for the blond youth's Colt.

"You're next," he drawled, and advanced a step toward Pecos, who drew his hand quickly away from the .45.

From close to Joe's left came a gun's low-throated roar. A numbing shock paralyzed Joe's gun hand. The heavy Colt spun from his grasp. He wheeled, in time to see a stranger walk into the circle of firelight.

Alongside, Saygar said: "Nice work, Harper."

This was the Diamond foreman Blaze Coyle had spoken of with such open scorn and dislike. The mark of the killer was on Harper, Joe saw, for the man's hawkish, scarred face was as inscrutable as a rock slab, his pale-green eyes cloudy and expressionless. He held his gun carelessly, and, as he advanced toward Saygar, he drawled: "Thought you might want him whole, Mike."

With that casual proof of the expertness of Harper's aim, Joe knew he had lost. A moment later, Pecos had the groaning Whitey's .45 and Saygar was facing him, the light of cold fury in his eyes.

"Brother, let's see how fine you whittle down," Saygar said simply. Then he struck.

Joe took that first blow on the point of his turning shoulder, answering with a stiff uppercut that jarred Saygar to his boot heels. But the outlaw was sure of winning now. He merely shook his head to clear his reeling senses, and then came at Joe head down, slugging. And still Joe held him off, dodging the brutal drive of the outlaw's heavy fists, making the swift slashing of his own fists count. Two rapid jabs drove the wind from Saygar's lungs; another at the base of the neck threw him off balance. Joe was cocked on toes, arm drawn back for a finishing looping right to the jaw, when Harper stepped in and calmly tripped him.

Saygar hit Joe as the latter's knees struck the ground, hit him with all the drive of his heavy body behind his rock-knuckled fist. A bright burst of light blotted out Joe's vision. From then on he didn't feel the blows. His arms fell to his sides and Saygar beat him into unconsciousness with the ease of a man whipping a child.

When Joe lay at his feet, bleeding from nose and mouth, Saygar motioned to Pecos. "Roll him over the bank," he ordered harshly.

"Looks like I hit here at about the right time," Harper drawled, the glance he directed down at Joe tinged with admiration. "Who is he?"

"Joe Bonnyman."

Harper whistled softly. "There's a reward out on him."

"You want to collect it?" Saygar asked savagely, for the knowledge that Joe would have licked him still rankled.

Harper shrugged. "Do it your way, Mike," he drawled, and watched Pecos lift Joe by the arms and drag him the thirty feet across to the edge of the high bank that dropped into the roiling waters of the Troublesome.

Pecos hesitated there, plainly disliking his job. Saygar came over and said sharply: "What're you waitin' on?" Only then did Pecos give a quick thrust of his boot that rolled Joe off the bank. He didn't look down to make sure of what happened but turned and, the color gone from his face, walked over to see what he could do for Whitey.

Saygar saw Joe's loosely rolling frame swallowed by the black waters of the creek. A wicked down-lipped grin touched his heavy features. "Wonder where they'll find him?" he asked Harper, and walked over to the fire.

Return from the Dead

The numbing chill of the water brought Joe back to consciousness with a lung-constricting shock. He swallowed water and would have drowned but for the fact that his head rolled above the surface of the angry waters at that moment, letting his lungs suck in the air he was starving for. By the time his head went under again, he was enough aware of what was happening to him to hold his breath.

It seemed an eternity before he could command his muscles to move. He struck out feebly, trying to swim, but the strong current sucked him deeper under the surface. A jagged rock slashed the left side of his chest. One of his boots touched another rock. Panic hit him and his lungs seemed about to burst as he thrust out with that boot and again pushed his head above the water to catch two gasping breaths.

He managed to keep his head up this last time, only to find that he lacked the strength to fight the current. Time and again he would strike out for the looming shadow of the bank, but his arms flailed the foaming water with no visible effect. Once again, as he rolled onto his back, his head went under. He came up, gagging and coughing, at the fiery pain of water in his lungs. He glimpsed a rosy glow cutting the darkness far upstream, not then knowing that it was the light of the fire at Saygar's camp.

He fought now with a dull fear making him waste his strength. He felt that strength slowly going. At last he even lacked the energy to move his arms. When a wave sucked his head under, he didn't struggle against it. He relished the pleasing languor of exhaustion settling through him, wondering only what he would do when his lungs used up the last deep breath he had taken.

His lungs were beginning to crowd him again when, face down, his chest scraped the bottom. His first thought was that the current had sucked him under again. Instinct made him lift his head. It came above water and the tonic of the fresh, sweet air he drew into his lungs braced him.

Joe found himself lying belly down in a shallows where the water no longer moved in oily, fast-flowing swells but foamed whitely to each side, vaguely reflecting the sheen of starlight. He pushed himself up onto his knees and let the water foam about his thighs until his breathing came easier. Then, struggling to his feet, he started for the nearest bank. Once he stepped into a hole and went under, but now he had more strength, and three powerful strokes took him to the shallows again. He reached for the knob of a boulder and pulled himself up. Standing once more, he waded to within reach of the bank, stumbled, let himself fall, and lay there for long minutes, his strength slowly building.

When he finally drew his legs from the water and looked about him, he saw that he was on the east bank of the creek at the point where he had earlier crossed on the bay. Out there in the darkness he could vaguely make out the shape of the mounded island that divided the stream into two channels. Getting his bearings further, he knew that he had less than a quarter mile walk to his bay. And, knowing that Saygar might not yet have found the horse, he got on his feet and started for the knoll on the far side of which lay the outlaw camp.

It hurt him to walk. The throb of his head was less painful than the cuts and bruises all along his body. Only now did he realize what punishment he had taken while struggling against the stream. His lips were puffed and swollen from the blow Saygar had struck, his jaw ached, and, when he breathed deeply, there was a pain deep in his chest.

The farther Joe walked the less urgent it became for him to find the bay and get out of here. Now that he could think rationally, he saw that he had gained an advantage over Saygar and Harper. They would naturally think him dead. Their vigilance would be relaxed. And when that thought came to him, he stopped abruptly, trying to figure out how best to use his advantage. When he went on again, he angled back in the direction of the Troublesome's low roar, so as to circle the foot of the knoll and come in on the camp from the south.

His first glimpse of the camp showed him Whitey stretched out on a blanket near the fire, his right shoulder bare, Pecos and Saygar kneeling beside him. A whiskey bottle lay on the ground nearby. Whitey's face was lined with pain and he winced sharply once as Pecos wrapped his bullet-punctured shoulder in a rag. Beyond the wounded man, farther toward the outer margin of firelight, lay Reibel's inert figure; his gun lay beyond one of the outstretched lifeless hands.

Harper stood across the fire from the others, his back to the near corner of the lean-to. He stood with one hand hanging, thumb hooked from his sagging shell belt, a cigarette drooping from his mouth, idly watching the attention Saygar and Pecos were giving the wounded man.

Joe was careful to take note of each detail, of the three saddles and the stack of grub against the back sloping wall inside the lean-to, of the coffee pot and Dutch oven on the fire. He tried hard to see into the lean-to's back corner but there the shadows were too dense. He wondered if there were any rifles in there, remembering now another item he had planned on settling when he rode in here. It concerned that telltale sign that marked the gun of the man who had tried to bushwhack him, the print of the scarred Winchester butt plate Blaze had mentioned finding by the rock in the upper basin.

It took Joe a full five minutes to make his quarter circle of the camp and come down out of the trees toward the shadowy mound that was Reibel's body. He crawled the last twenty feet, his glance riveted on Harper, who faced his direction. The Diamond foreman still stood in that careless stance against the end of the lean-to.

Finally Joe lay behind Reibel's body. He was reaching over the dead man's chest, his hand groping for the gun, when he heard Saygar say: "How soon did he say Coyle would be here?"

Harper pushed out from the lean-to and flicked the stub of his smoke into the fire. "He didn't say. It was to be sometime after dark. Only he was to come with Bonnyman. Maybe he won't show up now." Harper sauntered over and looked down at Whitey. "How you feelin', kid?"

"Like hell." Whitey's look was bleak.

"It'll heal up," Harper said. "But it'll never work right again. You better take up another trade, friend."

The expression that came to the youth's face at that moment made it obvious how much deeper his wound had struck than the mere bone and flesh Joe's bullet had damaged. Tonight had seen him crippled more effectively than the loss of a leg would cripple a cowpoke. Whitey's life had been built around his skill with a gun. Now, with his right shoulder broken, his gun magic gone forever, he faced a future that was a void of despair.

Joe heard him say tonelessly: "Pass me the bottle, Mike." Saygar handed the bottle of whiskey across, and Whitey took three long swallows before he handed it back. Then, petulantly, he asked: "You goin' to leave me here?"

"You'll be in shape to sit a saddle by mornin'."

As Saygar drawled his casual answer, a look passed between him and Harper. Had Whitey seen it, there would have been little doubt in his mind about what was to happen to him. In the morning, Joe knew, Saygar and Pecos would desert their crewman to whatever fate, good or bad, lay in store for him. It was the law of the pack and Joe had seen it work before; there was no room for a cripple.

Answering Saygar's glance with a barely perceptible nod, Harper hitched his Levi's higher along his waist and said: "Time for me to be goin'. We'll be through here later for that money, Mike."

"I'll be here."

Joe had a moment's panic, thinking Harper was coming toward him. He took a chance, coming up onto his knees and snatching up Reibel's walnut-handled .45. He cocked it and the hammer *click* brought Harper wheeling around to face the sound.

"Don't move," Joe spoke quietly, his voice barely audible above the persistent low roar of the nearby creek. Yet Saygar and Pecos both heard it—Saygar's thick upper body turning, Pecos straightening and staring with face slack with amazement.

For a moment Harper stood absolutely motionless. Then his hands slowly lifted to the level of his ears. Saygar likewise put up his hands. Pecos was too startled to move: It didn't matter, for he wore no weapon.

Joe stood up. "Whitey, reach for that iron and you'll never know what hit you." He advanced toward the wounded man as he spoke, his glance running between Whitey and the others. A moment later he was close enough to Whitey to reach out with the toe of his boot and kick away the shell belt and holstered gun that lay alongside the blanket.

He stooped, picked up the belt, and slung it over his shoulder. With a motion of his leveled .45, Saygar and Harper turned their backs. Joe stepped in behind them and uncinched their belts, looping them across his shoulder as he had the first.

"Saygar, where are your rifles?" he asked flatly.

"Where you hid 'em day before yesterday," was Saygar's immediate reply, "up there in the timber by the cabin. We couldn't find 'em."

Joe said—"Stay set."—and backed over to the lean-to. He stooped down, cast a quick glance inside that showed him no rifles, and came back around the fire again.

"Where's your horse, Harper?" he queried.

Harper made no answer. It was Saygar who said: "Out by the corral. Off there." He brought his hands down, motioning into the northward darkness.

"I'll be gone a minute," Joe drawled. "Maybe you better not move."

The rope corral lay half a dozen rods out from the camp. He walked fast in reaching it and at once spotted Harper's saddled horse tied along its near side. There was a rifle in a scabbard on the far side of the saddle, and Joe took it down. He saw Harper's silhouetted shape take a step out from the fire and levered a shell into the rifle, lined it, and put a bullet into the ground a foot ahead of the Diamond man. Harper stiffened and lifted his hands again, not moving a muscle.

Approaching the fire again, Joe drawled: "Funny, but I had you pegged for havin' some brains, Harper."

His pulse slowed as he rocked the rifle's butt up and held it to the light. Then his hopes died. The butt plate was of smooth steel, marked with rust but unscarred by any line that would fit Blaze's description of the bushwhacker's rifle.

Joe stood there a moment debating what to do next. Saygar's story of not having been able to find the hidden guns up by Hoelseker's cabin had carried a ring of truth. It would be a simple matter to check his story later, when there was more time. Harper's Winchester wasn't the one.

Then who was the man who had tried to kill him, in fact left him for dead? Joe's thinking hadn't gone beyond this point, this meeting with Saygar. He hadn't found the rifle and he didn't believe he could make Saygar talk. What was he to do now?

"You gents ought to eat well for the next few days," he said tonelessly. "The county's goin' to be buyin' your meals and . . ."

A sound out of the darkness to his left made him wheel in that direction, lifting the rifle to his shoulder. His muscles tightened at the expected slam of a bullet, for what he had heard off there was the hoof fall of a walking horse.

Abruptly the tension drained out of him at the sound of a voice that called: "That you, Joe? If it ain't, whoever it is better reach for the stars. I got a line on your belt buckle!"

Joe lowered his rifle. "Come on in, Blaze."

Half a minute later, the red-headed Anchor foreman was standing alongside him, a wide grin slashing his homely face.

"Now ain't this a nice catch," Blaze drawled, eying the trio standing before him, the dead man, and the wounded outlaw. His look came around finally to Joe and he was visibly shocked at what he saw, his friend's bruised face and cut and swollen lips, the torn Levi's exposing a blood-reddened thigh, Joe's still wetly clinging shirt.

He holstered his gun, unbuttoned one cuff, and began rolling his sleeve. "Which one do I take on first?" he demanded,

"None, Blaze," said Joe. "We'll take 'em down to Yace. He'll do a better job."

"Yace! You go in there? Man, don't you know Yace has been hellin' around up here most of the day on your trail?"

"Then you'll take them in." Joe was looking at Harper and Saygar, seeing the outlaw's face set doggedly in an impassive way, Harper's in a faint arrogant smile. When he added—"I hope they'll give them a chance to talk before they string 'em up."— the gunman's smile faded.

Waiting for Trouble

The rider was close, entering the yard, before Ruth Merrill recognized him in the light of the lantern at the gate. It was Clark Dunne.

She turned from the window and stood a moment debating what to do, her pulse stirring to a quicker beat. In that brief interval, alone, her face mirrored the swift run of her thoughts in a sharp, calculating way. When she finally went to the door and stepped out to call him before he turned down to the corral, the look on her face was serene.

She told him—"I've been hoping you'd come back tonight."—as he came out of the saddle at the foot of the porch steps. Then, haltingly, she said: "Clark . . . I . . . I've been thinking."

Ignoring her words, he came on up the steps. He took her in his arms, kissing her on the lips and resisting the pressure her arms made to draw away. When he let her go, she laughed nervously and pretended to smooth down her flawlessly brushed hair.

"Clark! What if one of the men should see?"

"What if they should?" Clark's face was handsome under its smile as the lamplight from the open door struck it. He put his arm around her waist. "And now what were you thinking?"

She went serious, looking up at him with her head cocked to one side. It was a glance at once appealing and tender. "It's only this, Clark. Dad might not . . . might not have known what he was saying last night. It doesn't seem right that we should be getting married so soon after . . ."

She paused there, letting her thought complete itself.

He let his arm fall abruptly and stepped back from her, trying to see beneath her expression. "You've heard about Joe, haven't you?" he asked.

Her air of coquetry vanished before a run of cool aloofness. His insight had destroyed the calculated edge of her approach and he had his answer when she said accusingly: "What about Joe? Why would that make a difference?"

Something in him hardened. "Suit yourself about the weddin'," he said, for a moment forgetting that this independence in him was neither wise nor diplomatic.

A haughtiness edged into Ruth's look now. "Clark, I asked you about Joe. Please tell me."

"He was seen north of here this afternoon," he told her, willing now to pretend as she was pretending. "They're looking for him."

"I hope he gets away," she said directly. Then: "You won't mind waiting for a few days, will you?"

"No. It's probably better that way." He turned and went back down the steps and picked up his reins.

"Will you have supper here at the house?" she asked.

"I'd better eat with the men. We're expectin' word from Yace Bonnyman any minute."

Ruth let him go without further urging, a little frightened at not wanting him to be with her tonight and at showing it. Two hours ago one of the men coming down from the herd camp had brought her word of the renewed hunt for Joe. Since then her dismal world had brightened; it had also become complicated, chiefly by her promise to Clark. Now she was excited and wary, not knowing what to do but wait.

Until just a moment ago she hadn't consciously tried to picture her wants. But they stood out clearly now and Joe Bonnyman formed the core of them. She had come to the abrupt realization that Joe was the only man who mattered to her. She wanted terribly to see him; her hope that he would live through this seething trouble was a constant and heavy pressure on all her thoughts.

She watched Clark walk off into the shadows and turned back into the house, avoiding the main living room where her father's body lay in its simple pine coffin before the huge center fireplace.

The six men down from the herd camp had already eaten and were loafing along the front of the bunkhouse, enjoying their after-supper smokes, their talk running icily and low against their expectation of what the coming night might hold. At the side kitchen door, Clark called in to the cook—"One more plate, Jim."—and, having rolled up his sleeves, ladled out a basinful of water from the cedar bucket on the bench.

The cool lathering Clark gave his face and hands seemed to cleanse him of more than the dust and grime of this afternoon's ride. By the time he had toweled his face dry, he could look with some amusement on Ruth's poor show of affection. He was fully aware of her reason in asking that the wedding be delayed. Joe was much in her thoughts, he realized. Well, he wouldn't be there long. Tonight, tomorrow at the latest, and Joe Bonnyman would no longer be a threat.

He was halfway through his meal in the kitchen when he heard a horse running in along the road. He stepped to the door and saw a rider swing across the yard and come straight on for the bunkhouse.

It was an Anchor man, Ed Dennis. He came directly to the kitchen entrance, seeing Clark there, with a casual—"Hi, yuh, boys."—to the men outside the bunkhouse door.

Dennis's message was brief and he began it as soon as Clark had closed the door. The mesa men had lost Joe just below the pass at dusk. They were on the way back to Yoke now. They would take time out to eat there and start for Diamond around 9:00. Workman would take half the men and circle to come in on Diamond from the east. Bonnyman, with the others, would follow the basin trail in from the west.

"You've got the tough job," Dennis concluded. "The boss wants Harper tolled out into the open, if it can be worked, sharp on ten o'clock. That's where you come in. You're to ride straight in the road from the south. You'll likely get within range of the layout before you're stopped. Throw a lot of lead at it, and then hightail. The boss thinks Harper'll follow you. If he does, once he's clear of the trees, we'll have him on two sides."

Clark frowned, seeing the simplicity and workability of Yace's plan. It didn't seem to have a hole in it. Harper would naturally take the initiative once he saw he wasn't outnumbered, especially in view of what Clark had told him this afternoon. Clark's six men would look like easy odds to him. He wouldn't be expecting a trap because he was relying on Clark to arrange matters.

Misunderstanding Clark's frown, Dennis said: "If you're careful, none of you will even get scratched. The boss said not to get too close but to raise plenty of hell with your powder, then run."

There was nothing for Clark to do but agree. He did.

Dennis seemed relieved. He explained further: "The only reason you're drawin' on this job is because you ain't wore out like the rest of us. We ran the legs off a lot o' horseflesh chasin' Joe this afternoon. I'll sure be glad to turn in this jughead I got for that little paint horse."

"No luck with Joe?"

Dennis shook his head. "He played us for a bunch of suckers. Yace can't decide why. Well, I'll get on back. Oh, another thing. Lyans ain't due back in town until late tonight. They decided not to wait on him."

After the Anchor man had ridden off into the night with a peremptory—"Enjoy your rest while you can, gents."—to the idle Brush crewmen outside, Clark sat for several minutes deeply in thought. He was remembering something Dennis had said, a small but potent item of information, wondering how he could use it. Only when he felt the presence of the men gathered close to the door to the bunkhouse beyond, anxiously waiting to learn what news Dennis had brought, did he resume his eating. He intentionally delayed telling the men of the plans for the night in order to settle on one of his own.

What he was thinking made him glance toward the closed door of the kitchen. He decided finally, over his second cup of coffee, that it had been impossible for any of the crew to have overheard Dennis. Sure of that, yet not sure of one other thing, he left the kitchen and sauntered out through the bunkhouse to the door. There, he stood and took his watch from the pocket of his waist overalls and looked at it.

"Time to ride," he told them. "We're due to move in on Diamond at ten." He went on to explain how they were to decoy Harper away from the layout.

The willingness and speed with which the men got their guns, saddled, and were ready to travel was grim proof of the seriousness with which they were tackling this job. Shorty, the Anchor man who had been killed at Diamond this morning, had boasted many friends; several of these Brush men were among them. As one of them put it before they left the lower corral: "Dunne, I've notched every slug on my belt. If one of 'em hits a man, it'll tear a hole in him big enough to shove a boot through."

Clark had an impulse to go to the house to speak to Ruth. But the memory of her interest in Joe still rankled and he rode straight out of the yard without once looking toward the house.

They traveled at a steady trot, neither hurrying nor wasting time. Long past the time they should have raised the lights of Diamond, Clark signaled a halt, telling them: "They're expectin' us. No lights. We'll go along careful." He took out his watch, held it close so that he could see it in the faint starlight. "Twenty minutes. Plenty of time."

"We goin' right on in?" one of the men asked.

"Right on in. But slow."

When they went on, Clark was tense under the foreboding that there was nothing he could do to stop this. Earlier, when he saw Harper, he'd been optimistic over the possibilities of heavy casualties among the mesa crews. But because he hadn't been in on Yace's plan, his own was unworkable. The last twenty-four hours had put much power in his hands. Now he wanted more, and his whole thought was centered on tonight so weakening Anchor and Yoke and the other big outfits that, when this was over, he would come out stronger than they. It was possible, he told himself, if only he could find a way of getting word in to Harper.

They rode the high grass with their horses at a walk, the shoes of the ponies making but a faint slurring sound against the night's utter stillness. Ahead, the shadow line of trees that hid the Diamond buildings held a threat much greater than the presence of lights would have indicated; wakeful, watchful men were on the alert there, Clark knew. He was riding into a trap of his own planning.

Finally he could stand it no longer and said sharply: "Hold on! Something's wrong up there." His glance came around to the nearest man. "Alec, you and I will go on ahead and have a look."

"Careful, Dunne," said one of the others, as Clark and the man he had spoken to reined on ahead toward the margin of the locust grove, now less than 300 yards ahead of them.

Clark drew his Winchester from the scabbard and laid it across the horn of his saddle. Alec, close alongside, did likewise. Clark could feel the other man's tense excitement.

They reached the trees without being challenged. The channel of Clark's spine was cool with nervous perspiration. This, he told himself, was the hardest part. His pulse hammered as he saw he might make good his one slim chance.

Reining close in to Alec, he whispered: "You go right, off toward the house. Don't go in on it but take a look and get back here. I'll take the bunkhouse."

Once he had lost Alec in the darkness, he came quickly out of the saddle, looped reins over a low branch, and hurried back through the trees until he was even with the bunkhouse. There

he halted and whistled softly, the same call he had used in summoning Harper two nights ago.

There was a moment in which the night's utter stillness
remained unbroken. Then Clark heard the hinges of the bunkhouse door *squeak* faintly. A man stepped out of the door.

Clark came out of the trees, speaking softly: "Heads up,
Harper."

"Oh, it's you." The voice wasn't Harper's but Tillson's. He
came across to Clark. "Neal ain't back yet. We can't figure what's
slowin' him. We doused the lights a couple hours ago, just in
case."

Clark had his moment's worry over Harper's delay in
returning from Saygar's camp, then he forgot it in the face of this
other, more urgent, matter.

"What about Vanover?" he asked.

"Gentry's got him and the girl at the house. We had to hog-
tie Vanover. He tried twice to make a break for it."

"Get this and get it fast, Tillson," Clark said, knowing now
where his only chance lay. "Round up every man and hit for
the trees close above. Take the Vanovers, only keep them back a
ways. You and the rest stay close enough so you can spot anyone
movin' around down here. I want this place empty in ten minutes. Give me five of those ten to get clear. I've got a man with
me."

Tillson's suspicious glance searched Clark's face in the obscurity. "What's this addin' up to?"

"I'm not sure yet. Maybe, just maybe, it's goin' to be the
finish. Twenty or thirty minutes from now you may see men
movin' around down here. Wait until the guns cut loose down
here before you open up on 'em. But when you do open up, get
every man in sight. Harper's goin' to make it worth your while to
do the job right."

Tillson's drawl lacked its edge of suspicion as he said: "It's
about time we collected on something around here."

"You will tonight." Clark turned and faded back into the trees. He rode out the way he had come, cautiously, soundlessly. He came up to Alec so quietly that he startled the man.

"Not a soul stirrin' in the house," Alec breathed, watching the shadows. "What in tarnation can this mean?"

"They're out somewhere," Clark said, "maybe keepin' a watch on our crews. The bunkhouse is empty as a drum. Say!" He spoke the last word explosively. "This may be our chance!"

"How come?"

"We could go in there, fort up, and catch 'em when they come in."

Alec was silent a moment. Then he breathed: "By Satan, you're right. Let's go back for the others."

It was Alec who did the talking when they reached the others. His enthusiasm needed no prodding from Clark. The only question, voiced by one of the others, was: "What'll Bonnyman and Workman be doin' all this time?"

Clark shrugged. "They were to wait until we tangled with Harper, then pitch in and finish it off. If you ask me, they'll stay set. This is a surer way than the other, especially since the other won't work."

"How about roundin' up the others?"

It was Alec who said sharply: "And spend half the night findin' 'em, maybe even get shot because they think we're Harper's bunch? Uhn-uh. If we do this, we do it on our own. And right sudden. Maybe Harper's crew has drifted in while we been sittin' here talkin'."

That decided them. Clark's breath left his lungs in a sharp sigh of relief as another man said—"Come on."—and led them away back toward the trees. Later, if questions were asked, Clark would be able to say that he wasn't the one who had made the decision.

At the trees, they halted, listening a brief interval for any sounds that would betray the presence of men having come in during their short absence.

"We'd better take the bunkhouse, all but one man," Clark said finally. "They'll head for there or the lot behind when they come in. Alec, you take the house."

Alec left, and the others rode back through the thick-foliaged locusts until they were close to the bunkhouse. In a voice barely above a whisper, Clark told the nearest man: "Stay with the horses." Rifle in hand, he swung out of the saddle, setting an example for the others.

He was first in through the bunkhouse door, pushing it back, flattening to the wall a moment before he stepped on in. When the others had entered, he struck a match, glancing around the room in its brief flare, then whipped it out. Quickly, curtly he stationed his four men at windows and door. He climbed to the top tier of bunks and took the high, slitted window facing the barn lot behind, lifting out the sash and then giving them his last word: "This may be a long wait or a short one. Whatever you do, wait'll I give you the word before you open up. We want to be sure of this."

The minutes ran on interminably for Clark. His palms were damp with a nervous perspiration. The silence became oppressive, close to intolerable. Maybe he'd been right in telling his men that the mesa crews would stay set, not moving in unless they heard sounds of a fight. Maybe this was all wasted effort on his part. Tonight might bring no action at all.

He was thinking this, staring out across the wide lot toward the shadowy high shape of the big barn when he saw a dark shape move soundlessly in out of the gloom. Shortly he made that shape out as a man's crouched figure. Slowly the man circled out from the hill slope at the back of the lot, seemingly heading for the bunkhouse.

The Brush man at the side window whispered hoarsely— "Here they come."—and at that exact moment Clark heard the soft footfall of slow-walking horses come faintly from the end of the lot out of his line of vision.

Fire at Yoke

For a moment after hearing that low-voiced announcement by the Brush man—"Here they come."—Clark Dunne stood irresolute. In the past few days he had gone from robbery and the involuntary killing of a man to bushwhacking, to cold-blooded murder, but even now he could not contemplate the wanton blasting down of his own people without asking himself if there were any other way out. In a flash he knew the answer and his indecision passed. Dropping quickly off the top bunk, he went to the side window, peering out over the shoulder of the man who knelt there, his rifle half lifted. Four riders were in sight, halted now. One of the horses was a paint.

"That's them," Clark breathed softly. "There's that pinto horse of Harper's. The rest of you get over here."

His urgent whisper brought the others across the room at once. When they stood beside him, he said: "Each of you pick a man, left to right as you stand. Forget it's a man you're shootin' at. Be sure to bring him down. There's another farther out back I've spotted. I'll climb up to my window again and get a line on him. When I shoot, the rest of you cut loose." He wheeled away from them and climbed back to his window.

Clark's hand was shaking as he laid the sights of the carbine on the chest of the man he had first seen, now walking across and nearly out of sight to join the others. Moving his gun to follow the target, the barrel of his Winchester came against the sash he had removed from the window. Irritated at the obstruction,

213

Clark shoved it aside. It tipped over and fell sideward, down in behind the inner edge of the bunk's mattress.

He made a frantic stab of the hand, trying to catch it, then knew his action was wrong. In the last moment he tried to throw his sights on the man in the barn lot again. The *crash* of the splintering glass spoiled his aim, but he pulled the trigger anyway.

The man who had been his target—Sherman, Anchor's straw boss, he discovered later—lifted a strident shout that rang across the yard. The guns below Clark at the side window exploded in a ragged, deafening concussion. Out there, somewhere, a man screamed. A riderless horse plunged into Clark's line of vision.

Close on the heels of the rifles in the bunkhouse, others exploded from the timber on the hill close above, laying an uneven but insistent fire down on the men trapped in the barnyard.

Clark called harshly: "Stop! Don't shoot again! Its our own men!" He cursed long and loudly as he dropped down off the bunk, making good this final pretense of his having been innocent of anything but honorable intent in setting this trap.

The bunkhouse was silent a long moment under the realization of these men who were wordless with the stunning realization that they had fired on their own men. Finally one of them spoke, his tone awed and ragged: "Great Jupiter, I know I put a slug in his chest." It was the man who, back at Brush, had mentioned slotting the points of his bullets so that they would mushroom on striking a target.

"Alec, you had a long look at that pinto," Clark said savagely. "Whose was it?"

"Must've been Dennis's," Alec answered in a tired, lost voice. "And I saw him drop."

Never mind that," rasped Clark as the rifles on the hill were answered by a few shots out of the barnyard. Out there men were shouting, cursing, and at least two horses pounded away. "Someone's shooting down from the hill. It must be Harper's crew. They laid this trap and we walked straight into it! Get to the other window and see if you can pick off a man or two."

Three men went to the room's north window, one of them knocking out the lower sash with the barrel of his rifle. That man knelt, took deliberate aim, and fired, cursing saltily as he levered a fresh shell into his weapon. Clark, coming up behind him, also laid his sight on the flash of a rifle up in the trees and pumped two shots at his target before he moved quickly aside.

A bullet chipped a splinter from the window's sill, close to the Brush man kneeling there, and *whunked* into the wall across the room.

"Get back," Clark said flatly. "We'll have to make a run for it. It's every man for himself. We meet a mile south."

The rifles on the hill dropped one Brush man as they made the dash across to the locust grove where they had left the horses. Clark had a moment's panic when a bullet creased the front of his thigh. But once in the trees, out of breath and momentarily safe, he was grateful for that scratch. It would be proof that he had guessed wrong, like the others, fought with them, and come close to being cut down.

As he climbed awkwardly into the saddle, favoring his hurt leg, he heard a confused welter of sounds echoing out of the barn lot. Once he thought he caught Yace Bonnyman's voice booming over the others'. A thin smile came to his face as rifles once more threw back sharp echoes from the hill face.

He rode a quarter mile out on the flats, then turned west, putting his pony to a stiff lope, thinking to come up on Bonnyman's and Workman's men. But after ten minutes' riding, he stopped and listened. The night's stillness seemed complete until, in the direction of Diamond, a renewed burst of firing suddenly sounded. The mesa outfits had evidently stayed on to fight it out, probably because Bonnyman or some other bull-headed fool was unwilling to take his licking and leave.

"Hell with 'em," Clark breathed, and rode on toward Yoke, wanting to get a bandage on his leg as soon as he could; he could feel the cool wetness of blood down as far as his knee.

There was no light, no sign of life at Yoke when he rode into the yard. Even the big corral was empty, its pole gate standing wide. He went over to the house, got down out of the saddle, and tried the door. It was locked.

"Anyone home?" he called, listening for an answer.

No one came. The layout was completely deserted.

He had a thought that slowed the beat of his pulse until his chest ached. A dryness came to his mouth; he swallowed to clear it. Deliberately he stepped away from the door and down the porch to the nearest window. He lifted a boot and kicked in the lower sash. As the tinkling *clatter* of falling glass died out, he stood rigidly, listening again, this time for the sound of riders on their way in. But the night's utter stillness was complete except for the eerie chant of a hunting coyote far out on the mesa.

He stepped in through the window, groping in the darkness until he found the center table of the main room. His hand touched the big brass lamp there. He picked up the lamp, hurled it to the floor. The reeking stench of coal oil permeated the air.

He was shaking now in a trembling of excitement and rising fear. He went back to the window, listened once more. Still no sound to destroy the complete emptiness of the ranch. Turning back into the room, he quickly lit a match and dropped it on the dark, wet stain that ran across the worn rug. Flames leaped high from the match.

The barn was easier. A thick strand of loose dry hay hung down from the filled loft. All he had to do was light that and watch a leaping tongue of flame lick up along it to the mass of fire-hungry hay above.

Going back toward Diamond, Clark made a wide swing south, abreast the Middle Arizona layout, before he turned in toward it. The sound of rifles had died out. Diamond was seemingly as deserted as Yoke had been when Clark angled past the trees and lifted his horse to a quick run back toward Yoke. And now a rosy red glow cut the blackness of the night off toward Yoke.

Clark came up on three of the stragglers, Sherman of Anchor and two of his Brush riders, calling stridently when he saw Sherman swing a rifle around at him: "It's all right, Sherman."

As Clark came alongside, one of the Brush men said: "We been huntin' around for you back there. Thought they'd dropped you."

"I was fool enough to climb into the timber and have a try at 'em," Clark lied. "They heard me comin' and took me. I finally got away." He nodded off toward the strengthening glow of the fire in the distance. "What's that off there?"

"They fired Yoke," Sherman told him, his tone bitter and lifeless. "The rest have gone on ahead. We're too plumb wore out to hurry."

From then on no one said much.

The Rifle

Faintly, yet unmistakably, the sound of guns rode the night, insistent for a moment, then dying to an echoed mutter all but inaudible. Harper, in the lead and flanked by Pecos and Saygar and Whitey slumped over his saddle, stiffened as he caught the first of those far echoes. Blaze misread his change of posture and lifted his .45 from its holster. Then he, too, heard the faint thunder of the guns and his glance whipped around to find Joe, bringing his pony to a halt as his head cocked to a listening attitude. The quartet ahead had stopped now.

"We're too late," Joe said, low-voiced. "That's coming from Diamond, Blaze."

The silence ran on briefly, to be broken by a renewed and stronger rattling of gunfire as the breeze momentarily strengthened.

Joe's voice came over it crisply, urgently: "Take 'em on, Blaze."

He had lifted his reins to turn away when Blaze's sharp—"You don't go down there alone, brother!"—stopped him.

"What about them?" Joe said, nodding to the three outlaws and Diamond's foreman, all three with boots roped to cinches and wrists tied to the horns of their saddles. Whitey, being severely wounded, hadn't needed to be bound. Joe went on to explain patiently, as to a child, knowing his friend's stubbornness: "You said yourself that Vanover and the girl ought to be in on this. I'll get them and bring them along to Workman's."

"How? By askin' them jaspers please not to shoot at you? Hell, they're playin' for keeps!"

"Then I'll just go down and take a look." Joe touched the bay with spurs, lifting the animal into a fast lope as he went away.

Blaze cursed soundly, for the moment considering leaving his four prisoners in his anxiety to know what was going on at Diamond. But in the end, hearing the guns no longer, he said dryly—"Ain't it a shame you boys can't be mixin' in that?"—and motioned them on with a lift of his gun.

Joe knew the lower basin well. He hit the timber at a point where the going was even and the trees grew sparsely, traveling almost due south. But a mile below the basin he swung sharply east, crossed the trail leading to Diamond, and rode across a high ridge that put him into a more broken country. He crossed two small hill meadows, the lower one well-remembered because he had fenced it in and grazed his yearlings there the last summer he was on Diamond.

He struck a little-used wood road and followed its twisting course the better part of a mile. Then, leaving it, cresting a nearby flanking spur, he looked down on the big, cleared pasture that stretched to within a scant mile of Diamond.

He was leaving the trees to cross the pasture when a gun's hammering explosion ripped the night from the trees close to his left. That and a sharp, searing burn on his right side came simultaneously.

* * * * *

Fred Vanover and Jean had listened to the guns with a dull awareness of their helplessness and a feeling of dread. They had been prisoners since late afternoon, first at the house and now here at the edge of the trees bordering Diamond's big hill pasture less than a mile above the layout. Gentry, their guard, had been polite and considerate, but there had been no mistaking the dead seriousness in his threat when they had stopped here. "I ain't never had to put a gun on a woman. Don't make me now," he had said.

This afternoon Harper had neither explained nor apologized when letting them know that they weren't to leave the house. Since then, Vanover had repeatedly asked to see his foreman, but with no success. Some forty minutes ago Tillson had come to the house, unlighted since nightfall, and held a hurried, whispered conversation with Gentry. Directly afterward, father and daughter had been taken out, put on horses, and brought up here.

It was obvious to both Jean and her father that a trap had somehow been laid down at Diamond for the mesa ranchers. How that had been accomplished, Vanover couldn't even begin to guess. When the sound of the guns came, he said simply: "Jean, I wish we'd never come here. Men are dying down there and it'll be blamed on me."

"It won't in the end," Jean said and reached over to put a hand on his arm, giving it a firm pressure she hoped would ease the burden on his mind.

Gentry was somewhere behind them in the tree shadows near the horses. They themselves sat on saddle blankets close to the nearest trees at the pasture's edge. Time and again, after the guns fell silent, Vanover looked back there, trying to see the man. Only once did he make out Gentry's position, and that by the faint red glow of a burning cigarette end. They were waiting, for what they didn't know.

That waiting was becoming intolerable to them both when, at first faintly and then coming stronger, they heard the hoof mutter of a running pony echoing down from the near hill slope. As a rider came out of the trees barely 100 yards away, Vanover sensed Gentry's presence close beside him. The gunman breathed—"Not a move, you two!"—as the rider angled out from the trees, approaching.

Suddenly Vanover saw Gentry's hand lift and the gun in it fall in line with the rider. Recklessly, not considering the consequences, Vanover stepped sideward so that his shoulder jarred the gunman. At that same instant Gentry's Colt exploded deafeningly and close.

Afterward, Vanover couldn't piece together the violent action of those next seconds with any pattern of continuity. He heard Gentry's profane oath, saw the rider roll out of the saddle. Vanover tried to step clear of Gentry, but was struck down by a blow of the swinging gun that caught him on the right shoulder. As he went down, he heard Jean's cry: "Dad!"

His fall faced him toward the pasture at the moment the downed rider rolled onto his feet. He saw the rider's instinctive sideward lunge that took him out of the path of Gentry's second bullet. Then the rider's gun opened up in a prolonged and thunderous chant that drove Gentry over backward, his frame jerking rigidly three times at the impact of bullets before he hit the ground.

There was a moment in which none of them moved: Jean, Vanover, or the rider. Then the rider called sharply: "Sing out over there! Who is it?"

"Dad!" Jean cried. "It's Joe . . . Joe Bonnyman!"

She stood beside him a moment and he felt her uncertainty and hesitation. Then she left him and ran out to the man who had holstered his gun at the instant her voice sounded.

The thankfulness and gladness that had been in Jean's voice told her father as much as her leaving him to go out to Bonnyman. He knew something about his daughter he hadn't known until now. This afternoon, as she unhesitatingly told him of the reason for her absence, she had said once—"He isn't guilty, Dad. I . . . I know it."—and at the time he had detected a strangely intent note in her voice without understanding it. Now he understood both that and this other of a moment ago. Following her out to Bonnyman, he experienced a deep sadness, an aloneness in which he was strangely proud of the choice Jean had made.

When he came up to Joe and held out his hand, Fred Vanover had accepted something he had long dreaded. It wasn't as bad as his imagining had often pictured it would be. He said quite levelly: "We've got a lot to thank you for, Joe."

Over the next few minutes, he put his attention not so much to what was being said as to sizing up this lean, blond man with the bandaged head, the fatigue-lined but strong and clean face. He found that he liked Joe Bonnyman. He found, too, without knowing how he arrived at the decision, that he didn't believe Bonnyman guilty of the indictments laid against him these last three days.

They discussed the shooting down at Diamond, how they had been brought up here by Gentry, evidently to clear the way for the action below. And Vanover approved of Joe's directness when, explanations finished, the younger man said: "You and I could go down and take a look at things, Vanover. After that we head across to Anchor. You've got to talk with Yace."

* * * * *

The ragged remnants of the mesa crews passed Yoke and rode on to Anchor, only a few pausing to look upon the fiery inferno of barn and house that represented Slim Workman's near ruin. Tonight's defeat had been so complete that this added disaster came almost as something expected, even though no man among them could offer an explanation for it.

As Workman himself put it to Yace Bonnyman and two other Anchor men who rode with him: "All I know is I'm lucky to be alive."

The yard at Anchor gradually filled as the stragglers came in. One rider led a horse packing a body roped across the saddle. Another supported a wounded Singletree crewman who rode double with him, bent over under the torturing pain of a bullet-smashed shoulder and his sleeve and side reddened by his lost blood. A third came in with his right leg hanging loosely and his boot clear of stirrup. He had to be helped down out of the saddle and carried to the bunkhouse; a bullet had splintered his shin and they had to cut his boot from his foot.

Hardly a man had come away without at least a superficial wound, so complete and utterly devastating had been the ambush made by the combined Diamond and Brush guns. There were those who didn't return at all, five, as they made the count after waiting a full hour.

Clark Dunne's arrival was a signal for the owners and foremen to go into the house. They lit the lamps in the cavernously big living room and began their talk. Clark was humble, almost in tears, as he told them his story. If he had looked for anger or hatred in these men, he was not to find it; they were too stunned, too completely bewildered to do more than listen.

When Blaze rode in with his four prisoners, the crews left the bunkhouse and ringed the five ponies, roused out of their apathy. The others came down from the house and for several minutes there was a welter of confused talk, until Blaze finally drawled: "Someone take care of Whitey there. The rest of you can get it when we're inside."

Whitey was lifted from his horse and carried to the bunkhouse, fainting as they laid him on a bunk. Mike Saygar remained cool and uncommunicative as he was taken to the house. Harper, following the outlaw, appeared genuinely afraid. Pecos seemed dazed.

Vanover and Jean were well into the yard before anyone noticed them. A Yoke man recognized Vanover and bawled: "Workman! Bonnyman! Get out here!"

His cry brought several men out onto the broad *portal* of the house. Vanover rode across there, Jean following and said a few quiet words to Yace Bonnyman and Blaze. Then he and Jean joined the group in the big living room.

From a distance out the lane, Joe watched their reception with a feeling that was a blend of admiration and uneasiness. It took nerve for Vanover to ride in and face his enemies. Joe hadn't been at all sure that someone wouldn't lose his head and take a shot at the Middle Arizona man, for what little they had seen at

Diamond spoke eloquently of the complete defeat tonight of the Mesa Grande outfits. But Vanover had insisted on taking his part in all this. So had Jean.

Once the *portal* door swung shut on the men gathered there, Joe came out of the saddle, looped the bay's reins over the top rail of the meadow fence, and went on afoot. He was tired, as tired as he could ever remember being, and his body was sore to the touch in a dozen places. But his head was clear and no longer ached; he was thankful for that, for never had he felt the need for clear thinking more than he did now.

Joe knew he had several minutes before the beginning of the next step in the plan he'd outlined to Vanover. As he walked out the head of the lane and turned off toward the big corral, where he knew he'd find the horses, he was going back over that plan, wondering it he'd forgotten anything, wondering if it would net him what he hoped. In the end, he couldn't be sure.

This first step seemed to be going off all right. He had counted on the watchfulness of the crews being relaxed. As he walked in on the corral and made out the twenty-odd ponies tied outside it, he knew his hunch had been correct. Off there at the bunkhouse, men moved to and fro in the light of the door; doubtless they were busy with more important things than keeping a watch on their horses.

He started at the far end of the line and worked down it, examining each saddle gun. He would walk in on the horse, speak softly to it, lay a hand on the animal's neck, and then, with the other, feel the butt plate of the rifle or carbine that was thrust in the scabbard. Several rifle boots were empty; many of the saddles didn't carry one. But each rifle Joe did find he examined carefully, his groping fingers feeling for a butt plate scarred to the pattern Blaze had described.

The seventh gun he examined was a long-barreled .30-30 Winchester, on the saddle of a leggy mottled gray horse wearing Brush's jaw brand. Joe had never seen the horse before. His hand, running along the stock, felt the smooth walnut and he knew that the weapon was fairly new. His fingers ran up over the arced end of the butt plate, down along its face. Suddenly his hand froze, his forefinger running along the deep channel of a straight indentation cutting obliquely across the steel. He found it hard to breathe and his heart didn't seem to want to keep on beating as he drew the rifle from its boot and, stock up, felt of the butt plate again. Here was the gun that had fired the bullet at him up there in the basin three nights ago.

Joe rocked the rifle into the crook of his arm, went back away from the corral, and took nearly five minutes making a wide circle that brought him in at the back of the house, between the root cellar and the kitchen stoop. He pushed his way through a clump of barberry bushes toward a lighted window of the living room.

That window was open; Joe had asked Fred Vanover to be sure of that. Coming in on it, he heard the drone of voices. Joe leaned the rifle against the wall close to the window's edge, and drew his .45 from its holster.

The Accounting

When the door closed, it was Yace Bonnyman who confronted Vanover with: "This had better be good, damn' good! There are over twenty men out there who'd like to see you with a bullet through your guts, Vanover! Talk!"

Fred Vanover did talk. So did Jean, repeating once more Blaze's story of Joe's lying wounded in the cave for two nights and a day while she cared for him. She added more detail to her father's story of their being held prisoner by Harper's men since mid-afternoon, of Joe's killing Gentry in Diamond's hill pasture tonight.

A brief silence ran on after her words, a silence brought on by one more prop having been knocked from under these men. Slowly but surely they were losing the threads that had at first appeared to lead to a solution of this tangled mystery. In that silence Vanover walked across to the window, flanking the big center fireplace, and threw up the lower sash, saying briefly: "Let's have some air." This side of the big room was fogged with tobacco smoke and the stale, heavy air was hard to breathe.

Out of his sheer bewilderment and helplessness Yace said bitterly: "If only Clark hadn't gone in there!"

"Easy, Yace," Blaze drawled. "Clark wasn't to blame. Hadn't he said he'd rather be lyin' back there right now than facin' this? Hang it, it's dark as the inside of a hat tonight. Danged if I could have told Dennis's paint from Harper's. Clark was right for goin' in there and fortin' up when he found the place empty. It looked

226

like a perfect chance to him. You and Workman were wrong to move in before you got some sort of a signal from him."

"That's right, Yace," Workman said lifelessly. "It was me, I'll admit. I was overanxious when I sent that man across to you and told you I was comin' in. I thought maybe they'd taken Clark's bunch without a shot fired."

Blaze saw the acute pain on Workman's face and, knowing the torture the man was undergoing in addition to having seen himself burned out, said quickly: "No one of you is to blame. The only thing that whips me is how them hardcases knew enough to let you fall into your own trap." His glance slowly traveled the faces of these men he had always known as his friends. "Saygar was in the hills during the fight, so was Harper, so was Joe Bonnyman. Vanover was a prisoner to his own men. So, gents, one of us, one of us right here is a stinkin', yellow-backed, double-crossin' coyote! Diamond had help layin' that trap for us tonight and this sidewinder I speak of helped 'em. He's the one who killed Ed Merrill. He bushwhacked Joe. But it didn't come off, thank God. He's responsible for the five men who cashed in tonight, for Shorty gettin' shot out of his saddle this mornin'. Who is he?"

Their glances turned involuntarily to Yace Bonnyman who had always been their leader. But he didn't have it in him to lead them now and his eyes refused to meet theirs. His look traveled slowly over toward the open window, evading their glances. He saw something that made him stiffen. Then they saw what he had—Joe Bonnyman stepping in through the window with a leveled Colt in his hand.

No one in the room made a move. The only sound that came at that moment was Jean Vanover's barely audible gasp.

Then Joe was leaning indolently back against the wall to one side of the window, drawling: "Go right ahead, Blaze. You're doin' fine."

Blaze gave a slow shake of the head, seemingly not as surprised as the rest. "That's as far as I can go."

"Anyone else want a try at makin' his guess?" Joe looked at Yace, seeing his father's face drained of color. He couldn't read the old man's look, couldn't decide whether it was anger, shame, or plain outright puzzlement that put the tight-lipped expression on that lined and rugged face. "How about you, Yace? Still think it was me?"

"Who said I ever did?" Yace blazed hotly, and now his face no longer lacked color.

Blaze Coyle's slow-drawled—"Don't try and back-water, Yace."—jerked Anchor's owner up just short of an added outburst.

Joe smiled meagerly. Looking at the others, he said: "There's a dapple-gray horse with a Brush brand wanderin' around the yard loose. Whoever rode him in better go catch him up if he wants to fork his own saddle home tonight."

Clark Dunne stood up slowly out of a rawhide chair. "Mine," he said, and had half turned to the door when he suddenly stiffened and faced around again.

In that brief moment a change had come over Clark's face, making it handsome no longer, but thin-lipped and ugly. His hard stare settled on Joe and stayed there warily. Somehow he knew that he had stepped into a trap.

Joe was feeling the strength go out of his knees and his hand began trembling. So it was Clark! It had been Clark all along. The man who, next to Blaze, he counted as his best friend. Clark had tried to kill him. Clark had killed Ed Merrill. Of course, Clark would be the one who would have recognized the horse-hair hatband. Slowly, relentlessly the full force of Clark's guilt struck home to Joe as a crushing weight. A strong nausea hit him and the room wheeled before his eyes, so violent was the upheaval within him. Then, gradually, he got a hold on himself and faced this old friend who he saw now as no longer a friend, but a cold-blooded and merciless killer.

"So you're the one, Clark," he said evenly.

A light step crossed the planking of the *portal* and the heavy bolt of the door rattled. Joe's glance went across there, past Clark, as the door opened and Ruth Merrill came into the room.

She stopped dead still, her hand on the wrought-iron latch lift, taking in the scene before her. Her tawny, blonde hair was wind-blown and her face rosy with high color. At this moment she made a picture that brought back all the old hunger, the old worshipful feeling to Joe. He was a fraction of a second too late in lifting his gun. Clark's hand stab had become a smooth, fast uplift as he rocked his .38 into line. Joe pushed sideward and out from the wall and brought his gun around. But Clark's exploded as he was moving. A heavy blow struck him along the forearm; the heavy .45 fell from his convulsively opening hand.

He stood there, his numbed arm hanging at his side, staring into the round bore of Clark's Colt as Ruth Merrill screamed.

Clark wheeled in behind a chair, his move putting every man in the room well within his line of vision. His ordinarily smooth voice grated now as he rasped: "Reach! Every blasted one of you!"

As their hands lifted, Ruth Merrill said from the doorway in a breathless, bewildered voice: "Clark! What are you doing?"

Clark ignored her, taking two backward steps that brought her into view. "Mike, get that gun off the floor," he said tersely. "Harper, Pecos, grab guns!"

Saygar came lithely up off the horsehair sofa, stepped across, and picked up Joe's Colt. Harper wheeled in behind Slim Workman, yanked the man's gun from holster and pushed him roughly across to stand beside Yace Bonnyman. Pecos lifted Yace's gun.

Only then did the hard, wicked set of Clark's face break into a milder look. His glance going to Joe, he drawled: "Well, Ruth, you can have him. He's what you've been after, isn't he?" A twisted smile crossed his face. "I wonder if I'll let you have him. How would you like me to make sure this time, Joe?"

The arm was beginning to hurt now. Joe reached over with his good hand and took a hold on it, throttling the pain. "You're through, Clark," he said. "You can't get away."

"Can't I?" Clark taunted. "Can we, Mike?"

"It's been done before," Saygar said. "We can do it again."

Clark laughed mirthlessly and softly and his glance ran over Joe to Blaze and Yace. Some thought, as he looked at Yace, made his smile fade. "It's too bad this couldn't have come off the way I planned it, Bonnyman. I'd have made you look like a ten-cow man. In the end, I'd either have bought you out or run you out. There was my own spread, then Brush and Singletree. Workman, you'd have sold out to me, wouldn't you? That fire I set tonight cut you off above the pockets, didn't it?"

Slim Workman's voice was awed. "So you did that, too?" he breathed.

"You must've had it all planned," Joe said, "as far back as the night you killed Merrill."

"You killed Dad?" Ruth's voice sounded across the room, hushed and lifeless.

"I meant Ed, Ruth," Joe said.

"Both," Clark corrected him. "Ask Doc Nesbit about it sometime. All I had to do was keep the old man from takin' his medicine."

Yace Bonnyman cursed softly time and time again. It seemed to amuse Clark, whose smile returned. "I'd have had you in less than a year," he drawled. "Maybe in a month. The basin along with the rest. If it hadn't been for Joe uncoverin' Saygar's men, they'd have deeded their homesteads over to me."

At the door, Ruth breathed: "You're a cur, Clark. No, not that. I have nothing against a dog. You're . . ." She stopped there, speechless in her anger and humiliation.

"Go ahead, say it," Clark taunted. His glance ran between Joe and Ruth. "I wonder if I ought to let you have him." He seemed intent on deciding that.

Strangely enough, Joe's look went to Jean Vanover at this moment. She stood beside her father, across from Clark. Her face was pale. She was looking at Joe and something in her eyes made him say, with near anger: "We'll decide that for ourselves, Clark."

A nod from Clark sent Harper to the door. The gunman pushed Ruth aside roughly. So concentrated was the girl's attention on Clark that she didn't seem to notice the gunman.

"Mike, cover my back," Clark said, and turned toward the door.

At that instant Joe let his knees buckle and his body fall backward. As his weight left his legs, he straightened them. He fell back out through the window in a twisting fall. Saygar's gun ripped away the silence inside, his bullet flicking loose a splinter from the window's sill at the exact moment Joe struck the ground, heavily, on his good shoulder.

He rolled out of line with the window, one turning boot knocking the rifle there aground. His groping hand snatched it up as he come onto his knees, wheeling to face the window.

He levered a shell into the gun and shot with it at hip level as Saygar's sloping-shouldered frame blocked the opening. The outlaw gave a pulpy cough and an expression of utter surprise crossed his face. Then, as though too tired to stand, he fell out and across the window's wide sill, hanging there with his gun hand straight down along the outside wall.

Joe saw this as he was coming erect and turning from the window. He snatched the outlaw's Colt from the hand's death grip and ran for the near corner of the house. Losing his footing, he fell headlong into the prickly thicket of barberry. He rolled clear of the bushes, a lancing pain coursing up along his right forearm. The rifle forgotten, he got up and kept on.

Clark Dunne's vague, high shape was in the saddle of the gray, turning out from the shadows down by the corral. Joe halted, stood straddle-legged to steady his aim, and laid his sights on the gray's chest. He squeezed the trigger. The horse, beginning a lunging stride under spur, went down as his forelegs buckled. Joe saw the beginning of Clark's fall and started to run across there.

Over by the house a shot rang out and a man's hoarse scream sounded briefly before a second explosion cut it off.

Joe ran past the cook shanty and was close to the bunkhouse when a stab of flame from the corral showed him Clark's position in the rank of horses. Joe didn't hear the sound of that shot, but felt the air whip of the bullet along the side of his face. He stopped short of the rectangle of light issuing from the bunkhouse door, then wheeled back, and ran into the shadow along the side wall.

He put three strides between him and the back wall before be ventured beyond it. The corral lay a trifle more than 100 feet away now. Joe saw a horse rear and paw the air and heard Clark speak a sharp oath in the moment he stood watching. Then, recklessly, he ran in toward the corral.

Now he could make out a few details in the blackness. He saw Clark plainly, jerking loose the reins of the animal that had reared. He called—"No use, Clark!"—coming in on the side of the empty corral opposite that where Clark stood.

His voice made Clark Dunne turn quickly about. Clark couldn't see Joe yet. He leaned down, stepped in between the second and third poles, and was in the corral.

"Across here, Clark!" Joe called tauntingly, as he went into a crouch.

Clark's .38 exploded twice. A bullet sounded *thwunk!* into one of the pine poles a foot over Joe's head.

Lifting his Colt, Joe targeted the flame stab of Clark's gun there, his own gun only chest-high. He saw Clark pushed backward a step and come erect once more. He saw Clark's hand lift, and drove another shot at the man.

Clark folded at the waist, slowly, as a man would in favoring an aching stomach. His gun exploded once as he fell, wheeling sideward, but the orange wash of powder flame was pointing toward the ground.

Joe walked across to the corral, straddled the poles, and then stood looking down at the man he had once called his friend. Clark's face was upturned. He was smiling, his expression serene except for the sightless, staring eyes.

Joe said—"So long."—softly, and tossed his gun away.

He didn't know the others were coming toward him until Ruth Merrill came in beside him. Putting her arm on his, she said: "Joe, we can forget all this and make a new start. Can't we?"

She drew back at the look Joe gave her. It was cold, furious, not intended for her, but showing the aftereffects of what had just happened. She took her hand away and anger destroyed a measure of her prettiness.

"I don't have to do this, you know," she breathed.

"I know," he answered, hardly aware that she had spoken and not understanding her words. He turned from her then, wanting nothing so much as to be alone.

The others, witnessing the scene, let him walk on away. Blaze had hung back just beyond the wide *portal* with Jean and Fred Vanover. As Joe approached, he told them: "He's takin' it hard. Did you see the way he shook her off? Stay out of his way when he's like this."

Vanover and Jean stepped back into the shadows. As Joe came up, he saw Blaze and some of his sanity returned. He saw the Vanovers beyond Blaze and called: "That you, Jean?"

"Yes, Joe," she answered. "What is it?"

He hadn't known until now what it was. But now that he did know, he walked over to her. Oblivious of Vanover, he took her by the arms and looked down into her face. A torrents of doubts assailed him, but he spoke anyway, the core of him yielding a knowledge of something he hadn't been aware of until he had left Ruth near the corral.

"Jean, I'm on my way out. I'm bein' fool enough to ask you to come with me. I'm no good and you wouldn't be gettin' much. But I've got to know."

Gladness was in Jean Vanover's face. Her eyes shone with tears she tried to hold back. She said in a barely audible whisper—"I'd go anywhere with you, Joe."—and didn't wait for him to kiss her.

Peace for Mesa Grande

It was the same room of three nights ago, the lamplight blue with tobacco smoke, the street below filled with men as on that other night. And it was Yace Bonnyman, as before, who did most of the talking. Only this time Yace wasn't arguing. He was doing the thing he liked best, blustering, driving home to these others the force of his will. And this time there was no question of right and wrong.

"Then it's settled," he said. "Acme stays open. You run it, Vanover. You're goin' to make Workman and Staples low-interest loans so they can get on their feet again. But your outfit's through when it comes to cattle. Either let go of Diamond or we'll run you out. We'll burn the layout to the ground if we have to. Your gun hands are in jail now. We can do these things I say, and you won't stop us."

"That won't be necessary," Fred Vanover replied. "Diamond's changing hands. We're only handling the mortgage on it."

For the first time since the meeting had started, Yace's look went cloudy with anger. "No tricks," he flared. "Come out in the open with the details. We'll let the sale go through on only one condition . . . that the owner is agreeable to us. Who is he?"

"Your son and his wife are moving in tomorrow, after the wedding," Vanover stated quietly.

"Weddin!" Yace was stunned into silence for a moment. "Why wasn't I told about this?"

Blaze, at the far end of the table, said dryly: "No one thought you'd be interested."

235

"Well, damn it, I am! Where's Joe now?"

"He and Jean were down in the street in my rig when I left them," Vanover said. "Unless they've decided to drive out where it isn't so crowded, you'll still find them there."

Without another word, Yace got his hat and left the room, his solid boot tread thundering down the covered stairway outside.

Vanover's shiny new buggy was at the rail in front of The Antlers. Only the night light shone from the hotel windows, so that walk and street were dark. The white sling of Joe's bad arm was all Yace could distinguish as he stooped under the tie rail and approached the rig.

"That you, Joe?" he asked needlessly.

"It's me." His son's voice was flattened.

Yace could make out the girl now and he tipped his hat to her. "I . . . I got somethin' to tell you, Joe," he said haltingly.

"Same here," Joe replied. "I only heard about it tonight. Thanks for savin' me a bullet in the back. I understand it was you that knocked Harper over. Blaze said he was goin' to have a try at him, but that you grabbed your gun from Pecos, wouldn't trust Blaze to do it. That right?"

Yace nodded, his face coloring in his embarrassment. "Blaze never did have a good eye for a shot in the dark. Pecos just gave up after Saygar got it. I took my gun back, ran out, and nailed Harper." He scuffed his boots in the dust, looking down at them. Finally he burst out: "I got a lot to live down, Son. All I can say is I been pretty thick-headed. We're glad to have you stayin'. And if you'll let an old fool say it, you're a fine judge of women."

Before he quite knew what was happening, Jean Vanover had leaned down and kissed him on the forehead.

He wanted to get away quickly, but couldn't. There was something else he had to say. "Son," it came out finally, "there's no use in you gettin' in over your head with a bank on this thing. I've got so much money I don't know what to do with it. Why don't you use some of it before I'm dead and buried."

"We'll make out all right," was Joe's reply.

"Have it your way." Yace turned back onto the walk, the old anger against his son's stubbornness in him. Then he checked himself.

Going back up the walk to the stable for his horse, Yace pondered this fact he had never understood before, humble before the feeling of wanting to make it up to his son.

It was on the ride home that he thought of way to make Joe take that money. He had as good a right as the next man to give a wedding present. It was bad luck, so he understood, to turn one down.

The End

About the Author

Peter Dawson is the *nom de plume* used by Jonathan Hurff Glidden. He was born in Kewanee, Illinois, and was graduated from the University of Illinois with a degree in English literature. In his career as a Western writer he published sixteen Western novels and wrote over 120 Western short novels and short stories for the magazine market. From the beginning he was a dedicated craftsman who revised and polished his fiction until it shone as a fine gem. His Peter Dawson novels are noted for their adept plotting, interesting and well-developed characters, their authentically researched historical backgrounds, and his stylistic flair. During the Second World War, Glidden served with the U.S. Strategic and Tactical Air Force in the United Kingdom. Later in 1950 he served for a time as Assistant to Chief of Station in Germany. After the war, his novels were frequently serialized in *The Saturday Evening Post*. Peter Dawson titles such as *Royal Gorge* and *Ruler of the Range* are generally conceded to be among his best titles, although he was an extremely consistent writer, and virtually all his fiction has retained its classic stature among readers of all generations. One of Jon Glidden's finest techniques was his ability, after the fashion of Dickens and Tolstoy, to tell his stories via a series of dramatic vignettes which focus on a wide assortment of different characters, all tending to develop their own lives, situations, and predicaments, while at the same time propelling the general plot of the story toward a suspenseful conclusion. He was no less gifted as a master of the short novel and short story.